ABOUT

I had one very big reason to swear off men forever: My cheating ex-husband.

Our marriage may have been a total disaster, but it did give me my beautiful daughter Birdie. She's the only good thing that man ever brought to my life.

So, when I packed up the car and headed to the small town of Reed Point to start a new life with my little girl, I vowed that a relationship—and the heartache and destruction that would inevitably follow—was *not* part of the plan.

That was before I walked straight into Jake Matthews and my whole world turned upside down. Jake is six-foot-something and all muscle, with piercing hazel eyes and a smirk that can set you on fire. He's protective and sweet—and he's 7 years younger than me. And when he finally gets me in his bed, I realize what I've been missing.

Every time Jake's deep, moody eyes meet mine, every time he whispers filthy things to me, I almost forget all of the reasons this is never going to work.

My life is complicated. I have a stack of bills I need to pay, a little girl who has to come first and a past that I'm trying to outrun. A past that is threatening to catch up with me.

The new life I've worked so hard to build could fall apart when I'm forced to make the biggest decision of my life. Falling for Jake was never part of the plan, but now I may need to walk away from the man who has stolen my heart.

Copyright © 2024 by Lily Miller

All rights reserved.

No part of this book may be reproduced in any form or by any electronic or mechanical means, including information storage and retrieval systems, without written permission from the author, except for the use of brief quotations in a book review.

This book is a work of fiction. Names, characters, places and incidents are products of the author's imagination or are used fictitiously. Any resemblance to actual events or locals or persons, living or dead, is entirely coincidental.

Play For Keeps

Cover photo: Asha Bailey, Asha Bailey Photography

Cover design: Kim Wilson, Kiwi Cover Design

Editing: Carolyn De Melo

Publicity: Love Notes PR

PLAY FOR KEEPS

HAVEN HARBOR SERIES BOOK TWO

LILY MILLER

PLAYLIST

1. Enough Is Enough—Post Malone
2. '98 Braves—Morgan Wallen
3. Get to Gettin' Gone—Bailey Zimmerman
4. your place—Ashley Cooke
5. Up All Night—Jon Pardi
6. Thinking 'Bout You—Dustin Lynch, MacKenzie Porter
7. Bigger Mistakes—Mitchell Tenpenny
8. Miss Americana & The Heartbreak Prince—Taylor Swift
9. Better Than You're Used To- Tyler Rich
10. If I Know Me—Morgan Wallen
11. Town Ain't Big Enough—Chris Young, Lauren Alaina
12. Ridin' Roads—Dustin Lynch
13. Butterflies—Kacey Musgraves
14. Spin You Around (1/24)—Morgan Wallen
15. Came The Closest—Sam Hunt
16. Austin—Dasha
17. Bad At Love—Halsey
18. Chase Her—Bailey Zimmerman
19. Locked Up—Sam Hunt

*To the girls out there who have dreamed about finding their Jake.
This is for you.*

ONE

SIX WAYS TO SUNDAY

Everly

I'm kicking myself for taking this shift tonight. We're short-staffed, and the restaurant has been slammed since I started at 5 p.m. Between dealing with customers who have had way too much to drink and trying to keep a very demanding corporate group happy, I haven't had a second to breathe.

Only two more hours, I tell myself as I weave through the tables to deliver a gin and tonic. *Click, click.* I cringe at the distinct sound of someone snapping to get my attention. Don't people know that is the cardinal sin of eating at a restaurant? Turning to see who is beckoning me, I trip over a toddler who has suddenly appeared at my feet and spill the drink down the front of my shirt.

This is why I never work Saturday nights. But when Faith, a co-worker at Catch 21, called and practically begged me to cover her shift so she could go to a concert with a guy she just started seeing, I couldn't say no.

Hurrying to the back room to change out of my wet

shirt, I pass Violet, who is on her way back to the dining room with a tray of appies balanced on her hand.

"Wild out there tonight, huh?" she says, stopping to blow a loose strand of bleached blonde hair out of her eyes. Violet is four years younger than me, but when I started at Catch 21 after moving to Reed Point four months ago, the two of us quickly became friends.

"Yeah," I sigh, motioning to my soaked shirt. "I'm just changing real quick. Can you cover for me?"

"You bet. I've got you," she says as I move quickly down the hall. Once in the back room, I close the door behind me and make a beeline for my locker, where I thankfully keep a clean shirt on hand for situations like this. Peeling the top from my body, I take a deep breath, trying to calm my nerves.

As I'm tucking the fresh button-down into my skirt, I feel my phone vibrate in my pocket. I dig it out, hoping it's not a message from my neighbor Franny, who is watching my daughter Birdie for the night.

Birdie and I met Franny the day we moved into our small, two-bedroom apartment. There was a knock at the door, and I opened it to find an older woman with a warm smile and a pouf of violet hair standing there. She held a plate of sprinkled cupcakes and a glittery cat ear headband —the ultimate housewarming gift for a 7-year-old. That was it for Birdie, she loved Franny immediately. I did too. We just seemed to click. Since then, she has become like family. Sometimes I don't know what I would do without her—like tonight, for instance. When I called at the last minute to ask if she would stay with Birdie, she was at our doorstep five minutes later armed with craft supplies and a board game. It's definitely not the first time Franny has stepped in to save me. Sometimes I worry that we are taking up too much of her time, but Franny insists that with her own two kids now grown up and out of the house, she loves being able to hang out with Birdie.

Thankfully, the two of them must be just fine tonight, because the text isn't from Franny, it's from Willa, my best friend back home. I slam my locker door shut and then swipe to read the message.

> Willa: Hey Ev... Can you talk?

Something about it feels ominous, and I get a nervous feeling in my chest. But it will have to wait. I've left Violet to cover me for too long as it is, so I type out a short reply telling Willa that I'll get back to her when my shift ends and then hurry back to the dining room.

When I think about everyone I left behind in Brookmont, Willa is who I miss the most. Four months ago, I packed up Birdie's and my belongings and loaded them into my car. I tucked my sleepy daughter into the back seat beside the boxes of our things and made the two-hour drive to Reed Point while she slept. Getting to this small town was the easy part. The hard part has been settling into a new home—one that is nearly 5,000 square feet smaller than the gated mansion we left behind. I still feel pangs of guilt about uprooting Birdie from the life she knew, but if I didn't think it was best for her, I never would have done it. Thankfully, she has been quick to make new friends and doesn't seem to mind our cozy little home. And although some days she complains that she misses her dad, she's excited to live closer to her grandparents. When my parents suggested I move to Reed Point for a while to be closer to them, I was hesitant at first; I'd need to find somewhere to live because they wouldn't have room for us in their tiny, old house. Turns out, finding our apartment was a lot easier than I expected and I took that as a sign; it felt like fate. My parents have been worried about me for a long time so they're over the moon to have me and Birdie close by.

Still trying to push down the anxiety that Willa's text sparked, I swing open one of the dining room doors—and walk directly into the hard wall of a man's chest.

"Whoa," the hard body says, his hands coming to my shoulders to steady me. "I'm so sorry. Are you okay?"

I press a hand to my racing heart. "I'm okay, thanks. I'm pretty sure that was my fault. I should have been looking where I was going."

I look up to see a roughly six-foot frame towering over me. *Wow.* This guy is ridiculously handsome. He has thick espresso-brown hair that is short on the sides and slightly longer on top, a chiselled jaw and a neatly trimmed beard that is sexy as hell. The mystery man is tall with an athletic build, a broad chest, and muscled arms. I pause when I notice the stormy intensity of his gaze, and the way his green eyes trail down towards my lips. I recognize the appreciation in his eyes, and for a split second, I allow the tiny flutter in my chest. But then I remember that I've sworn off men. Forever.

"I guess the same could be said for me. I'm sorry again," he says in a smooth, low voice, releasing the light grip he has on my shoulders. I blink hard for a second. "Have a good night." Then he's walking past me towards the restrooms, leaving me with my pulse still racing and my feet rooted to the floor.

I wince in embarrassment. I'm not usually this much of a disaster, but this clearly isn't my night. I take a deep breath and head back to my section, trying to ignore the strange flurry of butterflies in my stomach. It's been a long time since I've felt anything like this.

Get back to work, Ev.

Remember why you need this job.

Five minutes later, I'm standing at the bar, waiting on drinks from Owen, one of the two bartenders on shift tonight. Violet sidles up next to me and asks Owen for a Diet Coke refill.

"Did you see table seven, Ev?" Vi asks, nudging me gently with her shoulder. She looks across the crowded dining room and my gaze follows hers, landing on a table where three guys are having dinner and drinks. I shrug, giving her a quizzical look.

"Okay, you obviously have no idea who *he* is." She raises a brow at me as she adds a lime wedge to the glass that Owen has deposited on her tray.

"Is there a reason I should know who *he* is?" I ask, admittedly a little curious.

"He's practically royalty in this town. His name is Liam Bennett. Big time attorney. His parents own the Seaside Hotel chain. And his brother is Miles Bennett, like *the* freaking Miles Bennett. The whole family is loaded."

I obviously know who Miles Bennett is. I see his face plastered across magazine covers every time I go to the grocery store. I've even watched a couple of his movies. But as for the rest of the Bennetts—Reed Point royalty or not, I've never heard of them.

Violet glances back over her shoulder at their table. "He's beautiful. I mean look at him. The man could give Liam Hemsworth a run for his money."

"*And* he's wearing a wedding band on his ring finger," I note, raising an eyebrow in judgment.

"Doesn't mean I can't look." Violet shrugs with a grin.

"But fine, how about the guy he's with then? The one on his right. No wedding band there." She nudges me again.

I humor her, glancing over my shoulder at the profile of a serious-looking guy at the table, my eyes wandering from his dark brown hair to a jawline that could cut glass. I look up again to find a pair of killer green eyes looking straight at me and I realize it's the guy I just walked into. A wave of embarrassment rushes over me and I snap my head back toward the bar.

Perfect. As if this night wasn't already a complete disaster, a customer just caught me lusting over him like a total stalker.

"Ooh," Violet teases as a blush creeps up my cheeks. "You think he's cute! Come on, admit it."

"He's a good-looking guy. So are plenty of guys in Reed Point," I say, trying to play it cool. "It doesn't mean I want to sleep with them."

"A 'good-looking guy?' Do you need a pair of glasses? He's *gorgeous*. Who wouldn't want one night with a guy that looks like that? He looks all broody and serious too. That's so hot. I wonder who he is."

I fight the temptation to look back in his direction. "I have 20/20 vision. And I don't do hook-ups."

It's true. It doesn't matter how attractive the guy might be, I am not into random one-night stands. Birdie is my number one priority and I'm not looking to make our lives any more complicated. She's been through enough as it is.

"It wouldn't hurt to have a little fun, Ev," Violet muses. "No strings, no commitments. Not every guy needs to be the one you're gonna marry. Sometimes you need to get under a man to get over the one you're trying to forget."

"Who said I was trying to forget someone?" I haven't talked about my past to Violet or anyone else in Reed Point.

I'm determined to make a fresh start here, and I don't want any baggage getting in the way of that.

Violet raises her eyebrows at me, looking like she's not buying it. "Whatever. You're missing out, girl. Also, I think he likes what he sees. He's looking at you like he'd like to rail you over a table."

"Vi!" I hiss. "You have no idea what you're talking about."

She picks up her tray and turns back towards the crowded room but then stops and flashes a mischievous smile over her shoulder at me. "I bet that man could fuck you six ways to Sunday if you showed him a little interest, Ev. You deserve a hot night with a good-looking guy. I say go for it."

I scrunch up my nose in response, but she's already making her way to a waiting table.

I pick up my own tray and get back to work, deciding to ignore everything Violet just said. Easier said than done. Her advice plays like a loop in my mind for the rest of my shift.

THREE LONG HOURS LATER, I'M LYING IN BED IN MY PAJAMAS eating a peanut butter and jelly sandwich. The apartment is blissfully quiet, with just the faint sound of rain hitting my bedroom window. Birdie is asleep in her little bedroom and Franny returned to her apartment when I got home a little after 11 p.m.

My feet ache from the shift at the restaurant, and I relax into the pillows behind me, happy the night is over. I grab my phone from the bedside table to send a quick text to Willa. It has been weeks since we last talked. She hasn't been far from my mind, but I've been so busy getting settled into the apartment, starting a new job, and finding a new school for Birdie.

> Everly: I miss you. Is everything okay?

I stare at the screen, frowning, worrying about Willa and feeling sad at the distance I've put between us. She is the only person I said goodbye to before I left town. She's the only person who really understands why I had to make this move—how badly I need some space and time to try to forget him and everything he had put me through. Willa saw firsthand everything I lost being married to Birdie's dad, the way my joy and self-worth and confidence slowly disappeared along the way. This move and everything that led up to it has been difficult, harder than anything I've ever gone through, but I know it was a move I had to make.

A text pops up on my screen and I quickly swipe the message to life.

> Willa: I miss you too. And I'm fine but I thought you should know I ran into Miranda. She was asking questions, threatening attorneys, waving her millions around like I give a shit.

The mention of my former mother-in-law has my heart racing. Miranda is as close to narcissistic as they come. She thinks she knows everything, and that her money can buy her whatever she wants. She never thought I was good enough for her son, who had a million-dollar trust fund before he even exited her womb. I could never live up to her expectations, and she made that painfully obvious in every one of our conversations. As far as she was concerned, her son could do no wrong. It didn't matter how much of an egotistical ass he was being, she would back him up.

Grant and I came from two very different backgrounds —my parents were blue-collar; his parents had a billion-dollar iron company. Some wealthy people use their money for good, but Grant's parents use it as a weapon. Everything they do comes with strings.

> Everly: What did she say?
>
> Willa: She wants to know when you're coming home. She wants to see Birdie.

I roll my eyes. Miranda didn't have much time for Birdie when we lived 10 minutes away, so I know that her sudden interest in her granddaughter has little to do with Birdie and everything to do with the fact that she no longer has any control over us.

> Everly: What did you tell her?
>
> Willa: I told her I didn't know but I'm positive she didn't buy it.

Willa has been by my side through it all— the night I met Grant, the day I married him and the afternoon he smashed my world into a million pieces. And even though I know it broke her heart a little when I took Birdie and left town, she supported me. She understood that I needed to go, to escape Grant and try to heal the wounds that I'd been suffering through for years.

> Everly: I'm sorry you had to deal with her. I'll talk to her soon. I just need some room to breathe.

> Willa: You never have to apologize. I am happy to tell Miranda where she can shove it. :) I'm always here for you. How's my Birdie?

I look over at the photo of my sweet girl that sits on my dresser. It was taken on her 6th birthday. She's wearing a Tinkerbell costume, with a pink plastic tiara perched on top of her mass of blonde curls. The look on her face is pure joy. I smile at the memory and feel a rush of gratitude that despite everything, Birdie is still such a happy, loving kid.

> Everly: She's doing fine. I think she believes the move is temporary.

> Willa: Well, is it temporary?

> Everly: I'm not sure. I'm really hoping I can stay the year I committed to. I just hope Birdie doesn't hate me for it.

I swallow hard. Birdie is my world. I have done everything I can think of to make this move as easy as possible for her. I'm making sure she gets lots of time with my parents, because they're crazy about her and that kind of unconditional love is exactly what she needs. What we both need.

I've also tried to make the new apartment feel like home for Birdie. Her bedroom is the first room in the house that I set up. I painted the walls a beautiful, soft pink, hung a canopy over her bed and set up her dollhouse in the corner by the window. All of her favorite things are there—her stuffies are on the bed, her ballerina music box sits on her bedside table, her collection of glass marbles is in a bowl on her dresser. But it just isn't her home yet. Hopefully in time it will be, but for now I know that she must miss her friends, her old school, and her dad, even if he was rarely ever present.

> Willa: She could never hate you. Just focus on getting her settled. What about you? Are you okay?

I pause, mulling over her question for a second. I haven't had time to even think about how *I'm* doing. Am I okay? I'm not, but I'd rather be here in this tiny apartment than living in that awful house.

> Everly: I'm hanging in there.

> Willa: I'm sorry you're going through this. Grant is an asshole. You're better off far away from him.

I watch as text bubbles bounce up and down on the screen until a second message from Willa pops up.

> Willa: How's the job? It's still hard to believe you're waiting tables.

> Everly: It's not that bad. It's been a good way to make friends. Although it makes me feel really old. I feel like I could be their mother.

> Willa: That's just because you are one. 34 is not old. It can't be, because I am also 34 and I KNOW you're not calling me old.

> Everly: You're the exception, Wills. You'll still be 25 at heart when they wheel you into the retirement home. But this old lady needs to go to bed now. Love you. I promise I'll call you soon.

LILY MILLER

> Willa: Love you too. Try not to worry. You got this.

We say goodnight and my heart aches in my chest. God, I miss Willa.

But Birdie and I are going to be okay.

TWO

IT'S A BEER, NOT AN ENGAGEMENT RING

Jake

Grayson sets his paddle board on the sand, then sits down beside me. "Got any cold ones in that backpack?"

"Maybe," I say, rooting around for the three cans I stuffed in the bag on my way out the door this afternoon.

"You're a hero," Grayson says when I hand him a Miller Lite. "And it's chilled too. This is why I love you, man. You always pull through."

"It's a beer, not an engagement ring. Don't make it weird," I grumble, setting my can down in the sand while I pull my T-shirt on over my head. It must be close to 85 degrees today and after a two-hour paddle, I've had enough sun for one day.

"I don't care what you say, you're a fucking life saver," Grayson says, cracking the tab on the can I just handed him. "Got any sandwiches in there too?"

I side-eye him. "Don't push your luck."

A moment later, Tucker drops his paddleboard and flops down onto the sand beside us. I toss him a beer, which he immediately opens and knocks back.

"That is exactly what I needed," he says, wiping his mouth with the back of his hand and settling back on his elbows.

Grayson, Tucker and I, along with our other buddy Holden, have been best friends for years. It feels more like we're brothers at this point. The three of them live on Haven Harbor, next door to the little home my Gran has lived in since I was a kid. Gran happens to be a card shark, so she invited the guys to play poker with us one evening. It turned into a regular game, and the four of us have been close ever since. When I say my grandmother is a card shark, I'm not kidding—she creams our asses every single time.

But things will soon be changing on the secluded coastal street. Gran will be moving out of her home on Haven Harbor and into a nearby assisted living facility. My sister Sierra and I hated having to persuade her to leave the home she's lived in for decades, but she lives alone and after a string of accidents and close calls and the onset of dementia, it felt like the only option. The only good news in all of this is that Sierra is moving back to Reed Point from Virginia Beach, where she's been for the last four years.

I'm fucking happy she's coming back home. We're close, always have been. I get why Sierra left Reed Point, but I didn't like her living 500 miles away. I know some people think I'm a ridiculously overprotective older brother, but when you survive a devastating loss like we did as kids, you can't help it. Sierra and Gran are the only family I have left.

"How's Gran? Is she still giving you shit about the move?" Grayson asks as he slips his shades on and tips his face to the sun.

"She's pissed." There is no point in sugar-coating it. "She isn't making it easy on us."

The movers are coming in two weeks. And after we

move Gran out, Sierra is moving into her small house. It only made sense since she needed to find a place to stay, and Gran didn't want to sell.

"It sucks, but you made the right decision, Jake. Don't beat yourself up over it," Grayson says, toeing sand in my direction.

I nod, then take a long swig from my beer. I know it's what's best for her, but it still isn't easy. Sierra and I owe Gran everything. I was only 12 years old when we went to live with her after that horrible night, and Sierra was 10. Gran raised us both, and I know I didn't make it easy on her. I was angry at the world for taking our parents from us. I was also shouldering a lot of guilt—to be honest, I still am. On the night of the fire, I had snuck out of the house. If I'd been in my bed, where I should have been, my parents wouldn't have been searching for me through the smoke and flames. They probably would have made it out in time. They would still be alive today. All these years later, it still haunts me.

"Gray is right," Tuck says. "It's for the best. Besides, Gran is a social butterfly. She'll be a big deal around there in no time."

"She's bringing her poker table with her, right?" Grayson asks. He's lying in the sand with a forearm held over his eyes to block the glare of the sun.

"I think so." I shrug. "We haven't talked about it."

"Well, she should. She could make a killing. Take those seniors for every penny they have left," Tucker jokes.

"Better than having to play cards with you fuckers," I tell them. "She could have played blindfolded and still beat you pussy players."

"What would you know about pussy, Matthews?" Tucker

says, calling me by my last name. "You haven't gotten your dick wet in a year."

Grayson laughs beside me, and I glare in his direction. The truth is, Tucker isn't too far off the mark. Unlike these guys, I've never been into meaningless hookups. They're all right if the sex is good, but then it's awkward as fuck afterwards; I end up feeling like a dick when I don't really want the girl to stick around. I wouldn't be against dating someone seriously, I just haven't had any luck finding *the one*. One of the downfalls of living in a small town—the dating pool is painfully limited.

"You okay today, Jakey?" Grayson asks as he sits up and brushes the sand from his skin. "You're even moodier than usual."

I must look as tired as I feel. I've been short-staffed all week at the contracting company I own, which means I've been onsite early every day at one of the houses we're remodelling. It's tough, physical work and my body is definitely feeling it.

"I'm fine. Just tired of putting up with you two dummies."

"Hey, maybe if you got your dick sucked, you'd be less grumpy," Tucker says with a grin.

"At least my dick is intact," I respond. "Yours is probably in the process of falling off thanks to an STD."

Tucker flips me off.

Having had his fill of bullshitting for the moment, Tuck changes topics and asks where we want to meet for our weekly downhill bike ride tomorrow morning. I let the two of them argue about which trail we should ride, stretching out and looking down the sandy beach. It's not too busy today. Unlike the bigger beaches in Reed Point that are always packed on sunny days, this smaller cove a little further up the coast tends to be pretty quiet.

My gaze lands on a girl who is sitting by herself on a beach blanket not too far from us. Her feet are buried in the sand, her long, brown hair falling down her back. I squint, trying to confirm it is who I think it is. My pulse picks up just a bit. It's her. The waitress from Catch 21. She's just as stunning as she was the night I ran into her at the restaurant a couple of weeks ago.

Her face is tilted toward the turquoise sky, and I take the opportunity to stare. She's wearing a tiny pair of denim shorts and a thin tank top, her golden, smooth skin on display.

Breathtaking.

I snap back to reality when a boy comes running down the beach toward her, chasing a soccer ball. She puts a hand to her eyes as her gaze follows the ball to where it lands not far from me.

She looks up, and her wide eyes meet mine.

I instantly feel goosebumps race down my spine at the memory of running into her at Catch 21. It was nothing, just a moment. I've been around plenty of pretty girls, but there was something about her that lit a spark in me. Something that made me want to push her up against the wall and kiss her. She's popped into my mind many times since then, and it's always the memory of those hazel eyes locked on mine. Just like they are right now.

She cocks her head, and her lips tip up at the corners in a cautious smile before she looks away, breaking eye contact. I take a deep breath, the same spark I felt that night knocking me off kilter again.

"See something you like?" Tucker asks, fixing me with a knowing smirk.

I shake my head. "I just recognized her from Catch 21. She's a waitress there. I ran into her the other night when I had dinner with Liam."

"And now your dick wants to run into her," Grayson says, and I realize that all three of us are staring at her like assholes.

"Guys. Stop fucking staring, it's creepy." I elbow Grayson in his side, and he mock-winces.

"Geez, you have a crush on this girl," Tuck says, swatting at Grayson's leg. "See that, Gray... our boy has it bad."

Thankfully, Grayson's phone lights up with a call and our conversation is put on hold. As Tuck picks up his own phone and starts scrolling, I tell myself to be cool, just act normal. I am not in the mood for an interrogation about a girl I don't even know. But it isn't as easy as it sounds. I'm itching to look at her. It takes every ounce of my willpower to keep from glancing back in her direction.

Eventually I crack. I can't help it.

The breeze coming off the ocean blows her long hair away from her face and I notice the curve of her shoulder, the smooth column of her neck. She's the kind of beautiful that knocks the breath out of you. She has olive skin, and I remember her eyes being a color I've never seen before—like a bright green moss mixed with a precious stone. Her body makes me want to run my fingers over every inch of it.

My pervy thoughts are interrupted when Tuck sits up, stuffing his phone in his pocket. "I gotta run, boys. I've got dinner with my dad tonight, which is obviously just an excuse for him to tell me all the ways he thinks I'm fucking up my life." He rolls his eyes. "Can't wait."

Tucker's dad is hard on him, always has been. Their relationship is complicated, to put it mildly.

"I don't know why you're still taking his shit. You're a

grown man. You don't have to, you know," Gray says. He stands up, then grabs his board. "I'll catch a ride with you, Tuck."

Brushing the sand off his shorts, he looks at me and then nods down the beach. "You should shoot your shot with her, Jake."

"Maybe," I say. I know the guys will give me the gears if I don't man up and at least talk to her. It's been a long time since I've shown any real interest in a girl. Two years and three months, to be exact. But if I do decide to approach her, I'm not stupid enough to do it while Tucker and Grayson are here to witness it. I don't need to give them any ammo if I go over there and strike out.

Besides, I'm not looking for anything serious so what's the harm in talking to her? If she's not interested, it's no big deal. *Right?*

I say goodbye to the guys and then knock back the rest of my beer as I watch them head across the beach to the parking lot. Then, before I can talk myself out of it, I stand up and walk down the beach towards her.

When I get closer, her gaze tips up to mine. *Damn. She's beautiful.* I force myself to swallow my nerves.

"Hey. I recognize you from Catch 21," I start. "I was there a couple of weeks ago. I was the guy who almost killed you when I walked right into you. Sorry about that. I should really pay attention to where I'm going…"

My pulse hammers beneath my skin. I walked over here without any kind of a plan, and now I'm standing here blabbering like an idiot. What was I thinking? I'm not a talker. I'm not outgoing. I smile at her, hoping that panic isn't written all over my face. I take a deep breath, and her scent —something citrusy like oranges or clementines—smells so good that it's all I can think about.

I crouch beside her, and as she glances out at the ocean, I take note of the thin chain around her neck with a tiny pendant resembling a bird.

A sparrow.

I want to know what it means to her. I want to know everything about her.

She looks at me, her lower lip pulled between her teeth.

"Jake. Jake Matthews," I say, filling the silence. She nods, absentmindedly twisting her hair around into a knot at the base of her neck. "Hi," she says, a cautious tone to her voice. "I'm Everly." She looks back to the ocean, and I wonder if it's a subtle hint that she wants to be left alone.

I'm deciding whether I should just cut my losses and go when a little girl with blonde hair comes skipping up the sand, plopping down onto the blanket beside Everly. I watch as she slips her arm around the child's back, pulling her to her side.

"Did you see me jump the really big wave?"

My heart sinks as I notice the clear resemblance between them. She has a daughter? I can't help but wonder if she has a husband too.

I take in the girl's olive-hued skin and wide, hazel eyes which look just like Everly's. She wraps her sandy arms around Everly's neck and casts a sideways glance in my direction.

"I saw, baby. It was the biggest one yet," Everly says, grinning at the little girl. Her whole face has lit up. The cautious expression from before is gone. She looks happy, relaxed.

"Can I do it again, Mommy?"

It *is* her daughter. I quickly check Everly's left hand for a ring, wondering if I made an ass out of myself by coming over here. There isn't one.

The little girl flops down into Everly's lap. "I think I can jump higher."

Everly smiles wide. "Let's see. I'll watch you from here."

The girl gets up and dashes for the ocean, Everly's eyes on her the whole time. She looks so genuinely joyful that I start to feel like I'm intruding. But then she turns her gaze to me and the last thing I want to do is leave.

"You have a daughter," I say, stating the obvious.

"I do."

"She's cute. How old is she?" I ask.

"Seven." There's a pause, but then she adds, "Her name is Birdie. And yes, she's very cute. She's sugar and spice, that one. She keeps me on my toes." *Birdie.* That explains her necklace.

Everly smiles, but before the conversation goes any further, her phone chimes on the blanket next to her. She picks it up, swiping the iPhone to life.

"Sorry, it's my neighbor," she says as she types out a message. "I asked her to watch Birdie during my shift tonight, so I just need to make sure she knows the time."

"Catch 21?"

Everly nods as she types, her bottom lip caught under her teeth. Every couple of seconds, she glances towards the ocean, where Birdie is jumping in the small waves lapping against the shore.

I study her, wanting to know everything I can about her. Where did she grow up? How long has she been in Reed Point? Where is Birdie's dad and how does he fit into the picture? Are they still together? Does she still love him? I want to know it all.

Will I ever get the chance to ask her?

I've been attracted to plenty of girls in my lifetime, but this feels different. This spark that flashes in my chest every time her eyes meet mine, like a live wire behind my ribcage. The scent of her—lilacs and citrus surrounds me, practically soaking through my skin.

Everly drops her phone back on the blanket and gives me an apologetic look. "Sorry," she repeats, her teeth sinking into her bottom lip again. *Shit.* My dick perks to life every time she does that. She really needs to stop doing that.

"Don't be," I tell her. "I get it. So, how long have you worked there?"

"Catch 21? Not long. Six weeks, give or take."

"Do you enjoy it?"

"I mean, it's a job. I'm grateful to have it. I'd do anything to provide for Birdie," she says, still watching the little girl on the edge of the ocean. "It's fun some nights, not so fun on others. I'm telling myself it's an adventure. It's how I'm choosing to look at it."

"That's a great way to look at it." I swallow, then decide to just ask her the question that I can't get out of my head. "So, your husband can't watch her tonight?"

She gives me a pointed look that tells me there was nothing subtle about the way I asked that.

"If you are wondering if I'm married, you could have just asked."

"Fair. I'm wondering if you're married."

She smirks and shakes her head, holding up her bare ring finger. "Not married. No boyfriend either, which is why my neighbor is kind enough to help me out when I have a night shift."

"It must not be easy doing it all by yourself."

"It's okay," she says with a shrug. "It's for the best."

Everly picks up a broken seashell, rolling it between her fingers. I can sense the tension in her. It's clear that she doesn't want to talk about it any further than that, so I shift the conversation back to the day, the beach, Reed Point. Safe and easy topics, the things people talk about when they're getting to know each other. She waves to Birdie as she talks and the way her entire face lights up is mesmerizing.

Birdie is adorable. Her strawberry-blonde hair is held back in two long, messy braids. Every time she smiles—which she does often—she shows off the space where she's missing her two bottom teeth.

Everly's eyes are never far from her daughter, which gives me time to take her in. She's gorgeous. She's wearing barely any makeup—mascara and maybe a little bit of lip gloss. Her full lips look soft and pillowy.

I want to kiss them.

And now I'm thinking about where else I would like that pretty mouth.

I run a hand through my hair. Why am I so fucking curious about this girl? I may as well ask for her goddamn Instagram handle, that's how intent I am on finding out every single thing about her. *This is fucking ridiculous.*

"Is Reed Point home?" I ask.

"It is now," she nods, twisting a bracelet she's wearing around her wrist. "We moved here in March."

"What brought you to Reed Point?"

"I was ready for a change" she says, and again I can see there is more that she doesn't want to open up about. "And my parents live here, so it will be good for Birdie to spend time with them."

I resist the urge to ask her more. I want to know where home was, and what really made her move here. But it doesn't feel like it's my business. I don't want to scare Everly off. I already get the sense that there is an invisible timer ticking down the seconds of our conversation. Sure enough, a second later our time's up.

"Well, we should get going. It was nice talking to you, Jake."

I stand up, brushing the sand from my legs. A voice inside my head tells me I should walk away—she's not interested, she has a kid. *Read the writing on the wall, Jake.* But a bigger part of me needs to take the chance. To get her number, to keep talking. There is still so much I want to know about her.

"Yeah, I guess I should head out too. Hey, Everly, do you think we could—"

"Jake, it was really nice to meet you," she interrupts. "You seem like a nice guy." *Fuck. Nice guy.* I know a brush-off when I hear one. Everly gives me an apologetic smile and I know what's coming. She's not interested. "My focus is Birdie right now. It's just the two of us and it's... complicated."

I nod. "Yeah, of course." But as I say it, I take note of the way Everly's gaze rakes over my chest and down to my board shorts, appreciation in her eyes.

"Birdie, time to go!" she calls, bending to gather their blanket and shake the sand off of it. I watch her, wishing there was something I could say to change her mind. But I know I don't stand a chance.

Everly is the first girl I've felt a spark with since Jade. I'm hooked and she's not interested. *Fuck my life.*

"See you around, Everly."

"See you around."

Birdie appears beside us, and Everly wraps a towel around her shoulders and then picks up her bag. She gives me a little wave and I watch as the two of them walk to the road, trying to ignore the feeling that I just missed out on something good.

THREE

YOU CAN'T MISS THE OBVIOUS BULGE

Everly

Six hours after falling into bed after my night shift at the restaurant, I wake to the sound of my alarm clock blaring from my bedside table. I groan and force myself to get up, my legs still sore from being on my feet serving tables all night.

I'm exhausted, but six hours will have to do. I need to get Birdie up and fed so she isn't late for school.

I pad down the hall to her room. The house is quiet, Birdie still sound asleep, and as I quietly push her bedroom door open, my heart sighs when I look at her perfect little sleeping face.

She looks even younger when she's asleep, so tiny and innocent. My heart aches. I wish she didn't have to go through any of this. I wish I didn't have to uproot her from the life she knew, from her home and her friends and the routine that felt safe and familiar. I feel a rush of anger at my ex for making it impossible to stay with him. He made it impossible for us to be a family.

I am partly to blame for the way our marriage imploded. I was a fool for believing Grant loved me when he had been upfront with me from the very first day we met. He told me he wasn't looking for anything serious, that he didn't "do" relationships. But to me, it always felt like more. It felt like the kind of whirlwind romance you read about. Grant called and texted me all day, every day. He took me on dates to nice restaurants, introduced me to his friends. We slept at each other's apartments almost every night. We even cuddled after sex. It felt like we were in a serious relationship, but as I was falling hard for him, he was falling hard for half of Brookmont. Behind my back.

I was young, and maybe I was just being naïve. I overlooked his character because I was enamoured with his charm. My friends were all in happy, committed relationships, and I was happy to have someone who paid attention to me, who showed interest. Grant had made me feel less alone.

He was handsome and smart and came from a wealthy family. Everyone in Brookmont knew the Billings, for better or for worse.

His parents seemed to like me well enough until they found out I was pregnant. As soon as that news broke, they told him to drop me. They were convinced I got pregnant on purpose to trap Grant. In their words, "A girl like that only wants one thing with a guy like you. Money."

To Grant's credit, he defended me at first, but his family's accusations cut deep. I could get over being called a gold digger, but I couldn't understand how they could so easily just toss their own grandchild aside. They quickly decided I wasn't good for Grant, and over time he seemed to agree. At the very least, I wasn't *enough* for him. He thought he could have his cake and eat it too—me waiting for him when he came home, and whoever else he wanted when he went out. It went on like that for years. Finally, I stopped trying and accepted the fact that he didn't want me. When I suggested a divorce, he didn't argue. I stayed at the house for a long time— too long probably—to make the transition easier on Birdie.

Just thinking about that ugly time in my life makes me feel sick. And now here I am, a single mom struggling to build a new life. All because my husband couldn't keep his dick in his pants.

Just then, Birdie's wide eyes slowly flutter open, and the anger that had started to take hold of me melts away. It's moments like these that my nerves are a little less frazzled and my soul feels a little more at peace. I sit on the edge of Birdie's bed and gently smooth her blonde curls from her forehead.

I take in her long, dark eyelashes, her button nose, cherub lips, the freckles on both of her cheeks. I press my palm to the side of her face, running my thumb softly over her jaw.

My baby.

My whole world.

We have a new life ahead of us. For the first time in a long time, I am in control of what happens next.

"Good morning, Mommy." Birdie rolls to her back, stretching her arms over her head.

"Good morning, my angel. How did you sleep?"

She sits up slowly, reaching for her stuffed cat. "I dreamt about a castle and a princess. It was perfect. Did you dream about a princess too?"

My heart swells. "No baby, but I dreamt about the sweetest seven-year-old blondie on the planet who loves cats, swimming, and Amelia Bedelia books. Do you have any idea who that could be?"

Birdie squeals. "Me! You dreamt about me!"

"Every night, baby." I lean down and kiss the tip of her nose. "Now it's time to get up. You have school and I have errands to run."

"Maybe I could go with you instead? I bet there's nothing important happening at school today." She flashes me an exaggerated smile and bats her eyelashes, proving she could be an award-winning actress one day if she wanted. I enrolled her in summer school so she could meet friends before the school year began.

I tickle her under her chin. "No can do, pretty-girl. You are going to school. But if you're good, I might take you for a treat tonight after dinner."

Cutie-pop that she is, Birdie smiles her brightest smile, waving her hands in the air. "I'm gonna be so good, Mommy. I promise you."

My beautiful little Birdie.

I kiss her nose for the second time then remind myself we need to get moving. I have to get Birdie dressed, fed, hair done, shoes on and out the door. I've wasted enough time this morning thinking about the man who should be here with us instead of where he is, waking up in another woman's bed. Instead of dwelling on what I've lost, I choose to be grateful for what I have: my daughter. She's the only thing that matters.

Once I've dropped Birdie off at school, I make a stop at the grocery store to get a few things for the week, including some ground beef for tonight's tacos.

The afternoon passes quickly as it always does. I put away the groceries, do a load of laundry, unpack a few more boxes. I find a wedding photo of Grant and me tucked away in one of them and resist the urge to toss it in the trash. Whatever I might think of Grant, he's Birdie's father.

Later that night, after Birdie and I have cooked and eaten and tidied up, she reminds me about the treat I promised her this morning. We jump in the car and drive the three minutes to Birdie's favorite ice cream shop. She picks bubble gum in a waffle cone, just like she always does.

"That was the best ice cream in the world!" Birdie practically sings as I wipe the pastel pink remnants from her face and her hands. "Can I look at all the other flavors so I can choose one for next time?"

It's a school night and I should get her home, but instead of fighting her on it, I nod my head then watch her skip over to the counter and hop onto the bench so she's able to see the different flavors. I relax back into my chair with an exhale, tired from a couple of night shifts at the restaurant this week and the early morning wakeups with Birdie.

I can't remember a time I've ever been this tired, or my body ached this much. I was working as an assistant in a real estate company and going to college part-time studying communications when I met Grant. After I had Birdie, Grant asked me to quit my job. His family thought it was important he had a wife who stayed home, had dinner on the table, volunteered for whatever causes interested them at the moment. I knew I would miss my job, but I did what was asked of me. I didn't want to give them another excuse to dislike me. Besides, I didn't know how I could argue the point when I was living in a 6,000-square-foot home in a gated community, complete with a housekeeper and gardeners. Grant and I didn't need the second income.

We had it all. But apparently having it all wasn't enough for my husband. And Grant always got what Grant wanted.

The first time I came home and found him with another

woman in our bed, I was devastated. The second time, I was angry. After the third time, I felt numb. Ten years of broken promises and regrets, but I'd never regret the gift of my daughter.

I watch Birdie over the rim of my coffee cup, noticing yet again how much she looks like Grant. The resemblance isn't just physical. Birdie is confident. She's smart. She's funny.

A few minutes later, as Birdie continues her thorough investigation of every single flavor, I startle when I hear someone call my name.

I look up and see him.

Jake.

The guy from the beach.

The guy from the beach who is incredibly cute, sweet, and has a smile that can make you forget your own name. He frowns so perfectly too.

My God, he is handsome.

Jake is hot in a broody, rugged way. His hair is styled so it looks like he tried, but still messy enough that it doesn't look like he tried *too* hard.

Every angle of his face is chiselled—a sharp jaw covered in scruff, angled cheekbones, the perfect curve of his nose. The one exception is his lips—they look soft, and I find myself wondering what they would feel like on mine.

His piercing intense eyes are flecked with green the color of emeralds, and he looks at me with that gaze that seems to cage me in, and he'd kiss me fiercely, like he could never get enough.

Every muscle in Jake's body is perfected. He's well over 6 feet tall and lean, with broad shoulders. He's built like an athlete—even with his shirt on I can tell that his abs are cut with grooves and valleys, his arms corded and pecs just big enough that they stretch his T-shirt perfectly.

I doubt he looks that way by sitting at a desk wearing a suit all day. Or being the heir to his daddy's fortune. Jake is built like he works hard. Like he isn't afraid to get his hands dirty. I only wonder if he has a dirty mouth too.

He looks like he would. He seems cocky, in a good way. I bet he has a lot more experience than me. I've only been with one guy since I was 23 years old and let's just say the sex was underwhelming. I bet it wouldn't be with Jake. It's too bad I will never find out. A relationship is the last thing I need right now. And even if I was looking for someone, I get the feeling Jake is a lot younger than me. I doubt he's looking to get tangled up with a single mom and her kid.

I smile at Jake, realizing I've been staring.

"We need to stop running into each other. It's becoming a habit," Jake says with a grin as he approaches my table. I feel a blush creep up my cheeks. It's been a long time since I've talked to a guy like him, I'm out of practise. I grab Birdie's sweater from the table and hold the fabric against my chest as if it's a shield.

"A coincidence," I correct him, then accidentally drop the sweater to the floor. Before I can bend down to grab it, Jake scoops it up and hands it to me. A wash of goosebumps marks my skin when his hand touches mine.

I breathe hard, taking another look at him. Jake is wearing a pair of dark navy basketball shorts, white crew cut socks and Nike runners with a long sleeve Queens College T-shirt. He has the sleeves pushed half-way up his forearms. He looks fit, and young. I would guess he's still in his twenties.

Still, I like his look ... very much. The basketball shorts leave little to the imagination. There is no way they can hide what he has underneath them. You can't miss the obvious bulge.

Jake grins again and continues looking at me with his piercing brown-green eyes. Those damn eyes. Can he tell how much his stare is getting to me? My skin heats. It's *a lot* to have someone who looks like Jake hold your gaze a little too long.

"Maybe," he shrugs, shoving his hands in the pockets of his athletic shorts. My gaze drops down, following the motion, drawn to his forearm and the vein that runs the length of it. I tear my eyes away, meeting his.

"What are you doing here? I mean... sorry, that came out wrong. Let's start again." I laugh nervously. *What the hell is wrong with me?*

"Coffee," he says, nodding at the big espresso machine behind the counter. "I was just grabbing one to go."

"Right. That makes sense." I press my fingers into my temple and shake my head, shooting him a small, apologetic smile. "I'm sorry. I'm just tired. It's been a long week."

"Don't be sorry. You seem to have a lot on your hands. It can't be easy." He scrubs the back of his neck. "I know you said your focus is on your daughter, and I absolutely get it. But maybe a night out would be fun. The offer still stands."

"Jake," I sigh. "I don't have time for fun."

But when Jake smirks and his eyes darken, I feel my resolve weaken.

Green eyes burn into mine.

I give myself a silent lecture. *Birdie is your focus.*

My eyes drop to his mouth. I wonder what it would feel like to kiss him. *What is wrong with me?*

Get your things, Everly.

Learn from your mistakes.

Get Birdie and go.

But I stay where I am, not even the slightest movement.

Just then I feel a tug at my sleeve and look beside me to find my daughter's big eyes staring back at me.

"Is that your friend from the beach, Mommy?"

Birdie. She's looking up at Jake, curiosity written all over her face.

Shit. This is bad.

FOUR

ARE YOU EVEN THIRTY?

Jake

What are the chances?

For the third time in less than three weeks, Everly and I have ended up in the same place at the same time.

I don't know if I believe in fate, but I can't help but think that every planet and all the stars aligned for Everly and Birdie to be here tonight, and for me to end up in an ice cream shop, of all places.

I worked late at a job site today, spending an extra couple of hours finishing the moldings on a staircase. The contracting company I own has never been busier, so I've been working long hours. I was way too tired to cook dinner, so I stopped at Sushi Box on the way home. On the way back to the car, I passed the ice cream place and decided to pop in to grab a coffee.

I saw Birdie first at the counter. I immediately searched the room until my eyes landed on the woman who has been invading every one of my dreams lately. You can't miss her, not a woman that looks like that.

I am so fucking attracted to her; it almost doesn't make sense.

Everly's eyes go wide when she looks up and spots me and I don't miss the way her cheeks pinken.

"We need to stop running into each other. It's becoming a habit." She seems puzzled for a second before a small smile tips the corners of her lips.

Her long honey-brown hair is pulled back in a ponytail, showing off her pretty face. She's wearing an oversized sweatshirt that ends halfway down her thighs and a pair of black bike shorts. Her legs are bronze from the sun. She's petite, no taller than five-foot-three. I spot the sparrow pendant around her neck.

"A coincidence," she answers. *She isn't going to make this easy.*

Her citrus scent envelops me, and a memory of our time at the beach flashes through my mind. Since that day, I've thought about her sweet scent way more than could possibly be considered normal. I've thought about how she made me feel, desperate to get to know her and also filled with desire.

No one has ever made me feel like that. *Ever.* I didn't think it was possible. But the way my pulse is racing is proving me wrong.

I'm breathing in that fucking scent, acutely aware of how close I am to her when, suddenly, her daughter is at her side, her eyes bright and full of excitement.

"Is this your friend from the beach, Mommy?" Her little voice is so damn cute as she looks up at me, eyes wide.

"He was just stopping in for coffee, baby," Everly says, ruffling her daughter's hair before looking at me with uncertainty. "You've got five more minutes then we need to get you home."

Everly busies herself with tidying her table. She wipes a drop of ice cream from the tabletop, then crumples the napkin and tosses it into her empty cup.

"Do I have to go to sleep when I get home?" Birdie asks, resting her head against Everly's shoulder.

"Straight to bed. It will be well past your bedtime."

I stand beside them, disappearing into the background like wallpaper as I listen to them chat.

"Fine," Birdie says with a pout, then looks from her mom to me. "But *is* he our new friend? Should he come to our house on the weekend and have dinner? And Franny too?"

Everly's eyes fly to her daughter, sending her a warning glare to mind her manners. "We're busy this weekend."

"Are we going to Gramma and Grandpa's?" Birdie asks.

Everly nods, sweeping her hand over her daughter's curls. "They're excited to see you."

That seems to be a good enough answer for Birdie. She adjusts the cat ears on her head, then turns her attention back to me. "Do you like my cat ears? I wear them every single day. Cats are my favorite animal, but mom says I can't have one because they take work."

I crouch down so I can look Birdie in the eye. "Those are the coolest cat ears I've ever seen. And your mom is right. Cats do take a lot of work," I say, looking up at Everly, who's watching me with a look of surprise on her face.

"But they can catch mice and Mommy is really scared of mice. I told her if we got a cat, she would never have to be scared again."

Everly is looking at her daughter as if she hung the moon and the stars. We share a small smile before my eyes are back on Birdie. "Do you know what else they can do?"

"What?" she asks.

"They can jump up to six times their length."

Birdie's mouth falls open, and then she gasps. "Wow."

Everly arches a brow at her daughter, then at me, then shakes her head with a soft smile. "Birdie, your five minutes is almost up. Time is ticking."

My family is small and neither my sister nor me nor many of my friends are parents yet. Honestly, I've just never really been into kids. They always seem to be talking or crying or yelling. But Birdie? She is the cutest thing I've ever seen and, surprisingly, not a deal breaker for me.

Especially with a mom like Everly.

Do I really want to see where this could go?

It sure as fuck feels that way.

"Was that okay?" I ask quietly, standing as Birdie skips away.

"It's fine. But look, being friends with my daughter isn't going to get you anywhere with me. I already told you that she is my focus right now. I need you to know that."

"I was just trying to be nice. I'm a nice guy, Everly. You would see that if you got to know me."

Everly inhales and drops her gaze to the floor. "Jake," she whispers. "I barely have time to wash my face these days. And I have a pretty good feeling you're a lot younger than me—"

"I don't care."

"How old are you? Are you even 30?"

"No."

She snorts at that. *Fuck. She thinks I'm a kid.* "My God, Jake. You are *young*. You should be out having fun, not hanging out with a girl with a child. Frankly, we just don't make any sense."

"I disagree." I stare back at her, chewing the inside of my cheek, and decide that as much as I want to push her, I won't. "Fine, then what about friends? Can we at least do that?"

She folds her arms across her chest. "So how old are you? For real, I want the truth."

"Does it matter?"

"It does to me."

"Fine. I'm 27."

She shakes her head and blows out a breath. "You are too young. I'm seven years older than you, Jake. And like I said before... my life is complicated. I'm not sure how good of a friend I can be."

I couldn't care less about Everly's age. Am I surprised? Fuck, yes. She looks at least eight years younger. But the fact that she's older is nothing but hot to me. Especially since she looks like *that*, and my attraction to her is so strong.

"I'm busy too, Everly. I'm fine with an occasional, friendly text. Maybe a cup of coffee here and there. Yeah?"

If I don't get her number tonight it might kill me.

She inhales a deep breath before quickly glancing at Birdie, who is back at the ice cream counter. Then her eyes are back on me. "My pace?" she clarifies in a quiet voice.

"To start." I smile. "Hopefully I work my way up to a real date one day. But no pressure. Give me your phone."

She chews her bottom lip as she studies my face, and it's fucking cute. "Why do you want my phone?"

"I'm sending you a *friendly* text."

"Fine." She digs her phone out of her purse, unlocks it and hands it over to me, watching me with her eyebrows pulled together.

I nod. *Friends*. It's certainly not what I actually have in mind, but I'm hoping with some time I can change Everly's mind.

When I've finished adding myself to her contacts, I hand

the device back to her and then send her a quick message from my phone. Her phone chimes in her hand.

"I'm not sure how you got me to say yes to this," she says, shaking her head as Birdie skips over to us and grabs Everly's hand.

"Maybe we'll see you again," Birdie says to me. "Maybe we can have ice cream next week."

Everly clears her throat. "Okay, Birdie. Time to go."

As Everly and Birdie head for the door, I can't stop the smile that spreads over my face. I'm not exactly sure what I want to happen next, but I do know I want more time with her. Maybe if I'm lucky she'll give me the chance.

"Bye, Everly. Bye, Birdie." I raise my hand in a wave.

Everly pulls the door open, then stops and looks at me over her shoulder. "Bye, Jake."

I follow them outside, watching as Everly puts her arm around Birdie's shoulders and they walk down the street to her car. They turn the corner and are gone.

Adrenaline pumps through my veins. I tell myself to keep my hopes in check, but I can't help but feel excited.

After all, I got her number.

This isn't over yet.

FIVE

ALL NIGHT SEX FESTS

E verly
As I pour myself a glass of wine, I wonder what the hell I just got myself into. Was it a mistake, agreeing to this *friendship* with Jake? Honestly, I'm not sure.

He wore me down. The truth is, he caught me when I wasn't quite thinking straight. Watching him be so sweet with Birdie, it caught me off guard.

He didn't seem at all nervous to talk to her, which surprised me. He's a single guy in his twenties, I assume he doesn't spend much time around children. Flirting with hot girls and taking them back to his place for all-night sex fests, sure. Swapping cat facts with a 7-year-old? Now *that* I didn't see coming. But I have to give Jake credit—he definitely made an impression on Birdie. She couldn't stop talking about him the entire car ride home.

Watching a gorgeous guy like Jake be so adorable with my daughter seemed to immediately melt whatever resistance I had built up to letting him in my life, even if it's just as a friend. I'm beginning to think I have Jake pegged all wrong. Maybe he isn't some young, hot, immature player.

He isn't my ex and watching him with Birdie proved that. It was kind of hot watching him with her. *Damn Jake Matthews for being so sweet.*

But it doesn't matter. Birdie gets attached to people, and I can't have her heart broken when he stops coming around. Sure, it was only an unplanned run-in, but 10 minutes is all my daughter needs to form a bond with someone. Aside from that, I also don't need the stress and total mind fuck that comes along with dating. I've been down that road before and it left me broken. The overwhelming feeling of rejection is still fresh in my mind. So, for now I need to keep our circle small. I have enough on my plate without the distraction of a relationship that will only lead to disappointment in the end.

Leaving Brookmont after building a life there—going to college, getting married and having Birdie—has been the biggest and hardest decision I've ever made. It's one that I never saw coming.

Prior to that, Grant had announced that he was relocating to North Carolina for work. For an entire year. When I got upset and told him I was worried how it would affect Birdie, he grumbled that she'd get over it. Then he told me I needed to get over it too. That was finally it for me, the last straw. I began looking for apartments in Reed Point the next day.

Even after our split, I stayed living in the house with Grant. I divorced my husband, but I never moved out. Instead, I moved to another wing, so I didn't have to see him. It was the last place I wanted to be, but my only focus was Birdie. It was hard enough that her parents were breaking up, I wanted there to be as little disruption to her life as possible. And I didn't want her relationship with her dad to suffer.

But here was Grant, moving four states away without even a discussion. Without a second thought about our daughter.

That's when I decided to finally take my mom's advice and move back to Reed Point. Grant said he didn't care what I did when he was gone, so I put the move in motion. I found the little apartment, enrolled Birdie in summer school to keep her busy, got a job. We were finally getting settled when Grant called a couple of months later and told me his plans had changed and he was returning to Brookmont early. He didn't offer any more explanation than that, but of course he expected Birdie and I to come running back too. I tried to explain that it wasn't that easy—I signed a one-year lease, and Birdie had made new friends and was excited about school. When Grant realized that I wasn't going to come back just because he told me to, he cut me off financially before I had even gotten the last box unpacked. That didn't shock me. He could throw a fit bigger than Birdie. As it turns out, there's nothing he wants more than the thing he can't have. It's been *years* since he has shown either Birdie or me this much attention.

Grant rarely showed any interest in our daughter when we were a family. He regularly skipped dance recitals for late night meetings at the office and traded bedtime stories for drinks at the country club, but all of a sudden, he seems to have remembered that he's a father.

At first it was text messages asking us to come home, trying to persuade me to return to Brookmont. When that didn't work, the pleading turned to outrage. He left voicemail after voicemail demanding that I terminate my lease and accused me of having a boyfriend. I didn't, but the fact that he could bring that up after all his years of cheating and all of the countless women he's hooked up with since our split blew my mind. He threatened to sue me for full custody of Birdie and warned me that he'd spend every cent he has to force me to come back home.

Home? What home? I didn't have one.

Eventually, I will go back to Brookmont, but for now I need space.

I take my wine to my couch and sit with my feet tucked underneath me, looking around the tiny apartment that I rented sight unseen. It's not perfect, but it's the nicest space I could find on short notice.

The living room has a big window that looks out on the park across the street, with a playground that Birdie loves. A coffee table sits in front of the couch, piled with my romance books and a vase of flowers that makes the room look a little more lived in. The walls are a pale grey, and I've hung a few of my favorite photos of Birdie. The kitchen is small, but clean. There's a dishwasher, a small pantry, and white cabinets with only a few noticeable nicks and scratches. It's homey, and comfortable. Mostly, I love it because it is ours.

Settling back into the worn couch cushions, I pick up my phone to check the time and notice an unread text from Jake.

My stupid heart skips. *Don't be silly*, I tell myself. I don't even know him. But I swipe the phone to life so fast you would think it caught fire.

> Jake: Just a friendly text. Don't go overthinking this. :) It was good to see you tonight.

I read the message at least 20 more times, not sure how to respond. I need to be careful he doesn't get the wrong idea. Friends is all we can be and even that feels reckless. So,

I like the text and close out the screen before I'm tempted to write something back.

I'm sure Jake is a great guy, but I'm not about to put my heart, or Birdie's, on the line to find out.

JAKE

I follow Grayson, Holden, Tucker, and our buddy Beckett to a booth in the corner of our favorite Mexican restaurant, Cocina Caliente. We're all wiped after a killer ride today, not to mention starving. The conditions were perfect for a downhill banger, and we spent longer on the trails than we had planned. If I had my way, I'd be out riding every day, but with Gran's move coming up this weekend and being down a few guys at work, I've been busy.

We all slide into the booth, which feels way too fucking small for five big dudes. Our waitress stops by our table, and we immediately put in our orders: tacos and burritos all around, and Tuck orders an extra side of tamales because the man is a human garbage disposal. It's gross.

"Stop rubbing your thigh against mine, Gray, you're not my type," Tucker grumbles, trying to take up more space in the packed booth.

"You wish, buddy," Gray says. "You want a thigh rub, I think Holden's your guy. Right, Holdey?"

"You're a fucking idiot," Holden groans.

"An idiot who's starving. I worked up an appetite out there." Grayson rubs his stomach. "I was feeling good on the bike today. Grandpa Jake, on the other hand, was slowing us down. Hell, I saw a 10-year-old peddling harder than Matthews."

"Fuck off," I grumble.

"What's with your grumpy ass today?" Grayson asks, struggling to take off his jacket.

"Your face," I grumble.

Holden cracks up. "That the best you can come up with? You seem hangry, Jakey. Do you want me to ask the waitress to bring you a little snack plate? Maybe a glass of warm milk?"

"Would you guys fuck off already? Shit."

Thankfully, our waitress doesn't take long. She's soon back with our orders, and we all dig in as soon as she sets the plates down on the table.

Beckett looks at me in between bites. "Seriously, man, is everything okay? You seem stressed. Tacos with the boys is not the place for mopers."

"I'm fine," I reply.

"You're not acting like it," Grayson chimes in. "You've barely said 10 words all day and you've had your face in that fucking phone. Does this have something to do with the girl at the beach? Whatever happened with that? Did you make a move?"

I inhale a long, hard breath. It's been four days since I ran into Everly and Birdie at the ice cream place, and I haven't heard from her since. I sent her a text, which she didn't respond to—a *like* doesn't count in my books, that's code for, "I don't want to talk to you, but I'm being polite about it." It feels like Everly is making it crystal clear that she is not interested in even a friendship with me.

"Yeah, we talked. Then I ran into her a few days ago, and she shut me down. She has a kid. She told me she needs to focus on her."

"Woah, Daddy Jake" Tucker says, shoving a tamale in his mouth. "I didn't see that one coming."

"You can take it easy with the Daddy stuff," I say, holding my hands up. "I've talked to her twice."

I consider telling them that Everly is several years older than me but decide against it. I can imagine what the guys would have to say about that. It doesn't matter to me anyways. I don't give a shit that she's older. I just really wish she would get in touch. Maybe I blew it. Maybe I'll never hear from her. It's fucking messing with my mind.

"I'll tell you what I think you should do," Tucker says, leaning over the table.

"Oh, hell no," Holden interrupts. "Literally nobody should take dating advice from *you*."

"Hear me out," Tuck says, wiping his hands with a napkin. "You know where she works, yeah? So, you go in for dinner, make sure you're sitting in her section and when you leave, you give her a big, fat tip and leave her a note."

I raise my eyebrows. "Okay, Tuck. Humor me... what should I write in this note?"

"I can't wait to hear this," Holden laughs, tapping his hands against the table like a drumroll. "Let's go."

"It's simple, dummies. You tell her you can't stop thinking about her, and then you ask her out on a date."

"So, are there boxes on this note? Is she supposed to check yes or no like she's a fucking middle schooler?" Holden asks. "Man, girls our age do not want *notes*. They want you to tell them every filthy way you can make them come. You are the wrong person to be giving our boy advice."

"Don't be so sure about that," Tuck says, dipping his tamale in hot sauce. "I bet I get more ass than any of you."

"Well, you're definitely getting more ass than Matthews, I'll give you that. We all are. Hell, I bet *that guy* is," Grayson says, nodding at a man across the room who looks to be around 80 years old.

"Why do you gotta be a dick?" I grumble. "Can I just eat in peace? I'm starving."

"What's going on with you and Aubrey?" Beckett asks Holden, and I'm happy about the change of topic. Holden has been dating Aubrey for months now, which is kind of surprising. In all the years I've known him, this is the first time I've seen him be serious about a girl. Aubrey seems nice enough, but if you ask me, she's not as into the relationship as Holden is. I get the feeling she's in it for a good time, not necessarily a long time. But Holden seems happy with her, so what do I know?

"We're solid," he tells Beckett. "Aubrey is great."

"Sounds like you're falling in love," Grayson says, taking a sip of his Coke.

I hold back a laugh. Grayson wouldn't know a damn thing about falling in love. Not that I should talk. None of us have much experience with relationships. Of the five of us sitting at this table, only Beckett seems to have figured it out —he married his wife Jules last year and couldn't be happier.

As for me, my only real relationship was with a girl named Jade. We were together for two years before she dumped me and moved to a different country. So yeah, not exactly an expert when it comes to love.

"Calm the fuck down," Holden protests. "No one is falling in love. She's a cool chick. We're taking things slow."

"Bullshit. You've practically moved in with her," Tucker says. "I think you've slept at the house maybe once in the last three weeks. Whether you're ready to admit it or not, you're fucking whipped over the girl."

Tuck would know. He and Holden have been roommates

for years, living in a place on Haven Harbor next door to my Gran's house. Out of all of us, the two of them are the closest, probably because they are the most alike. You wouldn't know it by looking at them—Holden is a pretty-boy, all-American type, while Tucker has an edgier look with his tattoos and longer hair. But they're both always up for a good time, they're both baseball fanatics and they both like to play the field. Literally and figuratively.

"I like living with her more than I like living with your ass, that's all," Holden deadpans, tossing his napkin on his empty plate. "She's not a slob."

Tuck shrugs. "Sure, buddy. If that's what you need to tell yourself."

We pay our bills and head outside, and I take the opportunity to check my phone again, hoping there might be a text from Everly. There's not. It's driving me crazy that we haven't talked. Do I send her another message? I don't want to push her or come off like some crazy stalker, but at the same time I need her to know I'm interested.

Before I can talk myself out of it, I fire off another text to the girl I haven't been able to stop thinking about. Suddenly, Tuck appears beside me, looking over my shoulder.

"Ever hear of fucking privacy?" I ask, trying to shield my phone from him.

"Everly," he coos. "Is that her? Beach girl?"

"Would you mind your own business?" I tell him, tucking my phone back in my pocket.

"It *is* beach girl! You making plans with her? Is that why your grumpy ass was in such a rush to get out of here?"

"I'm not fucking grumpy. And it's none of your business. Leave it."

"Wait. I thought you said she turned you down?"

"She did." I clear my throat. "But I convinced her we could be friends."

I can tell by the look on Tucker's face that he's loving it. His eyes widen and his mouth forms the shape of an "O." Then the fucker laughs. "Friends? Oh, shit."

"Yup, something like that."

SIX

NEATLY INTO THE FRIENDS ZONE

Everly

"My love bug!" my mom exclaims, greeting Birdie and me at her door. "I'm so excited to see you."

"I'm excited to see you too, Gramma," Birdie says, skipping into my parents' modest, split-level home. "Where's Grandpa?"

"He's in the kitchen, baby," my mom tells her. "He's been waiting for you." I step inside and wrap my arms around my mom. "It's so good to see you, Everly," she whispers into my hair. "You look good."

"Thanks, Mom." I pull back from her embrace, taking in her slender frame. "So do you."

Her thick hair is cut short in a tight bob at her shoulders, her hazel eyes crinkled at the corners. My mom is the polar opposite of my former mother-in-law, Miranda. Grant's mom is cold, manipulative, and always focused on climbing the social ladder. My mom, on the other hand, is warm, kind and one of the most supportive people I know.

I've been trying to make a point of seeing my parents often since Birdie and I moved to Reed Point. When we lived in Brookmont, we made the trip out to visit them a couple of times a year at best, and I know it broke my mom's heart that she saw so little of us. It was always an argument between Grant and I, but his calendar was usually packed, and he didn't like the thought of Birdie and I making the drive on our own. Whenever I did plan a trip to see my parents, it seemed like a dinner party or black-tie event would come up at the last minute. Grant enjoyed these events far more than I did, but me being the good wife, I went along with it.

My mom gently squeezes my arms, pulling me from my memories. "How's my baby?" she asks, concern on her face.

I inhale a deep breath and decide how much I want to tell her. Truthfully, some days it's overwhelming, but I'm also happier than I have been in a long time. It has been a dream of mine to be able to share weekly dinners with Birdie and my parents, to watch my mom teach Birdie how to garden in her backyard. I know that moving here was the right thing to do, but some days it's been really hard. I'm exhausted, in every possible way.

"As good as I can be, I guess," I say.

"I'm worried about you, sweetheart. I don't know how you're juggling it all. Why won't you let your dad and I help you more? You know we are happy to."

Even though she knows I would never ask, I tell her what she wants to hear. "I will, Mom, if it gets too much. I promise."

The reality is that I need to prove to myself that I can do this all on my own. I can support Birdie and myself without my ex's money. No matter how tired or stressed I am, I'd still rather be working at Catch 21 and living here than be back in Grant's mansion in Brookmont.

"Come here," my mom says, reaching an arm around my

shoulder. "I made your favorite soup. Let's go sit down at the table."

She steers me into the kitchen, where Birdie is already sitting on my dad's lap playing a game on his iPad. My heart swells at the sight. Real. Pure. Love. With no strings. This is what I've always wanted for Birdie.

"Those two and their games," my mom says, looking fondly at them.

"There's my girl," my dad says, looking up from the iPad as I round the table and give him a kiss on his cheek. "I'd get up to hug you, but Birdie and I are a little busy here."

"Yeah, I can see that," I say, ruffling Birdie's curls.

"She's been telling me some very interesting stories," he says, giving me a knowing look over the rim of his glasses.

"Oh? What did you hear?" I take off my sweater and hang it on the back of my chair. It must be 85 degrees in here and the fan in the corner is doing absolutely nothing. I sit down, feeling immediately at home in the old kitchen. Not much has changed since I left for college. The cabinets are still a heavy oak with exposed hinge hardware and the walls are sponge painted a mottled beige.

"We can talk about it later," he says with a wink.

I cock my head at him, trying to figure out what on earth he's talking about. And then it dawns on me that Birdie has probably told him all about her new friend, Jake. My girl loves to tell stories.

I think back to the text message Jake sent me today. The one I still haven't returned. The text was innocent enough, falling neatly into the friend zone. *How was your week? Mine was a doozy so I hope yours was better.* I feel bad for letting another text from Jake go without a response, but in my defense, I read it while I was at the park with Birdie. That was a few hours ago, though, and I have no good excuse now for leaving him on read.

I shove the guilty feeling down, turning my attention back to my family. My mom asks Birdie if she can go check on the lettuce in the garden out back for her, and my daughter is off her chair and racing out the door in a split second.

"I think that was a yes," my mom says with a laugh. Birdie loves spending time in the garden at my parents' place, it's one of the reasons she is always wanting to come visit.

My dad leans forward on the table, that curious expression still on his face. "So, Birdie tells me you two made a new friend by the name of Jake." He gives me a look that I've seen a million times before. The one that says, *You better know what you're doing.*

I hold up my hands. "Whatever you're thinking, it's not that," I tell him. "We just met Jake. You know Birdie; she knows someone for five seconds and suddenly they're her new best friend."

"That is true, but she made it sound like there's something going on with the two of you. I don't want to stick my nose in your business, honey, but you know this will make things even more difficult between you and Grant. I doubt very much he would be okay with you dating."

I sigh. "I get that, Dad, I do, but there's nothing going on with me and Jake," I say again, a feeling of frustration building inside of me. "But let's say there was... am I supposed to allow Grant Billings to run my life forever? He and I are not together anymore. Don't get me wrong— I'm not looking to date anyone right now, but I *am* done with my life revolving around Grant."

My dad nods sympathetically. "Just be smart about

things. I know you will be. If you do end up falling for this guy and he's good to our Birdie, I'm not trying to talk you out of it. You deserve a second chance."

"Yes, honey. Grant cannot be allowed to take your happiness from you. He has already taken too much," my mom adds, placing her hand over mine.

I'm reminded of all the ways Grant pushed me to the point of breaking, until I felt like I was dying inside. I did everything he asked of me, and it still wasn't good enough. There was virtually nothing I could have done to stop him from sticking his dick inside of every beautiful woman who threw herself at him.

I'd met Grant at a mutual friend's birthday party. We spent most of the evening talking and laughing, and when he offered to drive me home at the end of the night, I let him. When he asked if he could see me again, I said yes, even though he told me he wasn't looking for anything serious. Pretty soon I was spending most of my free time with him. As far as I knew, we were in a committed relationship.

Eight months after we started seeing each other, I found out I was pregnant.

"Your mother is right, sweetheart." My dad brings me back to the present. "Do what makes you happy. Just be careful with Birdie's heart. She gets attached easily."

Ever since I ran into Jake in the ice cream shop, he's been all I can think about. I imagine his eyes—those eyes a dozen different hues of green—and his smile, especially when he smirks. Physically, I'm very attracted to him, but more than that, I love talking to him. Just being around him feels... intoxicating.

But my mom is right. I can't let Birdie get close to Jake, only for her to be heartbroken down the road when he decides he doesn't want to be in our lives. I have enough to deal with as it is. Jake Matthews is a distraction I can't afford right now.

Two hours later, after a delicious dinner and a second helping of my mom's homemade apple pie, it's time to leave. As I slide into the driver's seat, I feel my phone buzz in my pocket and my mind immediately returns to Jake. But when I pull my phone out and swipe the screen, I find a message from the last person on earth I want to talk to.

> Grant: You've had your fun, now bring Birdie back home. I'm tired of this bs.

I ignore the text, my jaw clenched so tight that I feel a headache coming on instantly. You would think I'd be better by now at not letting his rage texts get under my skin. But I'm not. Lowering myself into the car, I rest my head against the leather seat while tears prick at my eyes. Easing out of the driveway, I roll down my window and turn the music up in the car as a distraction. A warm, summer breeze hits my face as I drive, and I breathe in the scent of lilacs and linden trees as I try to calm the urge to scream.

Once we are back at our apartment, I park the car and try to put on a happy face for Birdie, but for the rest of the night I'm lost in my own thoughts. I'm happy here in Reed Point where the memories of my marriage aren't constantly haunting me. But it's *a lot*. Grant, his mom, paying the rent on this tiny apartment, making a home for us, my job, Birdie. It all feels like an impossible balancing act, and I am just so exhausted. The alternative is I could move back to Brookmont, but the thought makes my stomach twist.

Maybe I just need to take a break from it all, just for a day. Do something fun. I think back to the texts that are waiting for me from Jake. Maybe he's the fun I need.

. . .

JAKE

It's Thursday afternoon, and I'm back on a job site installing hardwood flooring, my T-shirt soaked with sweat. The good news is that we're back to a full crew tomorrow, which means I can get back to the office instead of breaking my back on my hands and knees. I'd forgotten how demanding this work is, and I had underestimated how exhausted I would be after a few weeks of it. The bad news? I'm in a shit mood.

Halsey pumps through the speaker of my site super's phone while he installs a bathroom vanity. The song, *Bad At Love*, is about falling hard and fast for someone, and although I'm not at the point where I'm falling for Everly, the song still annoys the shit out of me. I haven't heard a word from her. She's obviously not interested. She made that painfully clear when she didn't return the second text I sent to her. I need to forget about her and move on.

Unfortunately, I can't get her out of my head. I obsess over our conversations, thinking about what I could have done or said differently. I sit in traffic and wonder what she and Birdie are doing. I close my eyes at night and picture Everly. This isn't like me. The only time I felt anything close to this was with the one girl who ended up breaking my heart.

I know what it feels like to be in love. I was with my ex, Jade, for two years. Jade is beautiful—ice-blue eyes, dark brown hair. More than that, she got me. She had lost a parent too. When she was nine, her mother died in a car accident. She was driving home from a work function when a drunk driver swerved into oncoming traffic. Jade was the first person I met who had suffered a loss like I had, and I think that made it easier to be myself around her. She didn't expect me to be happy all the time, she gave me space when I didn't feel like talking. She loved me for who I was. Until she didn't. The day Jade broke up with me I felt like I lost everything. She said we were young, that things felt too serious. She told me she wanted to see the world. Three weeks later she left for Europe, and I haven't seen or heard from her since. That was two years and four months ago.

For a while, I really thought she would come back to me. I thought that one day I'd get a call from her saying that she was back home in Reed Point, that she realized she had made a mistake when she ended things. I think some part of me still wants that to happen. Maybe it will.

The truth is— I saw a future with Jade. It's not easy for me to open up to people, but Jade was so easy to talk to that it just came naturally. We had a lot in common. We just fit. We matched up well in the bedroom too. The sex was mind-blowing. Jade didn't want a gentleman in the bedroom. No, she preferred it when I pinned her up against a door, tore her clothes off, and left marks on her skin. She was always game to try new things and liked being pushed past her limits. She loved it when I was rough with her, and the dirtier I talked, the better. Her kink was being praised. Sex with her was more like a marathon than a sprint, and sometimes I wonder if I'll ever be able to find someone like that again, someone who likes sex the same way I do.

Ultimately, I want the girl who's going to beg me to fuck her harder while I'm whispering the dirtiest shit into her ear, not the girl who wants to have sex with the lights off.

Checking the time on my watch, I get back to work, trudging between the kitchen and the miter saw I set up outside. I work for another two hours solid, only stopping when I get a call from my sister. I step outside to answer it.

"I'm almost all packed. Are you excited to see me?" Sierra arrives on Saturday, and despite the difficult task of helping Gran move out of her home, I'm excited to see her. Four years is a long time. Too long.

"I am, Si. I know Gran is too when she isn't losing her shit about the move."

"Yeah, I'm sure she's giving you an earful. I'm sorry I haven't been there to deal with some of that."

"You should be. She's been a peach." I sit down on a patio chair, groaning slightly as I stretch my legs out in front of me.

"Are you okay?" Sierra asks.

"Yeah, just tired. I've been working on site for the past couple of weeks and I'm fucking feeling it," I admit.

"How old *are* you?" Sierra teases. "Do you need me to get you a room next to Gran's?"

I toss my free arm over my head, stretching out my deltoid muscle, which is killing me too. "Just remember who's going to help you unpack. Keep being a brat and I'll fake an appendicitis."

She laughs. "Yeah, yeah. You wouldn't dare."

"Don't be so sure."

We talk for a little while longer about the move. It doesn't just mean a new house for Sierra, but a new job as well. She works for the Seaside Hotel company in Virginia Beach, and they have agreed to let her relocate here to Reed Point, but I know that Sierra will want to hit the ground running.

"Text me the route you'll be taking. And call me when you hit the road, so I know what time to expect you," I tell her. "And keep your phone charged in case of an emergency. Oh, and don't stop at any of those dodgy road stops, people get murdered at those things. And call me as soon as you get here."

"You do realize that I'm a grown-up, right? And that people drive on highways every day and get to where they're going in one piece?"

"Yeah, yeah. Just drive safe."

"I'll drive safe, Jake," she mutters, and I swear I can hear her roll her eyes over the phone. Sierra likes to complain that I'm overbearing and overprotective, but I think she's used to it by now. When our parents died, I became the person who always looked out for Sierra. I was the oldest, and I know it's what my parents would have wanted. My sister might not always agree.

She thinks I'm too serious, and she's probably right. But I've had to be. While most of my friends were hanging out at the beach, I was working two jobs to help my grandparents out. When I wasn't working or paddle boarding, I would lock myself in my room. I've always preferred staying in and watching movies over getting wasted at a party. Even before my parents died, I would sit and play video games for hours, perfectly happy. They used to have to force me to take a break. Looking back, I wish I had spent less time in my room and more time with my mom and dad.

My phone vibrates, and I do a double-take when I look down at the screen and see Everly's name.

> Everly: Hey, it's Everly.
>
> Everly: Can we still be friends? Sorry I didn't reply sooner.
>
> Jake: I think I can overlook it.

> Everly: That's good. I'm trying to overlook the fact that you pretty much sold my daughter on getting a cat and now that's all I hear from her.
>
> Jake: I guess I kind of did. Maybe I should buy her one. They are really cute when they're kittens.
>
> Everly: I would stab you.
>
> Jake: Ouch. So violent.
>
> Everly: That is how much I do not want a cat.
>
> Jake: You better hope I don't show up with a furry feline with a bow around its neck next time I see you then.
>
> Everly: Who said there would be a next time?
>
> Jake: Oh, there will be. :)

I stare at my phone with a stupid smile smeared across my face.

> Everly: I better run. Night shift. I'm walking, so I need to get going.

While I watch the three gray dots bounce, I roll my shoulder forward and then back, but the movement only makes it ache more.

> Jake: You walk home after a night shift? By yourself?

The gray dots appear. Then stop bouncing. Then appear again.

> Everly: Yes, dad.

She follows the text up with a bald-headed man emoji.

> Jake: You shouldn't be walking so late by yourself.
>
> Everly: My neighbor is watching Birdie for me, but she doesn't have a car and I feel more comfortable if mine is there in case she needs it. And I'm perfectly capable of looking out for myself.
>
> Jake: I know you are. I just want to make sure you don't die.
>
> Everly: I promise I won't die.
>
> Jake: Be careful, Everly.
>
> Everly: I always am.

I shove my phone back into my pocket, and that stupid grin from before is back. This girl makes me feel crazy things and I have no idea what to do about it.

It's after eleven o'clock and I've been standing outside of Catch 21 for almost an hour, waiting for Everly to get off her shift.

I didn't tell her I was coming—hell, I didn't even know I was going to stand here for this long. I have no idea what I'm doing when it comes to Everly. All I *do* know is that I want to see her.

I was out with the guys drinking—they were doing most of the drinking, I just had a couple of beers. I was too worried about Everly getting home safely after her shift. The next thing I knew, I was making excuses for leaving early and heading over to Catch 21.

The restaurant door swings open, and this time it *is* Everly. My pulse quickens and I smile as I take her in.

She's dressed in a pair of sweatpants and a crop top, her hair pulled back in a ponytail. She has a duffle bag slung over her shoulder. She spots me, and her lips part in surprise.

"Jake?" she asks, walking towards me. "What are you doing here?"

"I was out with the guys... and, well... I wanted to make sure you got home okay."

I hate that she walks home at night. I mean, I get that Reed Point is a small, relatively safe, affluent town, but it's dark and bad things can happen anywhere. Everly may be tough, but she can't weigh more than 110 pounds.

Narrowing her eyes at me, Everly folds her arms across her chest. My eyes track the movement down to her incredible tits before returning to meet her glare. I get lucky when she doesn't call me out on it. "I told you I'm not helpless. I'll be fine, Jake. I walk home after night shifts all the time."

She seems irritated, but if she thinks she has a choice in the matter, she is dead wrong. "Not tonight you're not."

Everly's head tips to one side as she looks at me, no doubt trying to determine how serious I am about this. I can see the gears working in her brain. If she thinks I'm going to budge, she's dead wrong. I see a flash of frustration in her pretty, moss-green eyes. "You're not the boss of me, Jake."

"No, I'm not, but I'm still going to walk you home."

"You're going to walk me home?"

Judging from the surprise in her voice, the reality of this is just now sinking in. The anger seems to pass, and for the first time since I've met Everly, she looks vulnerable. A knot forms in my throat as I wonder how this girl was treated in the past. Walking her home is hardly a big deal. Besides, it'll give me some peace of mind. I wouldn't have been able to sleep otherwise.

"Yup, all the way. Now, are you finished arguing with me? Can we go?"

Her lips tip up in a smile, and I feel my heart pound in my chest. She even looks beautiful when she's busting my balls.

"This one time, Jake," she warns. "I mean it." I take her bag from her shoulder, noticing again the heady scent of her perfume.

"How was work?" I ask, slinging her bag over my shoulder. I let Everly lead the way, and we stroll down the dimly lit sidewalk. It's a clear night, and the moon is large and bright overhead.

"It was fine, but it's going to be good to get to bed. I'm up at seven tomorrow morning with Birdie to get her to school," Everly says, and I notice for the first time that she looks tired.

"Ouch."

"Yeah, I know. I've been a zombie since taking this job."

"Have you thought about trying out a different job? One that doesn't involve late nights."

"That's the plan, but I haven't been able to find anything that pays me as well. The tips add up to more than half my paycheck."

She has a point. Catch 21 is Reed Point's swankiest spot. The people who dine there have money, and they love to spend it. But it must be hard working nights when she could be at home with Birdie. An idea comes to mind, but I hesitate, sure she'll shoot me down.

"How are you with computers?" I ask her anyways.

She looks at me sideways. "Why do you ask?"

"Because I might know of someone hiring. It's a day job,

so you wouldn't have to worry about Birdie. I think it would be a good fit, and the pay would be the same or better than what you're making now."

Everly's eyes widen. "Really? What line of work?"

"An office administrator for a contracting company."

She stops and turns to face me. "Who do I contact?"

"You're looking at him. The job is yours if you want it."

I stand there, holding my breath, awaiting her response.

I've known this girl for all of a week, but it's long enough to know that she'll never accept my offer... not without a fight.

SEVEN

CALL ME A GOOD GIRL

Everly

"You want me to work for you?" I stammer. I was not expecting this.

"I need the help. You'd be perfect for the job. It's a win for both of us." He shrugs, his expression serious, and I am reminded of how sexy he looks when he's being all stern.

"No."

There is no way I could work in the same office as Jake every day—that idea has disaster written all over it. I am barely surviving the proximity to him now, standing next to him on this sidewalk. I'm hanging on by a thread.

He looks better than ever, wearing jeans that fit him perfectly and a short sleeve black T-shirt that showcases his corded arms. For the first time I notice the tattoo under his right sleeve. I wonder how many more I would find if he took off his clothes. I'd like to trace every inch of his body searching for them.

Just the thought causes my heart rate to dip in my chest. In my mind, I tour his six-foot-something body, from his ridiculously handsome face to the abdominal muscles I suspect are under that shirt. And then... further south.

I've spent almost 10 years with a man who wore Gucci loafers and always had a perfect side part. The thoughts I have about Jake, with his hair that always looks perfectly tousled, his muscular body, tattoos, and the dark scruff on his jaw, are downright obscene.

It makes me wonder what he's like in bed. Jake seems like the type of guy who would call me a good girl after ordering me to my knees with my hair wrapped around his fist.

And why does that turn me on so much?

"Everly?" Jake asks, snapping me out of my dirty thoughts. "Just hear me out and then I'll drop the subject, okay? If you took the job, you'd be helping me more than I'm helping you. Besides, how much longer do you think you can work those night shifts?"

That's a good question. Most days it feels like I'm burning the candle at both ends. "I'll figure that out when it happens."

He nods but keeps to his promise not to push it. We continue walking, streetlights glowing overhead. I can tell Jake has something on his mind. I tip my chin up to look at him. "I do appreciate the offer, you know. Tell me about what you do."

"I own a contracting company. We renovate and build houses."

"So, I was right!" I say, immediately regretting the words as soon as they fall from my lips.

"Right about what?" His eyes float down to my mouth briefly, and I chastise my silly heart for dipping in my chest.

"Oh, I just had a feeling you worked with your hands." My cheeks burn with heat, but I'm not sure if it's due to embarrassment or the fact that Jake is standing so close to me.

"Oh, I can definitely work with my hands," he says, and I can hear the smirk he must have on his face. There's no way I am going to risk looking at him to confirm, though. I might just spontaneously combust.

"I'll have to take your word for it."

"I can be patient," he says, and something about the way he says it makes me risk a glance at him next to me. We hold eye contact for a beat, and then he winks, giving me a lopsided smile.

There's that zap—that electrical current that always seems to be there between us. My heart hammers. It feels like I may never recover from that smile.

I chew on the inside of my cheek, trying to focus on anything but Jake, but the closer we get to my apartment, the more my nerves kick up. What will Jake do when we arrive at my doorstep? Will he try something, or will he stick to our pact of just being friends?

I'm not even sure what I want him to do, but I can hear my dad's words. *You deserve love. You deserve a second chance.*

I try to remember all the reasons that hooking up with Jake would be a bad idea. He's too young. It's not that he lacks maturity, it's that he should be dating someone closer to his age. A girl who isn't divorced, who doesn't have a child with a sociopath. I wouldn't wish my baggage on anyone.

We arrive at my apartment building, and Jake follows me down the boxwood-lined path to the front door, then inside to the elevator and up to the second floor. I think about protesting, about insisting he doesn't need to escort me all the way, but in truth I want a few more minutes with him.

By the time we stop in front of my apartment door, I'm

buzzing with nervous energy. I turn to face Jake, my heart pumping in my chest as he flashes me that boyish grin. But then his expression turns more serious.

"I'm glad you let me walk you home," he says, handing me my bag.

"Thank you for keeping me company."

I reach in my bag for my keys, hyper-aware of the sudden silence between us. Our eyes meet and his immediately darken, sending what feels like a million tiny butterflies fluttering in my stomach.

The look in his eyes says he wants to kiss me.

Do I want him to kiss me?

I am so into him, even though I keep telling myself I shouldn't be. The man makes me feel so good, and despite everything, I find myself hoping he does kiss me.

We're standing so close that I can feel an electricity buzzing between us. His eyes are on me, flashing with intensity. There's a heavy pause as I lock eyes with him, my heart pounding. It feels like he can see right into my soul. Like he knows exactly how I want him to touch me... and where.

My cheeks heat, and I wonder if he can see it in the dimly lit hallway. Anticipation hangs in the air between us.

Then suddenly the moment passes. Jake runs his hand through his dark hair, looking down at the floor, breaking the spell. "Well, good night, Everly. If you change your mind on the job, it's yours."

I plunge back to reality, frustrated with myself for getting my hopes up when kissing Jake is the last thing that should be on my mind right now. This would be so much easier if Jake wasn't so damn hot.

Your daughter is your focus, Everly.

Tell that to my stupid sex drive.

"Don't forget my number, okay?" Jake says with a smile.

"I won't," I tell him.

"Use it then. So you don't give me a complex."

My heart squeezes in my chest. How could a man that looks like that have a complex over a girl like me? None of it makes sense.

Jake's eyes are still on me, and my heart is in my throat when he takes a small step towards me, closing the distance between us. His strong arms wrap around me, and he pulls me close. He feels so good. We fit together perfectly.

He smells like pine and fresh laundry, and I breathe in the scent, allowing myself to enjoy the moment. Jake is warm and solid, and the weight of his hands on my lower back evokes an overpowering sensation of need and want. Not to mention the tingle between my legs that I haven't felt in years. It has been so long since I've been held like this by a man who makes me feel safe and respected, so I savor the feeling for as long as I can.

We finally break apart, and my eyes search his, trying to gauge whether he feels the same way I do. We're still so excruciatingly close to one another that I can feel the heat of his skin on mine.

I swallow hard.

"You need to get some sleep. I should go," Jake says, stuffing his hands into his pockets. I can see the apprehension in his eyes, and as much as I don't want him to go, I know he should.

"Good night, Jake."

Working with Jake has mistake written all over it. Tonight proved that being around Jake Matthews is just too tempting. Frustrated, I fumble with my keys in the lock, then finally push the door open, feeling Jake's eyes still on me the entire time.

Resisting the urge to look back, I close the door behind

me and then press my back against it, trying to fight off the rush of frustration I feel. It's partly due to getting a perfect job offer I know I can't accept, but also the fact that Jake didn't even try to kiss me. Did he not want to? Or was he just trying to stick to our promise of friendship and nothing more?

I shake my head, surprised at how quickly I am warming up to being much more than *friends* with Jake. That wasn't part of the plan.

EIGHT

I HOPE YOU'RE TAPPING THAT

Everly

I am going to die.

"So close, Ev. We're almost there," Violet tells me, looking just as tired as I feel. Her platinum blonde hair is pulled back into a slick bun and her lips are a matte red. She grabs a few cocktail napkins from the bar and adds them to the fresh round of drinks on her tray. "One more hour, but who's counting?"

I am. Every single minute. But that's what I get for taking an extra night shift.

The best thing about Catch 21 is the food. It's top notch. Unfortunately, that means that we are very rarely not busy. And tonight has been no exception. It was so slammed tonight that I didn't get a break and now my feet are screaming at me, and my back is in desperate need of a Swedish massage. Sadly, the only massage I can afford these days is one of those vibrating chairs at the mall and even that I would consider a luxury at this point.

Worst of all, I missed Birdie's end-of-the-month dance showcase tonight. I've never missed one of her recitals, and it kills me that I wasn't there to watch her. Thankfully, my mom stepped in to take her. That seemed to work just fine for Birdie, who was excited for her gramma to see the dance she's been working on. But I still hate the fact that I had to miss it.

I fill my tray with drinks and survey my tables, taking in the large open dining room, the wall of glass that opens to a patio with a view of the ocean, and the opulent gold chandeliers that hang from the ceiling. As the wife of Grant Billings, I would dine in restaurants like this one every weekend. And now? I'm embarrassed to admit that I can't even afford one of their signature cocktails.

A fancy night out for Birdie and me lately is hitting up The Olive Garden, and even that we can only afford to do once a month. But I don't mind. The freedom I now feel living in Reed Point away from Grant's controlling ways is better than all the expensive dinners in the world.

Thankfully, the hour passes quickly and then the night is over. Violet and I slump into chairs in the break room and slip off our shoes, stretching the arches of our feet. She pulls one foot onto her lap, massaging the ball of her foot. "Ughhh. Is it normal for feet to hurt this bad? My pinky toe has lost all feeling."

"I think mine are broken. Is it normal for feet to be this *color*?" I ask, bending over my knees to look down at my red, swollen, achy feet.

"If this is your way of asking me to carry you out of here, nope. Can't do it. I'm too tired," she teases, limping over to her locker to grab her change of clothes. To Violet's credit, she looks more alive than I do. To mine, she's four years younger and is not getting up at the ass-crack of dawn with a 7-year-old every day.

Once we've changed into our comfy clothes and

runners, we slip out through the half-full dining room to the front doors, waving a goodbye to Owen at the bar. He has at least another two hours left before he is out of here for the night.

I make it to the hostess desk when my eyes go wide and my heart rate skyrockets, feet rooted to the floor. "Oh my gosh."

"Oh my gosh, what?" Violet asks, grabbing onto my arm.

Her gaze tracks mine through the window to where Jake is standing. For the second time this week, he is waiting outside Catch 21 for me, and my body responds to the sight of him, sending a wave of heat shooting up my spine.

"Who is he?" Violet asks, craning her neck to get a better look. "Ooh, he's cute," she says, appreciating the view as much as I am. Jake is wearing a backwards baseball hat, light gray hoodie, and a pair of black athletic shorts. I am so into this look. "Wait. Holy shit! Isn't that the hot guy who was in here a few weeks ago?" she looks at me with eyes as wide as saucers.

I haven't mentioned Jake to her. I haven't mentioned Jake to anyone, minus the brief conversation I had with my parents. "Yeah. But you can stop looking at me like that. We're just... friends. It's nothing."

"*Friends?*" she says, eyebrows raised. "Well, whatever he is, I hope you're tapping that."

I gently elbow her in her side. "Stop it. I'm not tapping that. Not now or ever."

At least, that's what I keep trying to tell myself.

JAKE

. . .

My eyes land on Everly as she walks through the doors of Catch 21, and a smile forms on my lips because I'm a goner.

She's wearing what seems to be her post-work outfit—a midriff-skimming athletic top and a pair of loose sweatpants that hide her small frame. When she looks at me, it's like I can breathe again. Whenever I'm not with her, it feels like there's no oxygen left in the room. She looks like a dream. She's beautiful. Intoxicating. And she is so far out of my league, I'm not sure why she even talks to me.

I swallow the lump that has formed in my throat, trying not to let my nerves get the best of me. She heads straight for me, a girl with platinum hair in step beside her.

"Hey, you," I greet her, then immediately wish I had thought of something better to say.

She smiles as she tilts her head, eyeing me warily. "Hi, Jake." Her voice is soft and sweet, and I notice again the green and gold flecks in her hazel eyes. Her smile knocks the breath out of me. Everly is completely worth the wait.

I knew she had a shift at the restaurant tonight because by some miracle, she has held up her end of the bargain and has been texting me. The messages aren't coming as frequently as I would like them to, but Rome wasn't built in a day. It's a start.

"How was work?" I ask her.

She shrugs, adjusting the strap of her duffle bag a little higher on her shoulder. "It was fine. I managed to get through my shift alive. Do I need to ask what you're doing here?"

Everly shoots me a defiant glare, like she's trying to be upset with me for going back on my word. But technically, I didn't. I never said walking her home was a one-time thing. Those were her words.

"Probably not," I say.

Next to her, the girl she's with leans into Everly's side, nudging her gently with her elbow. "Who's your friend, Ev?" she asks, looking me up and down.

Everly clears her throat. "This is Jake. Jake, this is Violet."

"Hey. Jake Matthews," I say, extending a hand to her. "It's good to meet you." She shakes my hand with a strong grip. Violet is beautiful—tall and curvy with blue-grey eyes and pale skin. But she has nothing on Everly. There isn't another woman on the planet who comes close to her.

Violet's eyes twinkle with mischief as she leans closer, her voice playful. "Everly needs a little fun in her life, Jake. And you look like the perfect guy for the job."

Everly's cheeks blaze bright pink as she shoots her friend a *what the fuck* look. "I'm doing just fine, Vi, thank you very much."

"Yes, you're fine. You're better than fine, you're amazing. And you're also single." Violet shrugs. "All I'm saying is maybe the last guy's loss is Jake's gain."

"That would be fine by me," I say, flashing Violet a grin. I return my attention to Everly, who looks like she is plotting her friend's murder. "Are you two going out or can I walk you home?"

"Oh, no... we are *not* going out," Violet rushes to say. "She's all yours. I've got plans... with... my dog. In fact, I think Henry needs me now. See you, Monday, Ev?"

Everly levels a look at Violet while I try not to laugh. "See you Monday, Vi."

"Have fun," Violet calls in a sing-song voice as she heads in the direction of her parked car. The lights flash on a Honda CRV as she gets closer.

"I like your friend," I say with a smug grin plastered on my face.

"I'm sure you do." She rolls her eyes. "Don't listen to her."

"About which part?" I widen my eyes in mock innocence. "The part about you needing some fun in your life or the part about me being the guy for the job?"

"*Jake.*" She narrows her eyes at me.

"What?" I smirk, not able to keep a straight face. "Her words, not mine. But she's right. I could show you a good time."

"My god." Everly shakes her head. "I swear..."

"Come on," I laugh. "I'll stop. You ready to go?"

Her two front teeth scrape gently over her bottom lip. "No."

"What's the problem?"

"I have my car here." She gestures toward her black BMW. "Birdie is staying at my parents' tonight, so I drove."

Not the answer I was expecting, but I can work with this. It's late, but she's kid-free, and that's not an opportunity I want to pass up on. "Are you hungry? We could hit up Delila's Diner...they're open all night."

She scrunches her pretty nose. "It's a little late to eat."

"Not if you're hungry, it isn't. Come on," I say with a smile. "Let's get you something to eat."

I want her to say yes. Badly.

"Okay," she relents, and I barely resist the urge to throw a celebratory fist in the air.

"I'll drive. My truck is parked over there." I dig my keys out of my pocket, nodding towards my charcoal-gray F-150.

Everly stands, not budging an inch, while I reach towards her shoulder to take her duffle bag. She folds her arms over her chest. "This isn't a date, to be clear."

"Definitely not a date." I repeat her words back to her. It is *so* a date, who is she kidding? But I know better than to argue with her. Everly can't be pushed. I've learnt that much.

"Just making sure we're clear." She arches an eyebrow, handing me her bag.

"Crystal."

At Delila's, Everly and I sink into the avocado-green leather booth, and I can sense her relief at being off her feet. Apart from an older couple at a table near the door, we're the only ones in the place.

I take my hat off to pull my hoodie over my head. It feels like it's a million degrees in here. I don't know if they need to fix their air conditioning or if it's just sitting this close to Everly that has me feeling like I'm on fire. *What the hell is happening to me?*

Everly is one of the hottest girls I've ever seen. Sitting across from me in her comfy clothes, with barely any makeup on, she looks so much better than the women I often see in tight dresses and fake eyelashes, stumbling on heels they can barely walk in. On the drive over, Everly threw on a gray zip-up hoodie that she unzipped to her abdomen, revealing her pale pink athletic bra and perfectly proportioned chest. Somehow, I'm managing to keep my eyes above her tits. For the most part.

As I tug my baseball hat back on my head, I notice Everly checking out the ink on my right arm. But she doesn't ask about it. Instead, she looks to the menu as she reaches for her water glass.

"You know... I've never been to a diner before," she says

as she brings her glass to her lips, looking around the 70s-inspired restaurant.

"You mean I'm the first guy to take you to a diner on a d—"

Her eyes flick back to mine. "I told you, Jake, this isn't a date."

I smirk. Teasing Everly is my new favorite hobby. "I'm just giving you a hard time," I laugh. "You're cute, by the way, when you're all riled up."

She leans one elbow on the table, resting her chin in her palm. Fuck, she's cute. "And you aren't being honest."

She's right, I'm not being entirely honest with her right now— I'm not telling her how badly I want to kiss her or how I'm dying to touch her skin.

"Why do you say that?" I ask.

Her lips tip up in a wry smile. "You think this *is* a date."

Well, she's not wrong. But date or not, I'm not complaining.

"You're sort of right," I say, grinning back at her like a dummy. This whole *non-date* with Everly seems too good to be true. Like Christmas coming early. "I know it's not a date, but I wish it was."

I could have denied it, but what would be the point? I haven't been able to stop thinking about this girl since the day I met her. There's no question I'm into her. I just don't know if she feels the same way. I'm pretty sure she does, but she doesn't want to admit it.

I'll wear her down eventually.

Everly tucks a few strands of her long hair behind her ear, looking back at me like she's trying to figure me out. "My age really doesn't bother you?"

"Not for a second." I answer her honestly, locking my eyes with hers. I actually think it's hot that she's seven-years older than me, but I'm pretty sure she would shut down on me if I told her that.

Her playful expression is replaced by something else. She seems uncertain, like she can't quite tell if I'm being serious or not. I am *dead* serious.

The moment is interrupted when our waitress appears to take our orders. Everly decides on a turkey club while I go for the patty-melt. We sit in silence for a beat, the air still thick with tension from our conversation. Everly breaks the silence first.

"You didn't have to bring me here, Jake."

"I know I didn't. I wanted to," I say, my attention solely focused on her. She looks so heart-stoppingly pretty it actually hurts to sit here across from her and not touch her. I'm dying to kiss her, but I have to remind myself that kissing Everly is not on the menu tonight.

Everly and I have talked several times now, but she's still a mystery to me. There is still so much I don't know about her. But if I've learnt anything at all about Everly, it's that she needs to take things slow. She doesn't like to be pushed.

"I have to admit, it's nice to be out with someone who isn't constantly talking about Barbies or Peppa Pig," she says with a laugh.

"I don't know," I smirk. "Barbie is a legend."

She shoots me a dubious look. "Not you too."

I shrug. "I see a Barbie marathon with Birdie in my future."

Everly's eyes widen, and I immediately realize what I've done. *I'm such an idiot*. I wish I could take it back, but it's too late for that, so I do what feels like the next best thing. "Shit... I'm sorry. I didn't mean to overstep."

She drops her gaze down to her hands then back to me, exhaling a long breath. "Jake, you just showed more interest

LILY MILLER

in Birdie than her own dad ever has. You don't need to apologize for that."

Her honesty leaves me speechless. I stay silent, waiting like a tightly coiled spring to see if she'll tell me anything more about her ex. But she doesn't. He seems to be a topic Everly does not want to discuss, and probably for good reason. Based on what little I've heard so far, the guy sounds like a total asshole. I get the feeling there is a lot to that story, but I leave it, letting Everly set the pace. There probably isn't a point in getting into any of it now anyways. Everly is keeping me securely in the friend zone, but I'm still hoping she'll change her mind about that.

"Besides," she goes on. "Birdie would think that was the best day ever."

I smile, surprised at how happy it makes me to think that maybe I made a good impression on Birdie. "She's a cute kid." I trace the corner of my napkin with my finger. "And I really like hanging out with her mom."

Everly swallows. "I like you, too."

My body hums at her response, and the air in the diner suddenly feels charged with electricity. Everly usually has her guard up around me but for the first time it feels like she's built up the courage to be vulnerable.

"Tell me more about you," she says, just as our server returns with our orders.

I steal a pickle from her plate, grinning. "What do you wanna know?"

"Tell me about your family... where did you grow up? Do you have any siblings?"

I guess I should have seen the questions coming, but they hit me like a brick. My heart drops to my feet, like it always does when I'm asked about my family.

I clear my throat. "I grew up in Mayberry, not too far

away. But I moved to Reed Point with my sister, Sierra, when I was 12. Just down on Haven Harbor." I think about telling Everly more, but my throat tightens. I'm shit at sharing my feelings period, but talking about the night my parents died... I just don't do it. I can't.

"How about you?" I ask, shifting the conversation away from me.

"I grew up in Reed Point with my parents and my brother, Adam, then moved to Brookmont for college. My parents are your quintessential working-class couple, married for almost 40 years, still living in the same house I grew up in. Adam lives in California with his wife and two kids."

"What brought him to California?"

"Love, I guess? He's a pilot and met his wife on one of his layovers. She's from San Diego and when things got serious, he moved there to be closer to her. They got married two years later and the rest is history," she says, plucking a French fry from her plate. "His wife is the sweetest. She's the best thing to happen to my brother. He was a bit of a serial dater before he met her. We see each other once or twice a year when they come for a visit, but it's never enough. His daughters are close in age to Birdie, the three of them have the best time together. They always put on these elaborate dances, it's so cute. Oh! Speaking of... my mom sent me a video tonight and I haven't had a second yet to watch it." She pulls her phone from her bag. "It's of Birdie dancing tonight in her showcase."

She pulls up the video, and I smile at the way her face brightens. "Tell me this isn't the sweetest thing you've ever seen," she says with her heart in her eyes.

I expect her to just turn the screen to me but instead, she stands and comes to sit beside me, holding her phone in front of us. I can smell the citrusy scent of her, feel the warmth of her skin. I have to force myself to focus on the screen.

She hits play on the video of Birdie in a dance class. The camera is zoomed in on her, and she's beaming, dressed in pink from head to toe. I don't have to look at Everly to know that she's smiling.

"I may be biased, Ev, but she's the best one in the room," I say, watching Birdie twirl and jump.

"She loves it."

"Was this tonight while you were at work?"

"Yeah." She sighs. "First one I've ever missed."

I steal a glance at Everly and see the sadness in her eyes. "I'm sorry you missed her dance," I say, placing my hand on her arm, touching her for the very first time tonight. Her skin is soft and warm, and it makes me want to keep my hand there for as long as I can.

She turns to face me, and we both freeze, her green eyes gazing back at me through long, dark lashes. My heart thunders inside of my chest like a freight train. Her eyes drop down to my hand on her arm, and I feel her tense, but I leave it there, squeezing ever so softly. My eyes drop down to her lips, watching them part just slightly, and I wonder what would happen if I kissed her. Would she kiss me back?

Everything in me wants to find out. My heart stutters. My pulse sprints. Another second and my lips could be on hers.

"How's everything here? Can I get you two anything else?"

The waitress appears out of nowhere, and Everly pulls her arm into her side. She slides off the bench and stands, returning to her side of the booth.

"I think we're fine for now, thanks," I say, drawing in a

breath, trying to regain my composure, but I'm drowning. Being that close to kissing Everly and missing the opportunity feels like the biggest let-down.

I've never been this nervous around a woman before. Would Everly have kissed me back? If I do make a move, will I scare her away? Or will she flat-out reject me? The not knowing and trying to play it cool is going to kill me.

In other words, I am a total mess over this girl.

IT'S AFTER 1 A.M. WHEN I PULL UP BEHIND EVERLY'S CAR JUST down the street from Catch 21. I shift my truck into park and reach behind me for her duffle, handing her the bag.

"I hope I didn't get you back too late," I say, turning in my seat to face her.

Everly's eyes move to the clock on my dash, then widen when she realizes the time. "Wow, I had no idea how late it is."

I hope that's a good thing. *Time flies when you're having fun* and all that. We were at the diner longer than I expected, and it felt like neither one of us was in a hurry to leave. After the almost-kiss, the awkwardness quickly passed, and we took our time finishing dinner. We ordered coffee and split a piece of pie before I reluctantly paid the bill and we returned to my truck.

"What time do you have to be at your mom's to pick up Birdie in the morning?"

"Anytime." She shrugs. She said she can stay as long as she wants."

"That's great. You deserve a sleep-in."

"I won't argue with you on that."

Silence fills the truck, and it's noticeable. Conversation

between us is always so easy, but right now it feels different. I'm not sure what to do next. What I *want* to do is kiss Everly, but I know that would freak her out. Even a hug feels impossible thanks to the damn console being in the way. This is the first time I have ever wished I bought a smaller truck.

"Thanks for tonight," Everly says, unbuckling her seat belt. "I had fun."

"Does that mean we can do it again?"

She grabs her bag, her other hand already on the door handle. "We can. You were on your best behaviour." Her voice is cute, flirty. My dick responds with a twitch. It makes me want to push her a little.

"I was," I say. "But I don't have to be."

Everly tries to hide the grin that forms on her lips. "I'll text you, okay?"

"I hope so."

Everly had two more night shifts this week, and I showed up after both to walk her home. Aside from that, we've been texting multiple times a day. But that has been it. I still haven't found an opportunity to take her out again. Or to make a move. Every night I've walked her home has ended the same way—awkwardly. And it is starting to fuck with my head.

What the hell has happened to my game? I have none.

I haven't had too much time to dwell on it, because my sister and I have been busy moving Gran into her assisted living facility home. It was tough watching Gran say goodbye to the house she's lived in for so many years, and I was grateful Sierra was there to go through it with me. We went for tacos the following night to catch up and I gave Sierra the rundown on life in Reed Point. Now that she's getting settled into Gran's place, I told the guys to keep an eye out for her—from a fucking distance. Grayson, Tuck and Holden already know that my sister is off-limits. I'll break their legs and then their arms if they even try to go near her.

She'll have a chance to meet the gang tonight at my place, I'm hosting a Friday night cook-out. Tucker, Holden and Grayson are here, along with Aubrey and Beckett and his wife Jules, who works with my sister at The Seaside. Everyone is drinking, having a good time, but I'm feeling... off. The reason? Everly. We haven't talked at all today. And I wish she was here.

"You good, man?" Grayson asks me when he catches my eye from across the couch.

"Perfect." I take a long pull of my beer. I can tell I haven't convinced him, but he seems willing to let it go.

"Let's do some shots."

"I'll pass, man."

Grayson stands with his beer in his hand. "Why? Come on, Jake."

Because I'm fucked up over a girl. That would be the honest answer, but instead I just say, "I'm gonna finish my beer, then I'm hydrating. I've got shit I've gotta do tomorrow."

He gives me a look but thankfully decides against saying anything else, walking past me to the kitchen.

"Hey." Tucker swats my thigh with the back of his hand, lowering his voice. "Are you going to invite beach girl to Holden's cabin?"

Holden gets his uncle's cabin on the water every Labor Day weekend, and he invites us all up for an end-of-summer bash. He confirmed the plans tonight, and this year it looks like my sister will be coming too.

"Nah, we're not there yet," I say, picking at the label on my beer, inwardly laughing at the nickname for Everly. The thought hadn't crossed my mind, but I doubt Everly would want to go. Besides that, I can't imagine she would leave Birdie for three days. "We're nowhere close."

A crease forms between Tucker's eyebrows. "Things moving that slow?"

"Yeah. I've hugged her, that's about it."

Tucker shakes his head, smirking at my lack of game. "What are you waiting for, Jakey? Do you like her or not?"

"Of course, I do," I mutter.

"Then what are you waiting for? You still got your balls, make your move."

I nod my head, taking a sip of my beer.

But it's obvious Everly's life is complicated. Her ex, her kid, her job. What if she's not ready for me to make a move? Or worse yet, what if things aren't actually over with her and Birdie's dad?

I guess there's only one way to find out.

NINE

ZERO RED FLAGS HERE

Everly

After three episodes of *Peppa Pig*, two games of Snakes and Ladders, one dance party and way too much popcorn, I'm sitting on the couch with my feet up on the coffee table. Franny sits beside me, equally exhausted.

"Should I pour us a glass of wine? I think we earned it," Franny says, tossing a popcorn kernel in her mouth. "That girl has more energy than a Border Collie on a Saturday morning."

"You're telling me. How am I ever going to get her to sleep tonight?" I stand up with a sigh and retrieve the open bottle of red from the counter while Franny puts the pieces of the board game back in the box.

"Mommy, it's Daddy on the phone," Birdie says, trotting towards me with my iPhone in her hand. "I'm gonna answer it."

"Birdie—" I watch her tiny finger swipe the screen before I have a chance to take the device from her. Franny watches the scene unfold with a pained look on her face.

"Hi, Daddy." Birdie stands next to me in the kitchen, a look of concentration on her face.

I can hear Grant's voice on the other end of the call, and instantly the hairs on my arms stand on end. I don't need to see my ex's face to be physically affected by him. The sound of his voice is enough to send my anxiety through the roof.

I flash back to other phone calls between Grant and Birdie, when he would tell her that he'd been busy at work and then promise to make it up to her, to take her somewhere special. But then he wouldn't show. And I would have to watch her little bottom lip quiver, the tears falling one by one down her cheeks. No matter how many times he left her waiting, it never got easier. For either of us.

Was he always like that, from the start? Or did I ignore a bunch of red flags? He was confident and popular; I knew there were tons of girls who wanted a chance with him. I got stars in my eyes and imagined he was the man I wanted him to be. Looking back, I should have seen the warning signs. There were enough of them.

"I miss you too, Daddy."

"Yes, I want to see you."

"When?"

"Okay, here's Mommy."

Birdie extends her arm to me, my phone in her hands. I take the device from her and lower myself to sit on a kitchen chair. I hear Franny asking Birdie to show her something in her bedroom as she quietly leads her down the hall, leaving me alone with the devil.

The phone call lasts less than 5 minutes, neither one of us wanting to make small talk, and by the time I've hung up, we've gotten nowhere. Besides the fact that I want to choke him out. He wants to see Birdie tomorrow. *Tomorrow.* You've got to be kidding me. This is typical Grant, expecting me to drop everything to work around his schedule. He thinks the world revolves around him and his needs. Would it kill him to give me some notice? But what choice did I have? I know Birdie would like to see him. I reluctantly agreed to a visit when he told me he wouldn't be far from Reed Point, and he'd come to us. I told him we'd meet him at The Dockside, a lunch spot in town. There's no way I was going to invite him to the apartment —he would lose his mind, and the last thing I need is Grant judging me.

"You okay?" Franny asks quietly, walking back into the kitchen. "Birdie is in the tub."

"I'm fine. He's just infuriating," I say, pouring myself a glass of wine. I pour a glass for Franny too, then slide it across the table to her.

I feel safe to speak candidly with Franny. She's a good listener and she's never judgemental. "He wants to see her."

"When was the last time?"

"He saw his daughter?"

"Yes."

"Over four months ago," I mutter.

Franny sits up straighter in her chair. "Geez, that's a long time."

"He doesn't care."

"Maybe he was waiting for you to invite him to your new place?" Franny suggests.

I shake my head. "Grant Billings does not need an invitation to see his daughter. That man wouldn't let anything stop him from getting what he wants. Trust me... if he wanted to see Birdie, he could have driven the two hours."

"Has Birdie asked about him much?" Franny asks.

"Not as much as you would expect." I shrug. "I think she's distracted. When we're at my parents, she's excited to see them or when we go to the beach, she's happy to be there. She's busy. It helps."

"Or when she's running into Jake." Franny eyes me over the rim of her wine glass.

I feel my cheeks heat. "How do you know about Jake?"

"Birdie told me."

"Of course she did," I say, shaking my head. "It's not what you think. We're not dating."

"I didn't ask you if you were," she says, tilting her head to the side. "But if you wanted to, it would be okay. Not all men are like Grant."

Maybe she's right. But haven't I proven that I have terrible taste in men? I obviously am a horrible judge of character; after all, I didn't see the warning signs with Grant. What if I make the same mistake twice? I can't do that to Birdie. One day she will realize the kind of man her father is —never making her a priority, forgetting her birthday, putting everyone else before his wife and child—and it scares the life out of me to think that she might ever believe she isn't worthy of love.

"I'm scared to take that chance."

"You'll never know unless you do. And what a shame it would be to miss out on love. You have your best years ahead of you, Everly. You don't want to live them alone."

My mind wanders to Jake, as it often does these days. Jake, who has been patient, kind, and a perfect gentleman.

Zero red flags there.

I'm about to tell Franny that living alone beats having my heart — and Birdie's—crushed, but then Birdie walks into the kitchen with a giant towel wrapped around her little body. So even though the conversation is far from over, it's over for now.

I have the sweetest little 7-year-old to get ready for bed.

"When can we see Jake again?" Birdie asks as we're getting our shoes on.

"I'm not sure, baby," I say, tugging the laces on her runner. "He's probably busy with work."

"Mommy?"

"Yes, baby?"

Her eyebrows pull together. "Is Jake your boyfriend? I think I'd like it if he was."

It has been a while since Birdie has asked about Jake, and I wondered if she had forgotten about him. But of course, Birdie remembers everything and everyone. She never forgets a thing. One day that fact will bite Grant in the ass, but that will be his problem and not mine.

But today Grant Billings *is* my problem.

I told Birdie there was a chance we'd meet her dad for lunch today over breakfast and her smile lit up her entire sweet face. Meanwhile, my heart lurched thinking about Birdie waiting patiently for her dad to show up only to be disappointed when he doesn't.

As I sat and worried about every way today could go wrong and how I would handle it if that happened, Birdie ran to her room to make a card for her dad. And now it's time to go see Grant. If he shows up. So, I'm surprised that Birdie is suddenly asking me about Jake.

"Jake's not my boyfriend. He's just a friend."

"Why doesn't he visit us if he's your friend?"

"Would you like it if he came over to hang out with us?"

She nods her head. "I would really like that."

I smile at her big, generous heart. I try to picture Jake here in our tiny apartment, playing Candyland and being introduced to Birdie's extensive collection of Barbies. The image sets off butterflies in my stomach. But there isn't time to think about that now. Being late would aggravate Grant and that's the last thing I need.

So, I grab my keys and my purse, take Birdie by the hand and head outside to my car.

Ten minutes later, we're seated at a table by the window at The Dockside. The weather is cooler today, so instead of the air conditioning blasting through the vents, the restaurant has its glass doors open to a patio, which has a few picnic tables, a patch of turf and a small jungle gym for kids to play on. It's one of the reasons I like it here; I can enjoy my lunch while Birdie plays. I'm surprised when Birdie doesn't immediately ask if she can go outside.

The waitress is filling our water glasses when I see my ex-husband walk through the doors of The Dockside and spot our table. Birdie is sitting across from me with the card she made grasped tightly in her hand when she notices her dad.

"Daddy!" Birdie jumps up from her seat.

"No running through the restaurant," I remind her, moving her water glass into the center of the table before she knocks it over.

When Grant is a few feet away from our table, Birdie can't wait any longer—she pushes her chair back and runs straight into Grant's arms.

"Fuck my life," I grumble to myself, pasting a smile on my face for Birdie's sake. I stay seated as I watch Birdie with her arms wrapped around Grant's neck as he kisses the top of her head.

He looks to me and his grin fades to a passive-aggressive smirk. "Hi, Evy."

My stomach turns at the old nickname. I liked it once upon a time. Now, it's like nails on a chalkboard. "Hi."

He's wearing a perfectly pressed golf shirt and khaki shorts with a tan Gucci belt. His blond hair is styled in place with his signature side part, his skin bronzed from the tanning bed he has in his basement. He's wearing Italian leather loafers that I'm positive cost more than my rent. He looks the same. And so much like Birdie.

"How's my Jay-bird?" he asks our daughter, taking the seat across from her.

"I'm good, Daddy." She sits down and I help her push in her chair. "Here... I made you a card."

She hands him the brightly colored card she spent all morning making, and he glances at it and then sets it aside. "That's nice, Birdie," he says dully. I want to punch him in the throat. He waves a waitress over so he can order a drink, the card already forgotten.

I will never understand him.

"What's my girl been up to?" he asks Birdie once the waitress disappears.

"Well... I've made two new friends at school. One's a boy and the other is a girl. She's my best friend because she likes cats like me."

He straightens the silverware on the table in front of him. "You wouldn't like cats if you had one. They pee in a box, Birdie. They also shed and scratch the furniture."

Birdie's eyes drop briefly, but then she looks up again with a smile for her dad. I hate him. He's such an asshole. Just for that, I want to take her to the SPCA after this stupid lunch and let her choose five strays to bring home. *Dick.*

"But they can jump up to six times their length," she says, quoting Jake. I try to hide my smile. Birdie's eyes are wide, hopeful, as if she's hoping to convince her dad to love her favorite animal as much as she does.

"They also smell," he huffs. "How's school? I bet you miss Brentwood Academy."

I want to stab him in the eye with my fork, but for Birdie's sake I restrain myself. Grant paid twenty thousand dollars a year for his five-year-old to attend kindergarten with kids who had the same *pedigree*. I remember wanting to vomit when he said that to me. I argued that Birdie could get a good education in the public school system, which made him laugh. *My kid is not going to a public school*, was his response. And that was that. There were arguments I just knew I would never win and that was one of them.

"Grant, we should order. Birdie is hungry," I tell him. My patience is already waning, so I try to move things along.

"Fine," he says, picking up his menu.

We place our orders, and then Birdie is out of her seat and in Grant's lap. She probably knows it will be months before she sees him again so she's soaking him in. I can't blame her.

"Mommy is a waitress now too," Birdie says, watching a waitress carry an armful of plates to the table next to us. "She works at a fancy restaurant."

Grant's eyebrows shoot up. *This* is going to go over well. Luckily, I could care less what he thinks.

"She is, is she?" he gives me a mocking look, then shakes his head at me like I'm a piece of gum on the bottom of his shoe. I knew that was coming. It's a look I've seen plenty of times before.

I'm not having this conversation with him because I know exactly how it's going to go, so I change the subject, telling him instead about Birdie's teacher and all the great things she has to say about our daughter while we wait for our drinks.

"So where are you living?" Grant asks, cutting off my weak attempts at small talk.

"I found us an apartment here in town," I say. "Birdie likes it. We have a great neighbor, and there's a park nearby."

"So, you left the estate, where you and Birdie had everything you could ever possibly want or need, so that you could live in some shitty apartment in this shitty town? I don't get it."

I shake my head but try to maintain my composure. The guy is seriously clueless. If he thinks I would ever live under the same roof as him again, he's out of his mind.

I think to the night I finally decided to divorce him. I was at home in the kitchen making myself tea before bed when I got a call from a friend of mine who saw Grant walking into a hotel. He was with two women who I later found out he picked up at a bar. The three of them went upstairs to a room. It wasn't the first time he had cheated on me, but it was the first time someone other than me had caught him. I was humiliated. That was the final straw.

"Here y'all go. I hope you're hungry." Our server returns with our food, sliding the plates in front of us. I slice Birdie's hamburger in two and the three of us eat in near silence, the only conversation coming from Birdie, who talks a mile a minute about school and dance and her new friends. Grant listens to her but seems more occupied with his phone, which he keeps checking every 10 seconds.

"Can I have dessert?" Birdie asks once we've finished our meals.

"I need to talk to your mom for a second," Grant says. "Why don't you check out the swing set and you can have dessert after."

Birdie looks to me for approval. "It's fine if you'd like to go play," I tell her, ruffling her blonde curls, and then she's off through the open doors to the patio.

I can already tell this conversation is not going to go well. As soon as Birdie is outside, Grant's eyes narrow on mine and I notice the vein in his neck that looks like it's ready to explode.

"A waitress? Really, Evy? What do you know about waiting tables? You haven't cleaned a table in your life. I paid someone to do that for you, or have you forgotten?"

He is such an ass. I cooked dinner for him almost every night of the week and cleaned up afterwards. He just never bothered to notice. And the *someone* he's referring to is Ida, Birdie's nanny, and the family's housekeeper. I don't think I've heard him call her by her name.

"I'm not arguing with you over this, Grant. My job is really none of your business."

"We need to talk."

"Now? You haven't seen your daughter in over four months, wouldn't you rather spend this time with her?" I ask, annoyance seeping through my voice.

"I want my daughter back in Brookmont. I want to see my kid."

"I've never stopped you."

He huffs out a breath. "You live two hours away."

"And what was your excuse for never seeing her when you lived in the same house as her?" I deadpan.

"Everly," he bites back. "I'm not asking you. I am telling you."

"Grant, allow me to remind you... you agreed to this. Would you like to tell me why you're not in North Carolina?"

"Don't push me, Evy."

I sigh. "You don't get to tell me what to do, Grant. You have no power over me anymore."

He narrows his eyes at me. I've clearly struck a nerve. Grant is used to getting what he wants, but this time I'm fighting back.

"You have no idea what I'm capable of," he snaps, jabbing his index finger into the table. "I will call my lawyer the second I walk out of here."

"Don't threaten me, Grant." I sit up straighter in my chair. I refuse to be intimidated by him. I doubt that he actually cares about seeing Birdie more often. Grant just likes to win. And right now, he feels like he's losing. I doubt a judge would side with Grant. But the Billings have money, so the possibility of them fighting me in court isn't out of the question. My stomach turns at the thought.

"Then move back home and stop your childish behaviour."

"No."

"Do you hear yourself?" He glares at me. "You sound like a brat."

I couldn't care less what I sound like. I'm not moving back there. I knew having a conversation with him was going to be pointless. "You're an ass, Grant. I signed a lease. Birdie is settled into her new school, she's happy. We can figure out the two-hour drive very easily if you'd like weekly visits."

He rolls his eyes at me. I look past him, trying to stay calm, and my breath catches in my throat when I see a familiar face in the restaurant foyer. I'd recognize that man anywhere, even if his eyes weren't narrowed on me.

Jake.

A hostess grabs a couple of menus and signals for Jake to

follow her. He makes his way through the busy restaurant, his eyes on me the entire time. I know that Reed Point is a small town, but I can't believe Jake chose to come to this restaurant today of all days. I am sure he has all kinds of thoughts running through his head, and I want to go to him, to explain why I'm here, tell him about Grant before he gets the wrong idea. But I can't. Grant is looking for whatever ammunition he can find, and if he thinks he can use Jake against me, he will. I just want to get through this lunch without Grant flying off the handle.

"Who is he?" Grant sneers. My gaze snaps back to my ex-husband. He doesn't have the patience to wait for me to respond. "Are you fucking him, Evy?"

"He's a friend."

His eyes narrow. "Are you fucking your *friend* then?"

I clench my jaw so tight that my molars grind together. "That is none of your business."

Out of the corner of my eye, I see Jake sit down a couple of tables over, close enough that I'm sure he can hear this interrogation. I'm mortified. I sit uncomfortably across from Grant, who looks like he's ready to flip the table, praying he'll keep his voice down. He stares at me for a long moment, nostrils flared like he's ready for a fight. I can already tell my prayer is not going to be answered.

"So did you move here for him?"

"Lower your voice, Grant. The entire restaurant can hear you," I whisper through clenched teeth. "And I told you it's none of your business."

"It *is* my business when you take my daughter and move her two hours away. And now I find out there's some frat boy I've never met hanging around. Who is he, Everly? Or maybe I should go ask *him*."

Grant couldn't care less that he's in a room full of people. "I told you that he is a friend. That's it. Now drop it."

"You can't do this forever."

"Do *what* forever?" I ask, my eyes darting to where Birdie is still playing on the patio.

"Live here," he says with disdain in his voice. "Work a shitty waitressing job. It's an embarrassment. You're a Billings, for fuck's sake. Act like one."

I hear the legs of Jake's chair screech across the floor, and three seconds later, he's standing at our table, hands clenched into fists. "Everly, can we talk?"

Grant throws a wad of cash on the table then gets up. "Talk to your boyfriend, Everly. I'm going to say goodbye to Birdie. But we're not finished with this."

I can't stand him.

No, that's not strong enough.

I hate him.

It's hard to believe that there was ever a time I loved this man. I thought the world of him. How did he turn out to be so terrible?

Grant storms outside towards the patio where Birdie is playing. My stomach in knots, I watch him bend down to Birdie's level with his hands on her tiny shoulders. He says something to our daughter that causes her smile to fade. Then he kisses the tip of her nose. I watch them through the glass like I'm watching a movie.

"Sorry. Can you give me a minute?" I ask Jake, trying to stay as calm as possible.

"I'll be right here." Jake nods with a serious expression on his face. Very serious. Very intense. "I'm not going anywhere."

I reach the patio in time to hear Grant tell Birdie that he'll see her for her birthday. She's clearly upset that he's leaving so soon, but he promises her he'll make it up to her with a very big birthday present. She smiles, but I can see how disappointed she is. My heart shatters like it always does when she's hurting.

Grant pulls Birdie into a hug and then stands, taking a step towards me. He's so close to me now that I can smell his expensive cologne. "I want her in Brookmont. It's non-negotiable. I'll be in touch."

Grant turns, and I can see the muscle in his jaw tick when his gaze lands on Jake, who is now standing at the edge of the patio. I scoop Birdie into my arms and hold her close to my chest. She's on the verge of tears. I run my hand over her curls, kissing the top of her head as Grant storms through the restaurant doors.

TEN

I HAVE IT SO BAD FOR THIS GIRL

Jake

My chest tightens as I watch Everly soothe Birdie in her arms. I get it now. I get why her life is complicated.

Her ex-husband is an absolute piece of shit.

I couldn't take another second of him berating her, so without thinking I stood up and walked over to their table. The moment she looked up at me, I saw red. Her frightened hazel eyes and the tremble in her bottom lip told me all I needed to know. Adrenaline pumped through my veins. What the fuck kind of guy thinks he can talk to the mother of his child like that? And what was Everly even doing here with him? I had to remind myself to breathe. Stay calm. The guy's lucky he had the good sense to get up and leave. I would have had no problem shutting him up if he had one negative thing to say about Everly in front of me. It took all of my willpower not to knock the guy's lights out.

"Jake!" Birdie spots me over Everly's shoulder, pointing across the patio.

I see her damp cheeks. I also see the resemblance to her father. My heart twists.

As soon as Everly sets her down on the ground, Birdie is beelining it towards me, blonde ponytail swinging behind her. I can't stop myself from smiling. The rage I felt just minutes ago fades as I take in the excited expression on her face.

As Birdie stops in front of me, I sneak a peek at Everly, who is watching us from a few feet away. She's wearing a top that falls over one of her tan shoulders and a skirt that ends just above her knees, her dark hair swept up in a ponytail.

Beautiful. There is no better way to describe her. Her soft pink lips, those captivating eyes. She's perfect. Dammit...I have it so bad for this girl.

I bend down to Birdie's height, tearing my eyes from Everly. The little girl throws her arms around me, and I'm surprised at the flush of happiness I feel. "Hey, Birdie."

I sense Everly quietly watching us as Birdie pulls back from the embrace. "Hi Jake, are you having lunch here too?"

I clear my throat, doing my best to play it cool. I haven't spent much time with kids, so I'm unsure of how to act around Birdie; being around her always throws me for a loop.

"I am," I say, pushing to standing. I smile down at her.

"You could sit with us at our table." Birdie's eyes shoot to Everly. "We were going to have dessert but then my dad had to go." Her shoulders slump and I catch the way Everly's expression softens as she watches her daughter. My heart sinks. Everly is a good mom, but it can't be easy picking up the pieces that her ex leaves behind. "Or you could come over! Mommy, can Jake come over to our house?"

My smile falters. "Umm... I..."

"Please... Mom!" Birdie squeals, her face lighting up. She's wearing a pale pink dress along with the cat ears she had on the last time I saw her. This kid is freaking cute.

Everly takes a few steps closer, but she stops short as if needing to keep some space between us.

"I think Jake has other plans," she says, nodding towards my table. *Shit.* I completely forgot that I'm meeting my sister here for lunch. I glance back at the empty table, relieved for once that Sierra is late as usual.

"I'm meeting my sister for lunch," I tell Birdie.

Her tiny body deflates. "And we're going to my gramma's tonight. How 'bout tomorrow night? You could come over for dinner. Mom can make her best chicken and potatoes."

Everly's eyes widen, and she pulls her lower lip between her teeth. I can sense she's uncomfortable, so I decide to let her off the hook and tell Birdie I have plans so her mom doesn't have to be the bad guy.

But Everly surprises me when she says, "How about next weekend? It's fine with me if Jake would like to join us."

Before I can respond, Birdie is hopping up and down, a grin spreading across her lips. "You can make it, right, Jake? You can come over for dinner?"

I have a sudden image of Everly in an apron, and it makes my dick stir. I study her expression just to be sure she's okay with this. She's protective over her relationship with her daughter—I get it— and I don't want to overstep.

"If you're sure you don't mind..." I begin.

"Have dinner with us next Sunday," Everly says, giving me a small smile. "Come over at six?"

"Okay then," I say, looking back to Birdie. "Since it's okay with your mom, I'll be there."

"Yay!" Birdie jumps up and down, arms raised to the sky. But it's the smile on Everly's face that makes my heart skip two beats.

"We better go, Birdie," she tells her.

Everly seems to have moved on from the altercation with

her ex, but I'm definitely not over it. The angry way he talked to her keeps crossing my mind. How often does she have to put up with that from him? Is she really okay? I want to tell her that I'm sorry her ex-husband is such a jerk, but I have the sense to know I can't do that in front of Birdie. As if reading my mind, the little girl turns back towards the playground, which gives me an opportunity to speak to Everly alone.

"Are you good?" I ask, searching her face for a sign of how she's feeling.

Something flashes in Everly's eyes, but she quickly pastes on a small smile.

"I'm fine. It's nothing new," she says quietly, walking back to her table, grabbing her purse from the chair. The anger I saw in her when she was talking to her ex is gone. Now she just looks sad and embarrassed. I want to tell her she has nothing to feel embarrassed about. That her ex is the one who acted like an ass. But right now isn't the time to push it.

I watch her slip her purse onto her shoulder, then reach for some artwork that Birdie must have left on the table.

"You sure it's okay I come over?"

Her purse slips down her arm and I reach out to slide it back up to her shoulder, my fingertips grazing her soft skin. The pink in her cheeks glow even brighter at the contact.

"I'm sure, Jake." She smiles as Birdie comes running back to the table. "We'll see you Sunday."

I watch the two of them as they walk out of the restaurant— Birdie's hand in Everly's— with a sinking feeling that there is so much more to Everly's story than she's willing to tell me.

Maybe next weekend I can get her to talk to me. I hope she lets me in.

ELEVEN

THE BODY OF A GREEK GOD

Jake

My sister invited me for dinner tonight. She made the lasagna our mom used to make every year for my birthday. It's still my favorite. It feels like it should be a special occasion with all the trouble Sierra has gone to. There is warm bread in a basket and a lemon pie on the counter she made from scratch for dessert. When we were kids, she would spend hours in the kitchen baking with our mom. She is so much like her; it catches me off guard sometimes.

But as much as Sierra is like our mom, she was always daddy's little girl. The two of them were practically inseparable, always huddled together over a board game after we finished up with dinner. Occasionally Mom and I would join them, but usually it was only because I was forced to – or if they were playing Monopoly, that was my favorite.

Sierra serves me a square of piping hot lasagna on one of Gran's floral-patterned plates and we both take our seats. The first bite is incredible. The meat sauce tastes exactly like

Mom's used to. I close my eyes for a moment, the familiar taste bringing back memories.

I'm scooping a second mouthful of lasagna into my mouth when my phone chimes on the table next to me. I glance down to see a message from Everly. We've been texting back and forth for most of the day about nothing in particular, but this time my eyes immediately focus in on the word *emergency,* and I quickly swipe the screen to open the message.

> Everly: Sorry I didn't respond to your message earlier. I'm at Emergency with Birdie. She's okay but she fell off the monkey-bars at the playground. I think her arm might be broken.

I respond immediately.

> Jake: I'm on my way. I'll be there as quick as I can.

"I'm really sorry, Si. I have to go. Something's come up."

"Is everything okay?" She sets down her fork. "I saw you frowning when you were reading that text."

I push my chair away from the table and bring my plate to the sink. "It will be. It's nothing you need to worry about."

She gets up, wiping her hands on a napkin, then follows me to the door. "Jake, does this have anything to do with the girl you've been seeing? And when will you introduce me to her? I feel like I'm in the dark, and I want to know what's happening in your life."

Sierra walked into The Dockside as I was saying goodbye to Everly and Birdie the other day. It didn't feel like the right time for introductions, and after everything that just went down with Everly's ex, and I, I didn't want to push her by suddenly introducing her to my sister. She and Birdie were on their way out by the time Sierra got to the table, but of course Si gave me the third degree about them. I managed to dodge her questions.

"We're not seeing each other," I tell her now, grabbing my hoodie from the chair by the door. "We're not anything right now. It's just... it's her daughter. She thinks she broke her arm. She's taking her to emergency, and I said I would meet her there." I scrub my hand across the back of my neck. "Sorry, Si, but are you okay if we wrap up tonight a little earlier than planned?"

"Of course. Will you let me know how she is?"

"I will. And I'm sorry. Dinner was incredible. Tasted just like mom's. She'd probably get her feelings hurt if she knew how good you make it."

She smiles. "You know, I'm sure this girl means something to you, but if that's the case, shouldn't you be smiling more? Isn't that what's supposed to happen when you're getting to know someone? You've just seemed... pretty distant lately, and I don't understand why."

I sigh, stuffing my hands in my pockets. "She has a lot going on with her daughter." I look up to find Sierra studying me as if she's trying to figure me out. "She's just been through a lot, and I'm trying to be patient. That's it."

"Okay. I just want you to be happy. I worry about you."

"I'm okay, Si. I promise," I say, hugging her goodbye.

Twenty minutes later I'm jogging into the emergency waiting room area looking for Everly and Birdie.

"I'm looking for Birdie Billings," I tell the lady at reception. She asks if I'm a family member, and I don't even hesitate before telling her I'm Birdie's dad. I'm pretty sure her actual father won't be showing up tonight to challenge it. The woman checks her computer screen, points to the large double doors to the left of her and tells me I'll find her in there.

I push through the doors and find a nurse, who directs me to a curtained area towards the end of the hallway. I thank her, then follow her directions, sliding the curtain open a smidge to peek inside. Everly turns around and I see relief flash in her eyes when she sees that it's me.

"She's sleeping. It has been a day," Everly says in a low voice, looking exhausted. Her eyes are puffy, with dark circles underneath from where her mascara has smudged. Between the late-night shifts and early mornings, she's already been running on empty. She sags back into the plastic chair, lifting her hands to her face to cover a yawn. I can see she's barely hanging on.

"What did the doctor say?" I ask quietly, stepping into the room, looking at Birdie who looks so tiny lying there in the hospital bed, a gray blanket pulled up past her waist. Her little arm is wrapped in a thick tensor bandage and is bent at the elbow in a sling.

"Said she fractured the radius bone in her forearm. He took an x-ray, now we're waiting for someone to cast her. Thank goodness he doesn't think she'll need surgery."

"That's good," I say. "Poor thing. How long has she been sleeping?"

"About an hour," Everly says through another yawn, dropping her head into her hands.

"Here, I brought you dinner. I thought you might be hungry." I hold out a brown paper bag, and she smiles in response.

"What's this?" Everly asks, peering inside.

"I stopped at The Dockside on the way here. I got what I could. They were closing so there weren't a lot of options."

She looks up at me. "You didn't have to do all that."

"Judging by how long you two have been here, I figured you might need it."

She pulls the turkey clubhouse and a bottle of water from the bag, leaving the mac and cheese for Birdie. "Thank you. Really, Jake. I owe you."

"I can think of a few ways you can repay me," I grin, wanting her to smile again. I lower myself into the chair beside hers.

"You don't have to stay. We could be here for hours," she says as she unwraps the sandwich.

"I'm here, Ev, and I'm not leaving. I'll bring you two home. Before you say it, I know you can handle this without me. I know you're fine. But I want to stay."

I wait for her to protest, but instead she just nods and smiles at me.

She might be just fine without me.

I am anything but.

EVERLY

It's close to 10 o'clock when Jake pulls my car up in front of my apartment building. When Birdie was finally discharged, I tried to convince Jake he didn't need to drive us home because I didn't want him to have to leave his truck at the hospital. I knew it was pointless, but it made me feel a little better to at least try. It was a long day for all of us, but Birdie was such a trooper. Now she's fast asleep in the back seat of the car, sporting a new hot-pink fiberglass cast from her hand to her elbow.

Jake shifts my car into park, and like mirror images we both glance over our shoulders at a sleeping Birdie. She lasted two minutes before she was softly snoring, and Jake and I spent the rest of the 15-minute drive in a comfortable silence. My breath catches in my throat now, looking at this big, broody man who is so clearly worried about my daughter. I am realizing that Jake has such a soft side to him, one I never would have expected. Overprotective, confident, alpha with the body of a Greek God and a compassionate side? Yep, a guy like that is my weakness. Tingles skate over my skin at the way he looks at Birdie so adoringly, sending a zip of warmth through me.

Taking a breath to center myself, I brush the feeling aside trying to stop the feelings I have for Jake from bubbling to the surface.

He meets me beside the car, getting to Birdie's door first and opening it. "I've got her, Ev. You're tired," he whispers, carefully unbuckling Birdie out of her booster seat, gently scooping her into his arms like she weighs nothing. His six-foot something, carved like granite frame holding my baby in his arms as if she's his own makes my insides melt. My ovaries do a happy dance too. Birdie's eyes flutter open and her rose bud lips tip up in a smile. "Jake," she whispers, groggy from the medicine they gave her at the hospital and tired because it is way past her bedtime. "Will you tuck me in?"

Jake's big hand cups the back of her head while her legs wrap around him like a koala. "Of course I will, Birdie-girl." *Birdie-girl.* If that isn't the cutest. "Go back to sleep. I've got you." She lays her head down on his shoulder, his hand on the back of her head as he holds her closer.

My heart is in my throat and my eyes fill with tears that I swipe away. No mother ever wants to see her child hurt— today was a tough one— but seeing Birdie cared for the way she deserves to be, I am overwhelmed with emotions. I turn away, shutting the car door, trying to stop myself from swooning over the sight of Birdie in Jake's strong arms.

"Come here," he says reaching for my hand, lacing our fingers together. "Let's get you inside and to bed."

Once we're inside the apartment, I point to Birdie's bedroom and follow Jake as he carries her there. I pull back her covers and he gently places her in her bed, being careful not to bump her injured arm. "Do you want to change her into her pajamas or is she fine to sleep in this?" he whispers, looking over his shoulder at me. She's wearing a dress that is basically a long cotton t-shirt gathered at the waist.

"She's fine in what she's wearing."

Luckily, she doesn't wake as Jake pulls the covers over her and tucks her in. He brushes a lock of her blonde curls from her forehead. Jake doesn't have to be here with her. He didn't have to come to the hospital or wait there with us for hours. He didn't have to drive us home or tuck Birdie into bed. He's here because he wants to be. It's obvious that in the short amount of time he's known Birdie, he's come to genuinely care about her.

I kiss her forehead before we both leave her to sleep and head into the hallway.

"Go get ready for bed," Jake says, stopping in front of my bedroom door. "I'll make you a mug of tea."

I stare at him, speechless. I'm not used to being taken care of, and part of me wants to tell him he doesn't need to worry about me. But the bigger part is completely exhausted, barely able to keep my eyes open.

"Go, Everly," he says, before I can even attempt to protest. "It will help you sleep."

"You're spoiling me," I say, not sure what I did to deserve him.

He smiles as I turn towards my bedroom door. I need a

shower to rinse off the sterile hospital smell, and as soon as I step under the spray, I can feel the hot water start to soothe my tired muscles. I stay there for a very long time, before finally drying off and getting dressed into a T-shirt and sleep shorts. I'm climbing under the covers when I hear a soft knock at my door.

Jake appears in the doorway with a mug of steaming peppermint tea, setting the cup on my nightstand. "Feel better? I heard the shower going."

"Much," I say, pulling the covers up past my waist.

"Get some rest. You need a good night's sleep. I'm going to sleep on the couch in case Birdie needs something in the middle of the night."

"Jake, no. You can't sleep on the couch. Look at the size of you. Besides, you need to get your truck. It might get towed."

"My truck will be fine. I had a buddy pick it up for me. As for your couch, I've slept on smaller ones in college. I'll be fine." He tucks a loose strand of my hair behind my ear and the feel of his fingertips brushing against my skin sends chills up my spine. "I'll be here in case you or Birdie need anything. Just sleep, Everly." He tucks the comforter around me tighter.

"Thank you," I murmur before my eyes flutter closed and I fall into the deepest sleep I've had in a long time.

JAKE

Birdie grabs the loaf of bread while I crack three eggs into a frying pan. She climbs on to the chair she persuaded me to move into the kitchen so that she could make the toast, promising me it would be okay with her mom. I keep a close eye on her, praying she doesn't fall off and break her other arm. I can't believe I'm making breakfast with a seven-year-old. More than that, I can't believe I'm actually enjoying it. There was no way I was leaving last night. Everly needed a good night's sleep. Fortunately, she seems to have gotten just that. So far Birdie and I are the only ones awake.

I only got up once in the middle of the night to check on Birdie when I heard her tossing in her bed. She had to go to the washroom, so I waited in her bedroom until she was done and then tucked her back in. She fell back asleep quickly, but then woke me up around 6:30 this morning. I still had some time before I had to get to work, so Birdie and I decided to make breakfast.

I'm just finishing up the scrambled eggs when I hear the creak of a door and glance over my shoulder to find Everly. She looks rested, still in her pajamas with her hair pulled back into a high ponytail. She smiles when she sees Birdie and I in the kitchen.

"You're making me breakfast too? You must be a saint," she says as she walks into the kitchen, kissing Birdie on the top of her head. "How is your arm, sweet girl? Any pain? Did you sleep well?"

Everly strokes her hand through Birdie's curls. "It hurt a little when I woke up, but it's better now. Jake gave me my medicine from the doctor," she reports as Everly pulls her into her side.

"Um... what's this?" Everly asks Birdie, looking down at her broken arm.

"Jake signed my cast! He said I can get all my friends to sign it. Gramma and Grandpa too."

"And you let him sign it before your Mom?" Everly

teases her, tickling her side. Birdie's raspy laugh echoes around the small kitchen, making me laugh too.

"Don't worry. You can sign it too. There's lots of space." Birdie hops down from the chair, runs to the coffee table, and comes back with a Sharpie. After Everly signs her name, she gets back to work making toast. Her casted arm is making it a little more difficult, but she seems to be managing okay.

I slide the eggs onto a plate and turn off the stove, then pour a cup of coffee for Everly. "I've gotta get to work. But the eggs are made and Birdie's on toast, and there's extra coffee in the coffee maker. I'll text you later and see how things are going."

Four hugs from Birdie later, Everly walks me to the door. "Thank you for everything. I can't remember the last time I've felt this rested."

"I'm glad." I say, raking my hand though my bedhead. "Birdie will need another dose of medicine around noon."

"Okay... she didn't mind it?"

"I let her chase it with a scoop of ice cream," I chuckle. "Sorry about that."

Everly laughs and then goes up on her toes and hugs me. For a second, I foolishly thought she was going to kiss me. Wishful thinking. I hold her body to mine for as long as I can until I have to let her go.

I know it sounds insane, but I've never been as happy as I am when I'm with Everly and her daughter. And if being Everly's friend is the only way I get to be a part of their world, I'll have to accept that. But I sure as hell am going to try soon for something more.

I like a challenge.

TWELVE

GET IT TOGETHER. IT'S JUST DINNER

Jake

"Then cancel your plans" Tucker says on the other end of the phone as I race around my room trying to find the right shirt to wear.

"I'm not cancelling my plans."

He groans. "What's more important than the Yankees?"

"I can give you a list." I put him on speaker and throw my phone on my bed then take off my dark-blue T-shirt and toss it onto the growing pile of discarded shirts. What do you wear when you want to impress a girl? Everything I put on looks like I'm trying too hard, which I am, but she's not supposed to know that. I pull a light-gray one on instead, shaking my head at how wound up I am about tonight.

Normally I'd be all over beers and a game at Tuck and Holden's place. But tonight, I'm having dinner with Everly and Birdie. And I'm fucking excited about it. And nervous. "I gotta go. Have a beer for me tonight."

"Hold up, Jakey," Tuck gets in before I hang up the call. "What's going on tonight? You gotta date with beach girl? Please tell me you finally found your balls."

"Not exactly a date, but close enough. I'm having dinner at her house with her and her daughter."

"Shit, man," Tucker says. "That's a big fucking deal. You ready to hang with her kid?"

"Birdie is cool, I like hanging out with them. It's not a big deal," I say, not sure if I'm trying to convince Tuck or myself.

"So, it doesn't scare you... that she has a kid?"

It's a fair question. Not long ago, it probably would have scared me. But after the night at the hospital and breakfast the next morning, I can confidently answer it without hesitation.

"Not for a second."

I do realize that Everly having a kid makes things much more complicated. If things between us didn't work out, we'd have to be very careful with Birdie's feelings. But I'm getting ahead of myself. For now, Everly is still keeping me firmly in the friend's zone. If she would just let me in, I think we'd have a shot at something good.

"All right then," Tuck says. "I'm here for ya. Always will be."

"Thanks, man. I gotta run," I tell him, then end the call.

I swipe some molding clay through my hair and brush my teeth. After one last check in the mirror, I grab my keys from the hook by the door and head out to my truck. Ten minutes later, I'm standing outside of Everly's door with a small bouquet of flowers and a stuffed cat for Birdie that I found in a bin of stuffed animals near the till at the flower shop. I'm about to knock on their door when the door flies open. Birdie greets me with a smile as wide as a four-lane highway, her left arm in her hot-pink cast.

"He's here!"

"Birdie Marie. What have I told you about opening the door without me?" Everly appears in the hallway, wiping her hands on a tea towel. She smiles when she notices the flowers in my hand.

"These are for you. I hope you like daisies," I say to Everly, handing her the bouquet before turning to Birdie. "And this is for you, the bravest patient I know."

"A cat stuffy, Mommy! Jake brought me a cat stuffy!" Birdie says, holding the stuffed animal out for Everly to see. Then she pulls the cat into her chest and squeezes it. "Thank you, Jake. I love it."

Everly's eyes are on me. Weeks of seeing those light hazel eyes and nothing has changed... they still do crazy things to my pulse. A wave of heat creeps up my spine. I normally don't really *feel* things, but Everly is proving to be the exception to that rule.

My eyes trail down Everly's body as she walks towards the door, taking in her toned legs and slim waist. She's wearing a short, floral-printed skirt with a cropped, fitted T-shirt that reveals the smooth skin of her abdomen. Her chest looks fucking perfect too. My cock twitches in my shorts.

"Come inside." Birdie grabs my hand, pulling me inside as Everly smiles and closes the door behind us. I follow her to the kitchen, where she carefully places the stuffed cat I gave her on a stool.

"These are beautiful, thank you," Everly says, setting the flowers I gave her on the counter. "I'll just put them in a vase." She opens the cupboard above the fridge, standing on her tiptoes.

"Here, let me help you with that," I offer, rounding the bar. Everly steps out of the way, but the kitchen is so small she can't go far. I pull a vase from the cupboard, handing it to her, and a pretty pink flush creeps over her cheeks when our eyes meet. She startles when the oven timer goes off, then slips by me to grab an oven mitt from the counter. She lifts a pan of chicken and potatoes out of the oven, the scent filling the room.

"Why don't I put these in water for you?" I tell her, grabbing the bouquet.

"Birdie, do you wanna help me?" I ask, placing the vase under the tap. I turn the faucet, then jump when a jet of cold water shoots straight at me. "What the...!" Thankfully, I recall that Birdie is in the room and stop myself from finishing that sentence. Putting one hand out to shield myself, I reach for the tap again, turning it off. Beside me, Birdie is squealing with laughter. Everly hands me a towel, trying and failing to stifle a laugh as well.

"I'm sorry. I didn't think to mention that the tap is wonky. It's been like that since we moved in, I've just been too busy to ask my landlord to fix it. We've kind of learned to work around it. Duck and take cover, right Birdie?" Everly says to her daughter, who is still cracking up.

I do my best to dry off, then toss the tea towel on the counter. "Let me fix it. Do you have a wrench?"

Everly peeks up at me with an amused look in her eyes. Fuck, she's cute when she's having fun. Hot too, but I need to behave.

"Um... no?" She shrugs.

"Do you have a tool of any kind?"

"Why would I have tools? I wouldn't know what to do with them."

Good point. "I'm coming over tomorrow to fix this for you. You can't live like this."

"No, Jake, it's fine. I can call my landlord. You don't need—"

"I'm coming over tomorrow. It will take me 10 minutes.

Now, Birdie are you going to help me with the flowers?" I ask, changing the subject.

"Yes!" She hops on a kitchen stool next to her cat stuffy.

"Great. We're gonna need a pair of scissors."

I wrap my hand around the tap before turning it back on slowly to fill the vase. I unwrap the flowers while Birdie skips to a kitchen drawer to find the scissors. Then she does as I show her, taking each flower and carefully clipping the stem and then adding them to the vase.

"They're looking great," I tell her, tugging on the end of her blonde ponytail gently before looking at Everly. "Her broken arm hasn't slowed her down."

Everly chuckles, shaking her head. "Not one bit."

"I'm really good at putting flowers in a vase. Mommy loves having flowers in the house. Says they make people happy because they trigger our happy brain," Birdie says confidently, and I can't help but smile. I love hanging around this kid, she's hilarious.

I catch Everly watching us, and I wink at her, making the blush of her cheeks pinken even deeper. She looks away, busying herself with dinner. I love that I can make her flustered. The flirting has been pretty one-sided, but every time I'm with Everly her walls seem to come down a little more.

"Okay, now where should we put them?" I ask Birdie.

"I think the coffee table is a good idea. Mommy likes her flowers there," she says hopping off the stool. "I can do it."

"Are you sure? Even with your arm in a cast?"

"I'm sure."

I hand her the vase and watch the way she catches her bottom lip under her front teeth like her mom often does. She walks carefully towards the coffee table, then sets the flowers down.

"Ta da!" she exclaims, then turns and runs back towards

me. Thankfully I anticipate what she's going to do next and catch her when she jumps into my arms.

She squeals, wrapping her tiny arms around my neck while I tickle her sides making her giggle like crazy. "Jake!" She laughs and I tickle her a little more before I set her down to the floor. This kid. She is too cute for her own good. "I'm not really ticklish!"

I turn my gaze to Everly, who is laughing, watching Birdie and me from the kitchen. My heart tightens. My eyes drop to her mouth, drawn to her smile, and a warmth spreads through my entire body.

"Next time try her feet." Everly winks before carrying a stack of dinner plates to the table.

"I'll remember that," I nod with a smile.

I feel a wave of gratitude that they have let me into their little world. I am in awe at what an incredible mother Everly is, and Birdie is such a great kid. I want more with Everly, but for now this feels pretty damn good.

Birdie comes to stand next to her mom, and Everly bends to kiss the top of her head. "Dinner is almost ready, Birdie. How 'bout you go wash your hands?"

Everly gently squeezes Birdie's chin before she skips down the hall to the bathroom. As Everly finishes setting the table I ask her if I can help with anything. "Feel free to put me to work."

"Everything is ready but thank you. Now, what can I get you to drink?"

"I'll have whatever you're having."

"Two iced teas it is." She grabs a pitcher from the fridge and pours us each a glass. "Thank you again for the flowers. I love them. You know, you made Birdie's entire week by being here tonight."

"Getting the invite made my whole week too," I say, my

eyes glued to hers. Shit. I am in trouble. All I can think about is kissing her perfect pink lips, finally getting to know what they would feel like against mine.

The room suddenly feels too small. I've spent the better part of the past three weeks thinking about this girl. Would it be okay if I kissed her? Has she had a change of heart about being friends and nothing more? My pulse starts to pick up, but just then Birdie runs back into the kitchen. Before taking her seat at the table, she reaches for her cat and places him beside her plate.

"Daisy is eating with us too," she announces.

"Daisy?" I ask. "Is that her name? Good choice, Birdie."

"Like the flowers you gave Mommy," she says with a grin.

My eyes find Everly's, and that feeling, that longing, immediately returns. I'm starting to feel like I'm losing my mind. I need to know what she tastes like, and I need it to happen soon.

Get it together, Jake. It's just dinner.

But I want more. Yes, I want a lot more with Everly, but how do I get there? We have chemistry, that is undeniable. But we also have a lot standing in our way. Her ex-husband, for one. Then there's the age gap, which Everly seems hung up on. Oh, and until a few weeks ago I was still imagining Jade coming back from Italy asking for a second chance.

There is also Birdie. The kid is amazing, and she clearly is everything to Everly. I would never want to do anything, even inadvertently, that could somehow hurt her feelings.

Just a few months ago, I wasn't even sure I wanted kids. After losing my parents, it's not something I really saw for myself. I've always worried that my grief would impact my ability to be a good dad. I still think it will. But being around Birdie has me questioning all of that.

"Let me top you up," Everly says with the pitcher in her

hand. "Then we'll sit down to eat."

I am painfully aware of her proximity to me, of the curve of her hips and her smooth skin. I've lost count of all the times I've jacked off to those images of her or suffered through a cold shower in the last few weeks.

I feel like I'm 17 again. How much longer can I resist her?

"Cheers," she says with a smile, extending her glass to me.

I clink my glass with hers, locking eyes. The emotion I see in her eyes seems to mirror my own, and I wonder if maybe she feels the same way. She tips her glass to her mouth, her long, slender neck taunting me.

"Thank you for this," I tell her, taking a sip and then setting my glass on the counter.

"For what? A glass of iced tea?"

"For inviting me tonight."

She doesn't say anything in response, but the heat in her eyes is there. She swallows, and I sense the apprehension in her. She's holding back. Why is she still so nervous? Is it our age gap? Or is it that she's been burned before?

She has to know I'm nothing like her asshole ex. I wish she would just give me a chance to prove that to her.

Birdie tugs at my sleeve, interrupting my thoughts. "Jake, want to do something fun?"

"Like what?"

"We can play Nintendo." Birdie looks up at me with pleading eyes. "I have Mario Kart!"

"Right now?"

"Yes!"

Everly shakes her head, bringing dinner to the table. "After dinner, Birdie. We're going to eat first."

Everly scoops a serving of chicken, potatoes, and roasted cauliflower on Birdie's plate, and I try not to laugh when I see her scowl at the vegetables. Her expression speaks for itself.

"Mommy, can me and Jake *please* play Mario Kart after dinner?"

"If Jake's up for it, baby."

"Only if I can be Luigi," I tell her, spooning the cauliflower onto my plate.

"You can." Birdie nods. "Eat fast, Jake. Then we can play."

Everly raises her eyebrows at Birdie. "We will enjoy the meal I cooked and when we are done, and you've taken your dish to the sink, you can play."

"Okay," Birdie says. Then she leans into her mom's shoulder and whispers, but I can hear every word. "Mommy, should I warn him that I'm really good?"

Everly leans towards Birdie, but her eyes are still on me, a mischievous smile on her face. "I think you should surprise him. He won't see you coming."

Everly winks at me. And in that moment, I am positive that I want more nights like this with these two.

It turns out Birdie wasn't kidding. She beat me fair and square the first time, and then we split the next couple of games. Eventually Everly stepped in to point out it was well past Birdie's bedtime.

After some protesting, Birdie agreed to get ready for bed, but only after I promised I would read her a bedtime story. At first, I was nervous. Playing Mario Kart with her is easy—I'm a dude, I can play video games—but reading her a bedtime story is out of my wheelhouse. But after reading a couple of pages, my nerves eased.

Afterwards, I watched Everly tuck Birdie in beside her new stuffed cat, then she kissed her goodnight. I gave her toes a squeeze and then followed Everly out her door into the hall.

I've wanted to get to know Everly ever since that night I first bumped into her at Catch 21. After tonight, I know that I want Birdie in my life too. Part of me wonders if I'm moving too fast. Let's face it, I don't know the first thing about taking care of a kid. The crazy thing is… I really want to try.

Back in the kitchen, Everly sets two wine glasses down on the counter then asks me to grab the bottle of wine from the fridge. I crack the screw top then hand her the bottle and she pours us each a glass.

"Thanks for doing the dishes," she says. "It was nice to have the night off. You seem to be spoiling me a lot lately."

"Of course," I tell her. Everly has been through so much. If doing her dishes and tidying up her kitchen after dinner gives her a break, then I'm happy to do it. It's beginning to feel like I'd do just about anything for this girl and her daughter.

"I'm sorry that took so long. Birdie can drag a bedtime routine out for hours. Believe it or not, tonight was actually a sped-up version. I had to cut a deal with her to move things along."

"Oh yeah? What did she sweet talk you in to?"

She leans against the counter with a smirk. "An ice cream date… that I may have agreed to invite you to."

I grin at her. "If this is your way of asking me out on a date, Ev, the answer is yes. I give in, I'm all yours."

Everly grabs a tea towel from the counter and swats it at my hip. "Don't be smug, Jake Matthews," she giggles. "And stop being cute."

I wink, easily grabbing the tea towel out of her hands.

Her eyes grow wide as she watches me wind up the towel. She takes a step back, but I have her boxed in against the wall of the tiny kitchen. "Jake! Don't you dare. You wouldn't," she says through a laugh.

I keep winding the towel and Everly keeps on laughing. "Oh, I definitely would... unless you admit you want to take me on our third date?"

"*Third* date?" Her back is to the wall now. I have her trapped.

"Yep."

"How do you figure?"

"First was the diner. Second date is tonight. Third will be our ice cream date."

She narrows her eyes at me, hands on her hips. It's fucking adorable. "Jake, you agreed the diner wasn't a date."

"I lied." Then I gently smack the side of her hip with the tea towel.

"Jake!" She squeals, her hand shooting towards the polka dot tea towel as she tries to steal it from me. As she grabs hold of the fabric, my hands slip around her waist, pulling her back into my chest. We're both laughing as she struggles to get loose. I must have close to 100 pounds on her, so she can wiggle all she wants, but she's not going anywhere.

Our hushed laughs fill the kitchen. We're trying not to wake up Birdie but we're having too much fun. I squeeze her a little tighter. She laughs a little harder and squirms a little more, but it's a half-assed attempt.

Everly's laughter is like a song. I feel like I could listen to it for the rest of my life on repeat, volume on high in the car with the windows rolled down.

"Say it, Ev..." I hold her a little tighter.

"What do you want me to say?"

"You know what I want you to say." This is the closest I've ever been to her. Her back pressed against my chest, the top of her head under my chin. I'm probably too close, hyperaware of her slender body rubbing against me and my eager cock. I wonder if she can feel that I'm sporting a semi in my shorts.

"Fine, fine... it's a date, Jake." She says through a laugh as I release the hold I have on her, my skin buzzing from the feel of her against me. "A date between *friends*. Birdie isn't ready for anything more."

I wish she didn't tack on the word *friends* to the end of that sentence, but how can I argue? Birdie is always Everly's main concern, and I admire that about her. She's a good mom.

"We'll go on a friend-date then," I say, voice as steady as it can be. If it means I get another minute with Everly, then that's what we'll call it.

"Thank you, Jake. And thank you for everything this week." Everly's eyes meet mine. "It made all the difference that Birdie had tonight to look forward to. It's so hard to see her upset. She's my baby, you know? She doesn't deserve to be put on the back burner, where her dad puts her. Then she breaks her arm."

I clench my jaw before I say something about her ex and risk sounding like a total asshole. "She's a good kid. She's a handful sometimes, but she's sweet and kind and she deserves to feel like she's a priority."

I can tell she's upset by the way her shoulders tighten as she talks. My throat burns when I swallow down the anger I feel toward the man who somehow shares the same DNA as Birdie. How could any man neglect a kid like her? "Ev." I tip her chin up, so she's forced to look at me. "She's amazing. And she has you. Everything is going to be okay."

Her smile returns. "I may be slightly biased, but she is the best kid I know."

I love the way she lights up when she talks about her. I think back to what I witnessed between Everly and her ex at The Dockside. The way he spoke to her, the terrible things he said. The way Birdie's face crumpled when her dad left. I didn't want to bring it up when Birdie might be able to overhear, but I feel like we can't avoid talking about it forever.

"Do you want to talk about what happened at The Dockside?"

She flinches at my question. "I'm sorry you had to see that."

"*You're* sorry?" My tone turns gruff. "He should be sorry. Is he always that much of an asshole? Sorry, I don't want to overstep. But I hated the way he was talking to you."

She looks away and nods. I want so badly to pull her to me, to take her in my arms. But I don't.

Instead, I hold out my hand to her and wait for her to take it. She makes eye contact for a moment, like she's weighing something in her mind, then takes my hand. I tug her into the living room and we both sink down onto the couch, angling our bodies so that we're facing each other.

"Will you talk to me?" I ask, her hand still in mine. "If it makes you uncomfortable you don't have to. No pressure, but I'd like to be there for you."

Everly swallows hard, her expression pained. I give her a hand a squeeze, my thumb rubbing over the tops of her knuckles. I sit and wait for her to tell me her story. We're both silent for a moment, before she finally starts to talk.

"I married a monster."

THIRTEEN
TROPHY WIFE

Everly
My stomach tightens the way it always does when I think about my ex-husband. I wasn't planning to have this conversation tonight.

I listen for a moment to make sure there is no noise coming from the direction of Birdie's room, but after the excitement of Jake's visit tonight I'm sure she's sleeping soundly by now. I look down, to where my hand is still intertwined with Jakes, and try to think of the best place to start. I may as well go back to the beginning. Grant was a self-centered jerk from almost the day that I met him.

"Grant was a total playboy when I met him, but I had no clue. We met at a party. It was at a mutual friend's house. He was charming, confident, and handsome and I guess I was naïve and ignored the red flags." I pause and take a deep breath. Talking about Grant isn't easy, there is still so much pain buried in these memories.

"We were sort of a whirlwind right from the start, texting each other all day and all night. He told me he didn't really want anything serious, so I guess I should have listened to him. But at the same time, he was taking me out to nice restaurants, introducing me to his friends and family. We spent all our time together. It felt serious. It felt so much like a relationship... I guess I forgot he wasn't looking for one. I was stupid. I really thought he loved me until I found out later that I wasn't the only one he was sleeping with."

Jake flinches and squeezes my hand a little tighter but doesn't say a word. He doesn't need to... the look on his face tells me everything. His jaw is clenched, his dark eyes look thunderous.

I sigh. "Anyways, eight months later my whole life changed when I found out I was pregnant with Birdie. I remember just staring at the test in shock. And I was worried about how Grant would react, but when I told him he said that we should get married and raise our baby together. Honestly, I was relieved. We were young and I was so scared, I didn't see how I could raise a child on my own. So, getting married seemed like the best option I had. And back then, I didn't know the real Grant."

Jake's eyes haven't left mine. He holds my hand and listens to every word. I can tell that he's angry, but I also see the care and compassion in his expression when he looks at me. I wish I'd found a man like Jake when I was in my twenties. The kind of man who would make a great husband and father. The total opposite of the man I ended up marrying.

I draw in a shaky breath. "I never should have married him. Looking back, I know that I was never in love with Grant. I stayed for Birdie."

My confession hangs between us. "You never loved him?" Jake asks me. "Even before you married him?"

"No, not even then."

"Fuck," he mutters. "I'm sorry."

"It gets worse." A sick feeling swirls in my stomach. "I

was a newlywed and expecting my first baby. It should have been a really happy and exciting time, but they ended up being some of the hardest days of my life."

Jake's jaw tenses again, a muscle pulsing right below his ear. I've never seen him look this angry.

"We hid it from everyone until about halfway through the pregnancy, Grant kept coming up with excuses not to share the news. When we finally did tell his parents, it was a disaster. You'd think they would be excited to have a grandchild on the way, but they weren't. They accused me of getting pregnant on purpose to try to trap him. I was so humiliated."

I suddenly feel the urge to cry pricking at my throat. Even after all these years, it still hurts me to think back to that time in my life. Jake runs his thumb along the top of my hand, soothing me, giving me the courage to keep going. I inhale then exhale a long breath.

"I caught him with another woman two weeks before I had Birdie. I think deep down I knew it was happening for a while but seeing it with my own eyes destroyed me."

Jake squeezes my hand, catching my gaze. "He's an asshole, Ev. He never deserved you. You know that right?"

"I do now, yeah. But I didn't at the time. I was nine months pregnant and as big as a house, my new in-laws were still accusing me of all kinds of awful things and my husband was cheating on me. My confidence was at an all-time low."

"But then I had Birdie and Grant promised to change. He promised he would be a better husband and a good dad. And things got better for a little while. Right from the start, I loved being Birdie's mom. And Grant *was* around more. It felt like we were a family, and I thought maybe it could work. But it didn't last. By the time her first birthday rolled around, things were getting worse again. He was always working late, finding excuses not to be home. He was cold to me, and I was worried he was cheating again, but when I would ask him about it, he'd lose it." I sigh. "I finally had enough one night, years later, and brought up a divorce when a high fever sent Birdie to the hospital, and I couldn't get a hold of him. He wasn't responding to my calls or texts, and it pissed me off. She was never a priority in his life. Later, I found out there were four other women over the course of our marriage. I'm pretty sure there were probably more."

Jake's expression furrows, and he drags his free hand over his jaw. "I can't believe what he has put you through."

"We divorced soon after that, but to make the transition easier on Birdie, we never moved out, Birdie and I just moved to a separate wing in the house."

I married a man who didn't care enough to be faithful to me. That fact used to sting. Now that we're divorced, it's just... regret. Grant and I were never destined for forever, but despite everything, I don't regret a thing. Because without Grant, I'd never have Birdie.

Birdie is still too young to see the truth about her father. For now, I do my best to protect her, to make excuses for why Grant isn't around, but one day she's going to realize that he is an absent father and she'll have to carry the weight of that. Until then, all I can do is love her enough for the both of us.

"Why did you finally decide to leave?" Jake asks quietly.

I shrug. "I just reached the point where I'd finally had enough. I was tired of thinking about Grant's feelings when he had zero respect for me."

"And you came to Reed Point to be closer to your parents?"

"Yes. My mom had been suggesting it for a long time, but I didn't feel like it was really an option until recently." I tell him about Grant's move to North Carolina, and how it was suddenly cut short.

"That's why he was here the other day, he wants us to move back now that he is home. I've already told him that's not happening, and he's not exactly thrilled about it. He's even cut off all financial support to try to convince me to change my mind. So, now all we have is my salary from the restaurant and some savings."

The more I tell Jake, the more rigid his body gets. I am normally a pretty private person; I can't believe I've sat here and shared every ugly detail of my life. But Jake is easy to open up to. I feel like I've known him for much longer than I have.

"So, he cut you off when you refused to terminate your lease and come home?"

"He did. But if I'm being honest, I think it has been for the best. There are no more strings. He can't hold anything over my head," I say. "I can't believe I'm telling you all of this. It's so embarrassing."

Jake shifts in his seat, sliding closer to me. The expression is his eyes is so earnest, I feel it deep in my chest. "First of all, you have nothing to be embarrassed about. Just hearing what he put you through makes me want to put my fist through his face. He's lucky I didn't know any of this when I saw him last week; there would have been cops involved." Jake's voice is as sharp as a blade. "And second, you should be proud of yourself, Ev. It takes courage to do what you did."

"It hasn't been easy but it's worth it. I know I made the right decision to come here."

"Where is he now?" He asks. "Where did you live before coming to Reed Point?"

"He's in Brookmont." I inhale a long breath. "He's living in the home that used to be ours. We bought the house a year after Birdie was born. It's huge and it cost a fortune, and I hated it. It was all white—the walls, the cupboards, the couches, the furniture. It felt like living in a museum. But Grant never cared about my opinion. He only wanted a trophy wife who he could parade around at high profile functions. He could have cared less if I was happy or not." I swallow.

Jake cringes. "What an asshole."

"I know."

"So, I assume he fought you on the divorce?" Jake asks.

"It actually went quite smoothly. His parents, who are over-the-top wealthy, were all too happy to be rid of me, so they called in a favor with a judge they knew and had our divorce fast-tracked. I had to agree to 50-50 custody, which I didn't want to do—"

"They bullied you."

"Essentially." I tell him. "I knew I didn't stand a chance against their high-powered attorneys. I also knew that it didn't really matter because when it came right down to it, Grant wouldn't make the effort to see Birdie anyways. So, I agreed, just to make it all go away."

"I hate everything that you went through to bring you here," Jake says, his voice low. "But ... I'm really glad you're here."

"I am too."

I nudge my knee against his. "Thanks for listening. I haven't told many people about this." It's true. Only Willa knows the entire story.

"I really appreciate you telling me." Jake says. "You're an incredible mother."

The compliment feels equally wonderful and appreciated. More importantly it feels special coming from him because I like him. I like him a lot more than I should or ever thought possible. I have so many reasons I shouldn't think about him the way that I do, but my heart isn't listening.

I'm suddenly very aware of how close we are. I inhale a shaky breath, and the scent of his cologne fills my nose. Jake shifts forward, and his strong arms wrap around me, pulling me into his chest. I feel all of the tension in me disappear. I can breathe again in his arms. Jake is a safe place.

His hand massages my back in small circles while I close my eyes, fighting the tears that threaten to escape. I'm exhausted. This is the first time since we moved to Reed Point that I've allowed myself to let go and just... feel. I've had to put on a brave face for Birdie, to be strong enough for the two of us, but tonight it feels good to let go and lean on Jake. I like the way it feels to be wrapped up in his arms. I can't remember the last time I've been hugged like this. It's been years.

We stay like that, neither of us moving except for the rise and fall of our chests. I melt into him, my face tucked against his chest. He trails his hand down my ponytail. I want to stay like this forever.

Jake coasts his hands down my arms, and we pull apart slowly. His eyes find mine and he is looking at me with such adoration that my heart expands two sizes in my chest.

Then his gaze falls to my lips and all I hear is the sound of my heart beating in my chest. He must be able to hear it too. I hold my breath, waiting to see what is going to happen next.

Then, Jake's hand softly finds the edge of my jaw. I shiver at his touch, lost in his gaze. The space between us has been erased.

"I really want to kiss you," he murmurs, his eyes leaving mine to travel down to my mouth. I lick my lips absentmindedly and I feel his hand roam my leg from my knee up my thigh a few inches, making the space between my thighs ache.

Desire floods through me. I shouldn't want this—Jake is too young. But I can't move. I can't stop it. Also, every fiber of my being wants to lock my lips to his.

"I want to kiss you so fucking bad." He slides his other hand from my jaw to the back of my neck, drawing us even closer together. Then he tips his head and his lips fuse to mine, tasting me. Soft, a little uncertain. One feel of his tongue against my lips and I'm opening for him, my lips parting as his tongue slips inside to meet mine. With a sigh, he deepens the kiss, our tongues moving together—slow, lingering, and full of promises. Promises I'm not sure I can keep... but I don't want to stop.

My God, Jake can kiss.

I don't ever remember being kissed like this.

It's soothing, and bold and soft all at the same time.

The kiss is everything I have ever dreamed a kiss should be.

His grip on the back of my neck tightens as his mouth moves against mine, his other hand squeezing my thigh, making me moan against his lips. My skin tingles as he kisses me harder.

My God, his mouth on mine feels like magic.

My hands cling to his arms, afraid if he stops, I'll never feel like this again.

Before I have time to process what's happening, Jake

breaks the kiss. His eyes are hazy, a small smile tugging the corners of his mouth. I close my eyes as he gently swipes his thumb across my bottom lip.

I open my eyes, shaking my head, realizing what I've just done. Exactly what I told myself I wouldn't do.

"Ev..."

"Jake," I interrupt him, returning to my senses. "I told you, this can't happen."

Jake's dark eyes capture mine. "I know I agreed to friends. I've changed my mind."

FOURTEEN

SEXY LINGERIE AND BATTERY OPERATED TOYS

Everly

Four days later and I still can't get that kiss out of my mind.

It is seared so hard and deep into my heart that it has become one of the hottest moments of my life.

Apparently, I'm shit at hiding my obsessive thoughts about the way Jake tasted, the pillowy softness of his lips and how good it felt when he sucked on my tongue, because Franny picks up on the fact that my mind is definitely elsewhere. If she only knew the reason, I'd never hear the end of it.

"Earth to Everly!" she calls, laughing. "Everything okay?"

Thankfully, she is able to watch Birdie tonight while I'm at work. I already had to miss a shift this week when I took Birdie to a specialist appointment for her broken arm. The good news is the doctor said her arm looks like it's healing well, and she should be out of the cast in three weeks. The bad news is I lost a day's pay, which I really can't afford—especially with Birdie's birthday coming up soon.

Franny is looking at me now with a crease between her

eyebrows. "Where did you just go, because you weren't in the same room as me."

"I'm just tired. Early morning with Birdie today."

I hope that will satisfy her curiosity, because I'm not ready to open up about the real reason I'm so distracted. My mind wanders right back to Jake and to the memory of him and I on this couch, his knee touching mine, his tongue in my mouth. Heat flares over my skin, my thong soaked.

If *kissing* Jake has done this to me, what would it be like if we took things further? It's been playing like a reel in my mind for weeks now, taking me down a rabbit hole of fantasies. I've pictured him on my couch, legs spread, cock hard while I ride him. I've imagined him in the shower, my legs wrapped around his waist, my back pressed up against the tile wall while he fucks into me. I've imagined what he looks like underneath his clothes. Where does the tattoo I saw on his bicep end? Are there more? Does he have chest hair, is he circumcised, does he have a happy trail I could follow like a treasure map to a long, thick cock? The fine, soft hair on a man's pelvis is my weakness. The filthy scenarios I've dreamt up in my mind have been constant and dirty.

That one kiss with Jake has made me realize how much I was missing out on with Grant. I was inexperienced when I met him, and I was expecting sex to be one mind-shattering orgasm after another. I thought we would experiment with different positions, in every room of the house. But it turned out that not only was Grant a lacklustre boyfriend, but he was completely boring in bed too. He was a taker. He never took the time to get me off, and he wouldn't have been able to find my G-spot with GPS and a flashlight. From beginning to end, sex with Grant lasted 10 minutes tops, and after he climaxed, he'd roll over and go to sleep.

I tried to spice things up with sexy lingerie and battery-operated toys, but he never seemed to care. Nothing ever changed. Like everything else about my relationship with Grant, our sex life left me feeling lonely and unwanted.

And then I found out he was cheating.

Well, my condolences to whatever women Grant is sleeping with now. I would never want to have mediocre sex with him again. I want a guy who will wrap his hand around my throat as he fucks me into the mattress, someone who will whisper filthy things in my ear about all the things he wants to do to me.

"What time are you off tonight?" Franny asks, interrupting my daydreams yet again. I turn my face, hoping to hide my flushed cheeks.

"Later than I'd like," I tell her. "Around 11."

"Well, we'll save you some chili," she says, walking towards the kitchen to stir the pot on the stove. "This smells really good, Ev. I don't want you to miss out."

She offers me a weak smile when she sees my face fall. She knows how much I hate missing nights with Birdie.

"I'm sorry. I didn't mean it that way. You know what I meant."

"It's fine, I know. I'm just feeling a little frustrated." I sigh, standing up from the couch to grab my duffle. "I've never been away from Birdie this much and with her broken arm, I just feel guilty."

Franny rounds the kitchen island to put her hands on my shoulders, her brown eyes scanning my face worriedly. She pulls me into a hug. "I know, hon. I wish there was something more I could do."

"Jake offered me a job working for him," I tell her. "It's a 9 to 2, so I wouldn't have to worry about working nights or weekends." I hadn't planned on telling Franny about a job offer I can't accept, but I haven't been able to get it out of my mind.

"Oh honey, then why are you still killing yourself at the restaurant?"

I wish it was that easy. The job sounds perfect but working with the man I've been fantasizing about day in, and day out feels like a terrible idea.

A smile plays on her lips. "You really like him, don't you?"

"I do… and that's the problem…" I exhale a deep breath.

"Are you afraid of something happening if you're working in the same office together?"

"That's exactly what I'm afraid of," I admit.

"And would it be so terrible if it did?" Franny asks.

"I just think that bringing a man into Birdie's life right now is a risk I'm not ready to take. What if she gets attached to him and then things go south with us?"

"Then we'll all be here for her… and for you. Your parents, Violet, me. We're your family now," she says, patting my arm gently. "So, is that why I haven't seen Jake around lately?"

My brow raises and a laugh escapes me. "Are you spying on me, Franny?"

"I know he walks you home at night after work." She shrugs. "I've heard him in the hallway. I might peek through the peep hole sometimes. The man is seriously a work of art. Do you blame me?"

"I kissed him," I confess. "I had him over for dinner last week and after Birdie went to bed, he kissed me."

Franny's eyes go wider than saucers. "Ahh. So, *that's* why you've been so out of it."

My teeth sink into my bottom lip, hiding a smile. "I've been a little sidetracked ever since, I guess."

"Then I don't have to ask how the kiss was."

My cheeks blaze hotter than a stove. "Franny, it was the perfect first kiss. It could never be topped."

"Sounds like a once in a lifetime kiss to me."

I try to ignore the tingle that floats up my spine but when my heart follows next, tumbling in slow motion to the bottom of my stomach, I know she's right.

It was.

THE WEEK FLIES BY IN A BLUR AS I TAKE AS MANY SHIFTS AS I can at the restaurant to make some extra money. It's Birdie's birthday next month and she wants a new bike. I also need to sign the contract and pay for this season's dance classes that start in September since she's decided she likes the studio and wants to commit to a company program. It means she'll be dancing more hours, competing in the spring, and performing in a year-end recital. And dance isn't cheap. But she's made some great friends and I know the benefits of it firsthand. I grew up spending hours in a studio doing competitive dancing and I loved it. I want Birdie to have the same experience.

Being busy at work has given me an excuse to keep Jake at arm's length. Maybe if I wasn't so worried about falling for him, we could be spending more time together. He still shows up at the restaurant to walk me home when he knows I'm working late, but I've been careful not to cross any boundaries with him since *the kiss*. We're friends. That's it. I'm sure he wants to know where things stand between us. There were a couple of times I got the feeling he wanted to kiss me goodnight, but to his credit he's been giving me space.

I still haven't made good on the ice cream date I promised Birdie and Jake that night at my apartment. I've thought back to that evening so many times. It was so easy and comfortable. It was the polar opposite of the uptight, stupid dinner parties Grant liked to plan. In just a few short weeks, Jake gets me better than the man I married.

I turn my attention to Birdie, who is asleep in my arms on the couch. She fell asleep halfway through our movie, but I haven't had the heart to move her even though my arm went numb 15 minutes ago. I can't get enough of her little snores.

My phone lights up on the couch next to me and I groan inwardly when I see my mother-in-law's name on the screen. Using my free hand, I swipe to read the message.

> Miranda: Everly, I would like Birdie to come stay with us the weekend after her birthday. We are making plans to celebrate with the family.

I've never been away from Birdie for more than a night so a weekend without her makes me anxious. More than that, the thought of Birdie staying with the Billings without me scares me.

It's not that Grant's parents don't love her; they just have a very different way of showing it. They buy her things, but they rarely actually spend time with her. Anytime she's at their house, she ends up watching TV for hours by herself while their housekeeper makes sure she's fed and taken care of.

Honestly, Birdie would probably love a party. What soon-to-be 8-year-old doesn't want cake and presents? But part of me worries that Grant will find a way to disappoint her. He always does.

Will he even remember to show up? And if he does, will he bring his most recent flavor of the month?

The whole thing makes my skin crawl.

I look down at Birdie's sleeping face, listening to the soft sounds of her breathing. I'll talk to her about it and if she wants to go, I'll let her.

I cradle her sleeping body against mine for a few more minutes before I gently lift her, carry her to her bedroom and tuck her into her bed for the night. She stirs when my lips brush over her forehead, but she turns on her side, drifting quickly back to sleep.

The weekend at Miranda's is still weeks away, but I'm already dreading it.

Nobody has ever said parenting is easy.

FIFTEEN

WE'RE NOT THE FUCKING MAFIA

J ake
My poker game is shit.

I've lost seven hands in a row to Grayson, Tucker, Holden, and the card shark herself, my Gran. The only person playing even worse than me is Tucker, which isn't fucking surprising.

I'm off my game. And I know exactly why.

It has been almost two weeks since I kissed Everly. Two weeks of one-word text responses, quiet walks home after she works a night shift, and nothing more.

Everly is ignoring me.

And I fucking hate it.

I scratch my fingers through my beard, which is longer than usual. I'm a fucking idiot. I knew it was too soon to kiss her, but I did it anyway. Sitting so close to her after such a great evening together, my willpower was non-existent. And the kiss was perfect. It *was* perfect, wasn't it? It felt that way to me.

It was obviously too much too soon though. Everly made that pretty clear when she reminded me right afterwards that we could never be more than friends. I had every intention of going slow, but my resolve crumbled. Dammit.

It's been so long since a woman has made me feel this way. Jade was my only serious relationship. Since we broke up, there has been no one. It has been me and my hand for a while, except for one or two flings that aren't worth remembering.

But that day at the beach with Everly changed everything. I don't know why, but everything with her feels right. Jacking off to images of her in my mind was working in the beginning for a while until that night we had dinner at her house.

That night I wanted more. And now things between us are more complicated than ever. But I'm not giving up on us. I just need to figure out what I need to do.

"Maybe when you've been doing this as long as I have, you'll get the hang of it," Gran says matter-of-factly, knocking me from my thoughts. She stacks the pile of chips she just won on the table in front of her as Tucker groans and drops his head in his hands.

"Listen, you're lucky we even let you sit at the table with us," Grayson teases him. "Watch and learn from this woman right here. She's the GOAT of poker. She could teach you a few things."

Sierra planned this little dinner party for Gran tonight at her house, knowing that she was missing Haven Harbor and the boys after moving into her assisted facility home. Truth be told, they've missed her too.

"It sure smells good in that kitchen," Gran says from behind her cards. "I swear the cook at my place hates us all. You should see what he tried to get us to eat the other night."

"How bad could it be?" Tucker asks, throwing down a pair of kings.

"I don't even know. But the meat was green," she insists.

"Okay, that sounds terrible," Tuck says. "I'm busting you out of there next week and taking you to McDonald's."

Gran's eyes light up at the mention of the golden arches. She would eat three meals a day at McDick's if she could. Sierra and I take her there for lunch every year on her birthday.

"What else, Gran? You tell me what else is wrong and me and the guys will go down there and have a word with them."

"We're not the fucking mafia," I grumble. An image of me and the guys showing up in suits and gold chains pops into my head. Gran shoots me a glare. She has zero tolerance for cursing. "Sorry, Gran. My bad with the language."

"Now then. Since you asked," she says, turning towards Tucker. "My neighbor, Malcolm, next door likes to talk dirty. Says he knows how to work it."

"What! Whoa, Gran, this is TMI. I can't deal," I say, shaking my head. "For the love of everything, please stop."

She heaves out a breath. "I'm not dead, Jake. I still like the company of a man. But Malcolm comes on too strong. I don't really believe him. He's on the list for a hip replacement. How good could he really be?"

She shrugs her shoulders before laying down a royal flush. She reaches for the pot, sliding the mound of chips into her chest before reapplying her lipstick. "Be a doll, Jakey, and grab my sweater from the couch. All this winning is making me chilly."

Laughing, I stand to retrieve her cardigan. I stop when my eyes land on the framed family photo sitting on the mantel. My dad has his arms around my mom's waist, smile wide. My mom gazes down at Sierra, who's wearing a bright pink bathing suit. I'm standing next to my dad, my hands stuffed in the pockets of my board shorts, my expression serious. I remember the day it was taken. The beach was my mom's happy place, she could walk for hours along the sand, the tide rolling gently at her feet. That's partly why I love it too, I always think of her when I'm there.

Grief slams into me like a tsunami. It's been 15 years, but the loss of my parents is a pain that never goes away. My chest tightens. Grief is a wound. Over time it heals, but it leaves a scar. I was just a kid when my parents died in that fire; in the blink of an eye, our world changed, never to be the same again. I miss them.

Returning to the table with Gran's sweater, I see Sierra walking into the living room with drinks for us all. Grayson stands as soon as he sees her, and I don't miss the way his eyes are all over her as he takes the tray from her hands. I feel my jaw clench.

We've been here for an hour, and I've been acutely aware of how Grayson and my sister have been acting around each other the entire time. This isn't the first time I've noticed it since Sierra's return to Reed Point. I even confronted Grayson about it once, but he denied there's anything going on between them. And I trust him. Besides, he knows that if he tried to touch her, I'd rip his arms then his legs off and then find a creative way to dispose of his body.

I keep my eyes on them, pushing back my chair to stand as Grayson follows my sister into the kitchen, offering to help get dinner on the table. What the hell is going on with them?

"Sit down, Jake," Gran says. "I'd like to play some poker with my grandson."

I sit back down in my chair reluctantly. We're here for

Gran, I remind myself. I'll have to deal with this other shit later.

It's my turn to bet, but I can feel my jaw tic. I don't know if it's this growing suspicion about Sierra and Grayson that has me so stressed, or the frustrating situation I'm stuck in with Everly.

My mind has been pummelling me with memories of that kiss. When her lips met mine, every swipe of her tongue, the feel of her skin, the sounds she made. I haven't been able to stop thinking about how perfect she felt against me.

I'm also still bothered by the conversation we had that night about her ex. I hate that she was married to that asshole. I hate the way he treated her. It makes perfect sense now, why she's afraid to trust men. I understand why she's so hesitant to get into another relationship. There's no way she doesn't feel that spark between us, I'd bet everything on that. Hell, I find it difficult to be in the same room as her and not grasp the back of her neck and kiss the life out of her. But she went through hell and she's not ready to risk that again. She sees all men like her ex; selfish assholes who put themselves first who will take advantage of you.

Everly is scared to get hurt again. Worse yet, she's scared that Birdie will get hurt. That's what I'm up against.

This girl has woven herself into my life to such an extent that I can't imagine her not being a part of it. It's the way she smiles with her eyes, making you feel her happiness, or the way she looks at Birdie like she's the best thing to ever happen to her. It's the way she nibbles on her bottom lip when she's concentrating or worried that I'm going to tease her. Every time I close my eyes, I dream about kissing her again, craving that feeling of her body pulled in close to mine.

"I told you, this can't happen."

I've replayed her words in my mind dozens of times. Everly is scared, but I wish I could make her see that I'm worth the risk. I know we could be good together. I know what we have is special.

Sierra announces that it's time to eat, snapping me back to reality. We all take our seats in the dining room, squeezed together around the small table. We all dig in, the clatter of cutlery and laughter filling the room. I'm glad Gran didn't sell this place. It's not fancy, but it feels like home. And the view of the beach across the street from the living room window can't be beat.

After dinner, Sierra brings a homemade apple pie to the table, and it tastes just as incredible as it looks.

"Not everyone can make a pie this good," Gran tells her. "You have a gift like your mom."

The table goes quiet. The guys know that our parents died when we were kids, but they also know it's not something I talk about. I hate people feeling sorry for me. The silence at the table is deafening until the ever-unflappable Holden steps in to rescue us.

"So, did you hear about Tucker's run in with Norma at Seven Oaks?"

"Really?" Tuck shakes his head. "Do you have any stories that don't involve me? You're kind of obsessed, dude."

"What? It's a good story. Poor Norma wanted to die though. She was traumatized. Daisy witnessed the shit-show too."

Norma has worked at the Seven Oaks drug store in Reed Point for as long as anyone can remember. She's in her 70s now and knows everybody's business. Daisy has known Tucker all of his life, growing up in the house next to his. Their families are close friends.

"Tuck here," Holden says with a nod at Tucker. "Throws down a box of cereal, a jumbo box of condoms and a bottle of cherry-flavored lube at Norma's till. Poor Norma's jaw went slack, and I swear I heard her whispering the Lord's prayer under her breath. Daisy looked disgusted."

Grayson busts out a laugh. "Why didn't you go to Rexall? Everyone knows you can't buy that stuff at Seven Oaks. I don't think Norma has taken a sick day in 25 years. I hope you're ready for the whole town to know about your sex things."

Tucker rolls his eyes. "Do you have to call them sex things?"

"That's what they are," Grayson shrugs, shovelling a fork full of apple pie into his mouth.

"Norma needs to get a grip," Gran pipes up. "It's the 21st century, for Pete's sake. Does she think you're not having sex? And everyone knows cherry is the only flavour worth using." I drop my head into my palm in horror while the rest of the table cracks up.

After dessert, everyone takes turns hugging Gran before I leave to take her back to her place. It was a great evening, and I can see how happy it made her to see Sierra and the guys.

It's late, and I should head home and catch up on sleep. But my mind is racing. I'm unsettled, restless, and I know there is no chance I'll be able to fall asleep anytime soon. What I want to do is go to Everly's apartment, but I know that's not an option. So instead, I just drive, taking the road that winds alongside the cliffs above the beach. It's a quiet night, and I roll down the window to hear the sound of the waves crashing into shore.

I try to pinpoint what has me so bothered. It's Everly, of

course. It's always Everly. I'm crazy about her, but it feels like the line of obstacles in our way just keeps getting longer. It's more than that, though. It's also my sister. I'm so glad to have Sierra home, but ever since she's been back in Reed Point, there's been something off between us. And now I can't shake the feeling that she's keeping something from me. Is it Grayson? The thought of one of my best friends sneaking around with my sister makes my blood boil. I've known Grayson a long time, and he isn't a one girl kind of guy. But he wouldn't add my sister to his list of conquests, would he? He knows how protective I am when it comes to Sierra.

I pull a U-turn and head back towards Haven Harbor. I may not be able to do anything about the standstill with Everly tonight, but I *can* try to get an answer from Sierra. I feel like I'm going crazy, I have to do something.

Pulling my truck to a stop in front of my sister's house, I am relieved to see that the lights are still on. The front door is unlocked, so I knock as I push it open, then stop abruptly when I step into her place.

Grayson stands in the hallway, Sierra in his arms. That asshole is kissing my sister.

I see red, my hands tightening into fists at my sides.

IT'S A MIRACLE THAT I DIDN'T KNOCK HIM OUT. I DON'T recall exactly what happened, but I do know that I managed to stop myself from killing the guy. Sierra was in tears. They both swore they were going to tell me the truth. I find that hard to believe, since it turns out they've been together for two fucking months. Grayson says he loves her. I doubt that. He can't commit to a house plant, never mind a woman. My sister is the one girl I asked him to stay away from. I trusted him. I feel like an idiot.

Fuck him. Fuck all of it. If they expect me to give them my blessing, they're out of their minds. I'll give Grayson my foot to his face instead.

Back at home, I change into gym shorts and a T-shirt and head out for a run along the beach. My shoes pound the sand as images of the two of them flash through my head. By the time I get back to my place, I'm drenched with sweat and exhausted. Kicking off my shoes, I head to the bathroom for a shower. The hot water massages my muscles, easing the tension from my body. I'm towelling off when my phone vibrates on the bathroom counter. I'm tempted to ignore it, knowing it's probably my sister wanting to talk and I'm not ready for that. I pick it up anyways and am surprised when I see the name on the screen.

> Everly: Can we talk?
>
> Jake: Where are you?
>
> Everly: Home. Can you come over?
>
> Jake: On my way.

The message is shit timing, but let's face it— I miss Everly and if she wants to talk, I want to listen. Maybe it'll help distract me from everything else. My jaw is clenched tight the entire drive over to her apartment, and I take a deep breath before I knock on her door. My knees wobble a bit when my eyes catch on her.

She's wearing a pair of jeans and a white spaghetti strap tank top, her feet bare. Her hair is down in waves over her shoulders. Her normally bright smile is missing, but there's still a softness to her features.

"Hey." Her soft voice seeps into my core.

"Are you okay?" I ask, trying and failing to not sound like I'm worried about her. She puts me at ease with a smile.

"I'm fine. Birdie's fine. It's nothing like that."

I breathe out a sigh of relief. But, then what is it? This girl is going to be the death of me. I have no idea where we stand. It's been weeks since our kiss. And since then, she's gone out of her way to ignore me. A nervous feeling pulls at my gut.

Fuck. I shouldn't have kissed her. I shouldn't have asked her to open up to me about her ex. I did everything wrong.

Growing more anxious by the second about what she wants to talk about, I step inside her apartment, closing the door behind me. It's quiet, strangely quiet, and I wonder where Birdie is.

Everly stares at me for several moments, a veil masking the expression behind her eyes while I silently ask myself... what the hell does she need to tell me?

SIXTEEN

I HAVE A NEW KINK

Everly

I open the door and immediately notice the worry in Jake's eyes. My eyes track down the length of him to his low-slung joggers and fitted gray T-shirt. His hair is damp, and he smells like soap and clean laundry. Tension emanates from him.

I'm sure he's mad at me for ghosting him lately, and I guess I don't blame him. I freaked out. I needed space to sort out my feelings. Ever since that kiss I've been a mess of emotions, one minute angry at the way my life has turned out, and the next minute feeling like I'm seriously falling for this guy. This much younger guy. This guy who isn't Birdie's dad.

I think of the way Jake carried my baby girl to her bed the night she broke her arm, and of all the nights he has spent waiting outside Catch 21 just so I don't have to walk home alone.

"I'm sorry, Jake. After everything you did for us... I'm sorry. I shouldn't have shut you out."

He stares at me for a beat, combing his hand through his

hair, giving me the same look that he gives me when he's trying to be sweet. "You don't need to apologize. I'm the one who should be saying sorry. I shouldn't have kissed you. I knew the rule and I ignored it anyways."

My throat feels tight, and my voice breaks. "There's nothing you should feel sorry for." I stare at him for several heart beats, before inhaling a breath. "I liked the kiss. I didn't want you to stop."

My admission hangs in the air between us like a heavy fog. There's a nervousness in Jake's eyes that wasn't there when he walked in. He is quiet for a moment, and I can sense that he's contemplating the meaning behind what I've just said. Jake's eyes are glued to mine, and suddenly it seems ridiculous that I ever thought I could fight this pull between us.

"I got scared. I'm sorry, Jake. I told myself we could only be friends, that was the plan. But... I like you. I like you so much more than I ever expected to."

Jake reaches for me, his hand brushing my cheek, sending an electric current right through me to my core. "It's okay, Ev. I feel the exact same way. We're feeling the same things. Stop overthinking it."

Stop overthinking it? I know he's right, but it's not that easy.

"I love being around you," he continues. "And I love being with Birdie too. And when I'm not around you, I'm thinking about you. You're in my head, Everly."

"You're in my head too. I've tried to stop thinking about you, but you make it so hard."

He chuckles. "I'm not going to touch that."

I shake my head at him. His smile, his eyes, the way he's looking at me... it all feels like too much. In a perfect world, there would be no thinking twice. Jake and I would jump in with both feet. But I can't forget that there is so much at stake.

"What are you thinking about, Ev?"

How do I answer the question truthfully? I've tried to fight the feelings I have for Jake for weeks, but my resolve has slipped away. I've been scared to allow myself to fall for him, but more than that, I'm scared my daughter already has. She has to be my number one priority. I can't run the risk of having her heart broken.

"You know what I'm dealing with, Jake. You've seen it firsthand. There isn't a lot of room in my life for love. My life is a mess right now. I don't even know how long I'm staying in Reed Point. And then there's Birdie. She gets attached to people... I'm pretty sure she already is attached to you."

"I wouldn't be asking you for a chance if I wasn't falling for Birdie too. I swear to you. I know you two are a package deal." He takes a small step towards me, closing the space between us. "We don't have to put a label on it. We can take things slow... for as long as you want. But I can't fight this with you anymore. It's driving me crazy."

"What do you want from me, Jake?" I need to know exactly what he's thinking. Am I a one-night stand? Is he looking for a relationship? Does he understand that Birdie is my first priority? "Tell me exactly what you want. I need you to be clear."

"I want to be with you. Just you. We don't need the label, but I do want it to be just us." He pauses. "If we do this, there's no one else."

My breath hitches. I want all of that too.

If I knew this was going to work.

If I knew he wouldn't hurt me.

I swallow the knot in my throat as he takes one more step closer, his hands reaching up to my cup face.

"I promise you I'm not going to hurt you or Birdie. Give this a chance. I want to get to know you both better." Jake's thumb runs over the edge of my jaw, and I close my eyes, leaning into the touch. His other hand finds the curve of my hip, walking me backwards until he has me backed up against the door.

"What's stopping you from letting me in, Ev?"

He gently tips my chin to look at him and dips his face, so his mouth is inches from mine. I want him to kiss me. I want to tell him that I've thought about that kiss every minute of every day. The way it made me feel. The way *he* made me feel.

My breath hitches in my throat. "I don't want to get hurt again. And I don't even know how long we'll be in Reed Point. And there's Birdie. You're so much younger than me, Jake. We are in such different places in our lives."

"You don't need to be scared. I'm not interested in anyone but you. But say everything you need to say now, Ev. Ask me every question you need an answer to, because once I start kissing you, I'm not going to be able to stop."

I swallow hard at his words then draw a deep breath. "Why, Jake? Why me? When you can have any twenty-something-year-old you want."

Jake's fingers tighten on my hip as he tucks a strand of hair behind my ear with his other hand. "You say that like you're not the hottest woman I've ever seen. In my life. You make me hard every time you come near me. I don't give a fuck about our age gap. I don't want anyone but you, Ev. You're beautiful, smart, sexy as hell and my heart stopped fucking beating in my chest when I saw you for the first time. And I know you feel this pull between us like I do. It's not easy to find that with someone. I want you to admit you feel it too."

His words send goosebumps over my skin because he's right. I've never felt a connection like this. We're standing close enough that I can feel his chest expand against mine, and I swear I can feel his heartbeat through his t-shirt. But taking things further with him continues to make me nervous. "What if we're better off as friends? I don't want to ruin something good."

He lowers his gaze to mine, and his hand moves slowly to my lower back. He pulls my hips into his. "We both want more than just friends. Give this a shot. I know you want to."

Jake leans back a few inches, his eyes never leaving mine, searching for my answer.

I'm confused about so many things, but the one thing I know for sure is that I want him too. This desire inside of me threatens to unravel me.

Needing to touch him, my hands glide up to his chest to rest on the hard muscles of his pecs. He feels so good, but my body aches for more.

"I'm not going to hurt you," he breathes. "I know you're afraid, but I promise you, you don't need to be. And I'm just as nervous as you."

I look at him, surprised. "*I* make you nervous?"

He laughs softly. "I don't think you understand how nervous you make me. It's like I forget how to think when I'm around you."

I smile at him, taken aback by his confession. Just hearing him admit that I make him nervous makes me feel calmer. I am suddenly hyper-aware of Jake's proximity. Lust and need begin to override my fears, and I feel an overwhelming urge to give in and kiss him. His gaze pins me to the door, the hand on my lower back tightening as my body responds to him like it always does.

I'm falling.

Jake's eyes focus on mine, a deep, vibrant green. Heat expands through my center when he studies my lips reminding me there is definitely no shortage of chemistry between us. His fingertips ghost down the delicate skin at the back of my neck, making me arch into his touch. I swear I hear myself whimper. There's a pulse between my legs that throbs.

Jake moves closer. "Is Birdie in her room?"

"She's staying with my parents tonight."

There's a beat of silence. I draw in a breath, and goosebumps spread across my skin. Adrenaline spikes through me to my core. With every second he searches my gaze, my resolve crumbles a little more until I'm... done.

"When are you going to kiss me?"

Jake eye's flare. Dammit, will I ever get used to the intense way this man stares at me. He glances at my mouth, as he runs a hand to my throat. In what feels like tortured slow motion, he tilts my head so his mouth is inches from mine, so close I can feel his breath on me.

"Kiss me again, Jake. I haven't been able to stop thinking about that kiss," I plead. He pulls back slightly with a teasing smile before the hand that is wrapped around my throat glides to the nape of my neck, and he finally gives me what I've been aching for.

His mouth crashes against mine in demanding, needy kisses, and my lips open in eager desperation. This kiss is what I've been dreaming about, waiting for. Lust consumes me. His hand tightens on the back of my neck, holding my mouth firmly to his as I open for him, allowing his tongue to sweep inside. Stroke by perfect stroke, his tongue teases mine, kissing me like he's just as desperate as I am for this. As if I'm all he's ever wanted.

Holding my body tight to his, he consumes my mouth,

hungry for my kisses, his hand in my hair. I sigh against his lips, and he swallows the sound, my skin flickering to life like fireflies on a summer night. My body hums as Jake deepens the kiss.

He surprises me when he nips my bottom lip with his teeth. I whimper, loving the way he makes me feel. Jake is in control; he's taking what he wants. He's rough, and that's something I've been craving for a very long time. Almost as if he can hear my lust-filled thoughts, Jake takes hold of the roots of my hair, tugging the strands. I whimper at the mix of pleasure and pain, hoping this is just the start of so much more to come. Desire floods my veins; my nipples tighten and I'm breathless when he rolls his pelvis into me and I feel the hard outline of his erection pressing against my most sensitive spot.

"Do you believe me now?" he asks, his voice low and rough. My hips roll over the length of his hard on, making me want him more than I thought was possible. I want him naked. I want his skin against my skin.

I nod because it's all I'm capable of. My nerves are short-circuiting, and any restraint I showed when Jake knocked at my door is long gone.

My skin erupts in tingles when Jake sweeps my hair over my shoulder and sucks on my neck. His mouth is warm and wet, and it feels so good. I roll my hips over his stiff cock again, back and forth, over and over, chasing the friction I'm so needy for. I'm already so close, but it's not enough. I need more.

"You are going to ruin me." He murmurs.

"And I will be destroyed."

I am never going to forget tonight. Never, as long as I live. Men like Jake are the reason romance books are written. It's moments like this where two people give in to their every want and desire without caring about the consequences.

"You make me so fucking hard. Feel what you do to me." A moan escapes my lips as I grind over his length. I feel dizzy in the best way, limbs trembling, so close to coming and we haven't even taken off our clothes yet. I'm dangerously close to going over the edge when his lips brush across my jaw line, stopping at my ear, and he whispers in a breathy voice, "I want to strip you naked, Ev, and fuck you with my tongue."

I am already imagining it, vibrating from the inside out at his filthy words. I had a feeling I'd like to be dirty talked. I was pretty sure it would turn me on, and I can confirm that yes, I have a new kink. I'll be putty in his hands if he tells me that I'm a good girl.

Jake wraps a strong arm around my thighs, and without warning, lifts me over his shoulder. I gasp at the loss of friction between my thighs. "Jake!" I squeal, smacking his back, all plains of hard muscle.

"I told you what I'm going to do to you," he says as he carries me down the hall. "And I want to see you splayed out on your bed, legs spread wide while I feast on you."

Jake tosses me on my mattress, and I look up to see him standing at the foot of my bed with the hem of his T-shirt in his hands. His dark eyes linger on me as I slowly inch towards the headboard, leaning against the mound of pillows, waiting to watch him strip. Will he take everything off or just his shirt? Either way, I'm ready for the show, my tongue wetting my bottom lip. Jake's eyes travel over the wetness on my lip before he lifts his T-shirt over his head.

Jake is all taut muscles and golden skin, and I don't know where to look first—his broad shoulders, his six-pack that tapers into a delicious V between his hips, or the black ink covering his upper arm and part of his chest. The mystery of his tattoos is finally revealed. I take them in, lingering on the most striking one: a large clock with roman numerals. Jake is all muscle and golden skin.

I can't stop staring at a shirtless Jake Matthews.

"Tell me you want this," he says in a strong, low voice, eyes roaming over me like he's a man who knows what he wants. "I want to hear you say it. Tell me that it's me that you want."

Leaning up on my forearms, I murmur a breathy yes, then say the words that will change everything. "I want you to make me yours."

"Mine." He says, crawling onto the bed until he's hovering over top of me, his arms braced on either side of my shoulders. His hand slides over my abdomen to my chest, pinching my nipple through the thin fabric of my tank top while he kisses me. My skin erupts in white-hot heat, already addicted to his touch.

"You like it when I touch you, don't you?" My head tips back with a needy moan when his lips suck on my throat. "Like right here... *kiss*... and here, when I play with your tits... *kiss*." He pinches my nipple again through my T-shirt. "How about if I kissed you here?" His hand slides between my legs, over my jeans. "Would you like it if I put my face between your thighs?"

It is sensory overload. I widen my legs and angle my pelvis up to make room for him between my thighs. His tongue expertly sweeps inside my mouth as his hand roughly massages my chest. He continues to taunt me with his erection, grinding it into my wet center. Arousal flames through my body, straight to my core.

He breaks the kiss to slip my tank top over my head, smirking when he realizes I'm not wearing a bra. "Fuck, you are perfect," he says before sliding lower down my body, dragging his fingers down my throat to the center of my chest before taking a nipple into his mouth. "I want to play with these gorgeous tits while I go down on you."

I breathe out hard, grabbing his hair, needing something to hold on to. "I bet you're wet for me," Jake says in a voice laced with desire. "I bet you're soaked."

He isn't wrong. I've been sexually deprived for so long, it's not surprising I am drenched. I gasp when he flicks his tongue in an agonizing rhythm over my nipple, teasing the stiff peak until I'm writhing underneath him.

My God, this man's tongue. I can't imagine what he's going to do with it when he moves further down. With one last flick of my nipple, he kisses me chastely then moves down the length of my body, his big hands massaging and grabbing as he goes, handling my worked-up body like an expert. My head falls back against the pillow, savoring every touch. I want his hands everywhere. I want to be able to tell him what I want, what I need, what feels good. And it feels like I can ask for all of that with Jake without judgement.

I'm trembling in anticipation as he leans back on his knees between my legs and reaches for the zipper of my jeans. He unzips me, slides the denim down my legs, and tosses them to the floor, leaving me in only my black lace thong.

"Grip the bed sheets tight," he instructs, and I do what I'm told, fisting the fabric in my hands. "I'm going to lick you until you're trembling and begging me to stop."

Jake pulls the lace down my thighs, his inked arm flexing, a tattoo of a staircase winding around his smooth, golden skin like ivy. Then he licks a path up my thigh and presses a kiss to my center, where I'm already slick and needing him the most. My whole body goes up in flames when he licks a long, hungry line through my folds, his hands firmly holding my thighs open. He devours me, ravenously taking care of my needs.

I moan and whimper as he consumes me with his tongue, licking and sucking while I rock my hips over his face, back and forth, again and again. I move, desperately chasing my release. "More," I beg when he pauses with an intoxicated grin and runs the scruff of his jaw against my thigh before devouring me again. Edging me. Then eating me like I'm the best thing he's ever tasted.

I'm helpless, losing control. And growing wetter by the second. "Don't stop. I'm almost..."

I grip the sheets tighter as Jake inserts two fingers inside of me while sucking me with relentless, greedy moans. And then I'm breaking apart, a kaleidoscope of colors and bright lights rippling through me, heart pounding, body trembling, crying out, my body clenched around him.

I inhale a breath as Jake sits up, pulling my mouth to his in a slow, lingering kiss. His gaze is heated when he pulls away. "So fucking beautiful."

A lazy smile drifts across my lips as he guides his cock between my thighs, teasing my entrance. Jake's dick is hard and heavy. One hand is gripped tight around the base while the other shuttles up and down his shaft to the head, where he squeezes out a drop of liquid arousal.

My eager lips part and I open up my mouth to him. I stick out my tongue watching him swipe his arousal from the tip then I suck his finger into my mouth.

"So fucking hot," he says, leaning down to kiss me. His eyes an even darker green than normal. "I'm going to make you come again. But this time on my cock."

I'm dizzy from his filthy words. I'm drowning in blissful agony, waiting to see what he does next.

Jake grabs his wallet from his sweatpants, fishes out a condom and then returns to kneel between my thighs. He covers himself as his gaze coasts down to where I'm spread open for him. "So fucking pretty, and look at how wet you are for me."

He presses a finger into my arousal before lining himself up. "Tell me if you want me to stop."

"Please don't."

"Thank god," he says, sinking in. He pushes in slowly, but confidently, and I moan as he stretches me in the best way possible until he's all the way in.

"Look at you, taking every inch of me like a good fucking girl," he praises, and I'm already on the edge of coming again. This man and the things he says. This is what I've been craving. This is what I've been fantasizing about. A man who wants to please me in bed, who whispers the filthiest things in my ear as he fucks me. I've never been this turned on in my life. I feel like I'm holding on for dear life. I want to be Jake's good girl. So. Damn. Much.

He angles himself even deeper as he plays with my tits. I'm moaning, back arching, watching his abs flex with every thrust of his pelvis. His dark eyes are fixed on me, my hands gripping the muscle of his thighs. He groans. I shudder. A moan escapes my lips when he pinches one of my nipples, my body turning to liquid.

"Look at me, Ev. Eyes on me, baby."

I gaze into his eyes as his thrusts come quicker, causing every nerve ending in my body to ignite. His head falls back, a desperate moan escaping his lips, and I squeeze around him as he drives in and out of me in a quick, punishing pace. I can feel the size of him—Jake is big— but his size stretches me and strokes me at a perfect angle, owning my pleasure like he was made to please me.

My body starts to tremble when his finger works the sensitive spot between my legs in sweet circles. He doesn't stop. Jake slides into me, in and out, as his finger works me at a relentless pace. With every thrust, I am lost in the feeling, in the sounds our bodies make as they come together. And that is all it takes. I'm crying out his name, coming around his cock, and it's even better this time.

"Fuck." Jake's voice comes out in a growl. A groan shudders through him, and his abs tighten. His body goes rigid as he loses all control, filling the condom inside of me. His fingers tighten around my legs as he keeps pumping his hips through his release, taking everything he can. When his body stops shaking, he collapses on my chest, skin slick, our bodies still joined. He softly kisses my neck, and then his big arms wrap around me, holding me tight. We stay like this for several minutes before he finally lets me go.

"Don't move. I'll be right back." Jake walks into my bathroom giving me the best view of his ass. When he crawls back into bed after taking care of the condom and flicking off the light, he lies on his side, and I curl into him.

"You were worth waiting for," he whispers into my hair before gently pressing a kiss to the edge of my forehead.

I nuzzle in closer, placing my hand on his chest. We're wrapped up in each other's arms, in a tangled mess of naked limbs and bedsheets. My eyes grow heavy as I drift off to sleep.

SEVENTEEN
SEXUAL PREFERENCES

Jake

I woke up in Everly's bed. She was still sound asleep beside me, her long hair fanned out over her pillow and the soft curve of her shoulders. I tried to let her sleep, but everything in me wanted her back in my arms. I gently pulled her into my chest, her sweet little ass pushed up against my already excited to see her again cock. A soft little sigh escaped her lips when my dick twitched to life, but I knew she probably needed to rest. I was surprised I could even get it up after what we did last night.

We both couldn't get enough, waking up in the middle of the night for another round, then doing it again after that. It turns out that with Everly, I'm totally and fucking completely insatiable.

I still can't believe I'm in her bed. This was not what I was expecting when I showed up at her door, but I have absolutely no complaints about how our night went. But as happy as I am, I'm also a little nervous. Will she wake up and have second thoughts? Will she wake up and tell me that it can never happen again, that I'm too young for her, that she doesn't have the same feelings for me that I have for her?

I swallow the lump in my throat at the thought, breathing in the scent of her. I softly stroke her hair, which is a wild mess from having my hands tangled in it all night and press a soft kiss to her shoulder. We're both awake now, but neither one of us has made a move to get out of bed.

She will eventually have to pick up Birdie from her mom's and I promised the guys I'd go for a bike ride. But I don't want to think about any of that right now. All I want to do is stay in this bedroom, in this warm, little bubble with Everly in my arms for as long as I can.

Turning in my arms to face me, she looks up at me with sleepy eyes, her lips still swollen from my kisses. She's beautiful. Moving her hand to my chest, her fingertips run an outline of the clock tattoo on my pec.

"I think this one is my favorite," she says in a raspy morning voice. "It's sexy. But so are all of your tattoos."

She props herself up on an elbow, the bedsheets pulled up right below her shoulder blades. She traces the large hand on the clock before gazing back up at me. "What does it mean?"

There are a few reasons I got the tattoo on my 21st birthday. The nightmares I'd had for years, the ones I told nobody about, were not going away. I needed a way to channel that energy. It's hard to explain, but I think the tattoos were my way of taking control, a coping mechanism. In a strange way, it was oddly soothing. It was my first one, and after that I was hooked.

I draw a circle with my finger on the top of her shoulder and she shudders. "Have you ever felt like time passes, but you realize you haven't made any progress? Like you're stuck, or frozen?" Everly nods. "I got it to remind myself to keep going."

"I love that." She smiles softly before shifting her gaze to the staircase that winds around my bicep, outlining a spindle with her index finger. "And this one?"

The last thing I want to do is ruin this moment. Having Everly's naked body pressed up against mine is a special kind of bliss and I'm not ready for that to end. Her smooth, silky skin, the scent of her hair, the curve of her hip under the weight of my palm; I could stay cuddled into her forever.

"Why a staircase," Everly asks, dragging the tip of her finger over the ink.

"That one's a little more complicated," I tell her. "I got it for my parents."

She gives me a curious look. "Tell me about your family, Jake. Who do you look like? Your mom or your dad?" My stomach torpedoes to my feet, but when I look down at Everly, I realize I feel safe. She makes me want to let my guard down. But the wounds from my parents' death run so deep it's not easy.

"I look like my mom, but my personality is more similar to my dad's." I say, not ready to say more just yet.

"How? What's he like?" she asks, resting her chin on her forearm, which is draped across my chest.

"I can be quiet like my dad sometimes," I say, watching the row of goosebumps that pops up over her skin as I brush my fingers down her arm. "Some people think I'm moody, but I'm not. I just like time to think, to be by myself."

I can't explain it, but there's an ease I feel when I talk to Everly. I lift her hand to my lips and kiss each one of her fingertips. "I get that," she says, nodding. "It's smart. We all need time to relax and reflect. Time to re-center ourselves," she murmurs. "So, are you close with them? I mean, with your parents?"

The question makes my heart stop. It's been a long time since I've told anyone about my parents. Not many know the entire story. Everly shifts beside me, and when I look at her, she's frowning.

"Jake, I'm sorry. I'm being nosy. I didn't mean—"

"It's okay," I say, hating that she feels bad, but knowing we need to have this conversation. "It was going to come up sooner or later."

She sits up to lean against the headboard, dragging the bedspread with her and I join her, feeling even more naked than I already am.

"When I was 12, there was a fire at my house. It started in the middle of the night... it started in the laundry room," I say, a familiar anxiety creeping in. "A dryer vent was obstructed, and the machine overheated and caught on fire."

Fuck. I hate telling this story. But I need to suck it up. I need to tell her.

"Oh my God. What happened?" she asks, but I can tell from the look in her eyes that she already knows the answer.

"My parents died." There, I said it. The secret I keep locked up so tight.

"Jake..." Everly reaches for my hand, placing her palm over my knuckles. Her eyes are filled with compassion. She doesn't push. She gives me the space I need to tell my story at a pace that feels right. "I can't imagine what you've been through."

My chest aches remembering that night. I haven't forgotten a second of it: coming home to the flashing lights of the fire engines, the smell of fire and burning wood, my sister wrapped in a heavy wool blanket in the back of an ambulance. Because I wasn't there. I wasn't fucking there. And if I was... my parents would probably still be alive. They went back inside after getting Sierra out and wouldn't leave until they found me. But I wasn't fucking inside, and they had no idea.

The soft touch of Everly's hand on my knee brings me back to the present. I exhale the breath I've been holding. Things are about to get heavy. The memory of that night, the nightmares, my parent's funeral. Part of me wishes I had never brought it up, that we could just go back to talking about my tattoos. But I want to let her in. I scratch my jaw and meet her gaze again.

"My sister and I were devastated. I was a mess for years. We went to live with my grandparents after the fire and man, did I make their life hell." I shake my head remembering all the nights I came home late, all of the times I screamed and slammed doors. I went off the rails, but my grandparents never gave up on me. They were always there to comfort me when I was eventually able to calm down.

"It was my fault, Ev. I snuck out of the house that night. They couldn't find me inside... that's why they never made it out. They were looking for me."

She shakes her head, like she doesn't want to hear it. "Jake, don't you dare. Don't you blame yourself—"

"Ev." I stop her before she can go any further, sitting up in bed. I feel a sudden need to get up, to put some space between us so I can collect my thoughts. But she doesn't let me go. Everly grabs my wrist, tugging gently.

"Please stay." Her grasp on my arm is weak, but enough for me to know she's serious. "Please let me be there for you like you were there for me, Jake. I understand why you feel that way, but it just isn't true."

Then she's crawling into my lap, sliding her hands over

LILY MILLER

my jaw to frame my face. And she kisses me. The faintest brush of her lips, the softest sweep of her tongue. And I can breathe again.

My hands grip her waist, holding her in my lap, needing to keep her there. My fingers eventually skim down to her hips, tracing the curve of her ass. I savor the feeling of her warm, soft skin, and I soak her in, my entire body melting into hers. I'm reminded of what it feels like to fall in love with someone and I want to chase that feeling again.

She breaks the kiss after a beat, tilting her chin to my bicep, brushing the back of her knuckles over my staircase ink. "And the tattoo. It's to remind you to take one step at a time?"

I nod because saying anything right now feels impossible.

She sighs, then nestles into me, and I pull her into my chest. I feel her breath ghost over my collarbone, then her lips follow.

"I'm sorry, Jake. I'm so sorry you had to go through that."

I still miss my parents so much it physically hurts sometimes. My dad coached my baseball team when I was younger, he was the dad-joke guy, and all of my teammates loved him. He lived and breathed for my mom, my sister and me. I wanted to be just like him. *I still do.* My mom taught my sister how to bake, she'd watch movies with me in forts we'd make out of every blanket and pillow we could find in the house. There's no question there was a lot of love in the house I grew up in. My parents were the hopelessly-in-love type, always sneaking kisses or holding hands. They always looked at each other like they were the only ones in the room. It kills me that their lives were taken away from them. I *fucking* hate that reality.

It's not fair.

I'm not sure how many people find a love like theirs. Sometimes I wonder if that will ever be in the cards for me.

I'm knocked back to the present when Everly's phone chimes on the nightstand. She doesn't move, she stays right where she is, with her legs straddling my hips, her head on my chest.

Not even five minutes later, her phone chimes again, and she sighs. "It's probably my mom. I should make sure everything is okay with Birdie." Everly climbs off me, picks up my T-shirt from the floor where I left it last night and slips it over her head. Then she picks up her phone, checks the screen and drops it back on the nightstand.

"Everything okay?" I ask, puling the bedsheet up past my waist.

She stands up, wrapping her messy hair into a ponytail with an elastic she finds on her bedside table. My dick stirs. Why is it so hot watching her tie up her hair? "Everything is fine. It wasn't my mom."

She tenses when her phone chimes for the third time. This time she silences the ringer and places the iPhone face down on the table.

"Everly, who is that?" I ask cautiously. "Is it him?"

She looks mortified. A little angry, too. "Yes, it's Grant." She sighs, sitting back on the bed. "I'll call him later. Unfortunately, I cannot avoid my ex-husband forever."

My blood begins to boil. "Does he always blow up your phone like that?"

She drops her head in her hand and nods. "Grant grew up getting everything he wants. He's still the same, nothing has changed. Especially when it comes to me."

I hate that she has to deal with this guy. He clearly enjoys getting under her skin. I grab her by her hips and pull her in between my legs, her back to my chest. "He's a dick," I say, lacing our fingers together. "And for what it's worth, I think you are amazing. You are an incredible mom to Birdie; you work your ass off to give her what she needs." I pause to kiss the top of her head. "But he shouldn't be allowed to treat you the way he does. You don't deserve that."

I feel her lungs expand in her chest. "I wish it were that easy. I'm stuck with the guy for the next 10 years."

"I know he's Birdie's dad, so I'm not going to be an asshole about it, but if you ever need me to put the guy in his place, I'd be happy to. In fact, nothing would make me happier." I would love to put my fist to his face.

A small laugh escapes her, then she lets out a long sigh. "I'll remember that. You're a caveman, Jake." She wiggles her back against my chest.

"Oh, believe me. I'm a caveman. I am very protective of what is mine. Your ex does not want to make me mad."

Everly stills in my arms. "Jake, is that what I am? Am I yours?"

My chest bursts. Dammit, this girl kills me. She's absolutely fucking mine. Every night and every morning and that isn't going to change.

"You are mine," I say, confidently.

"You seem pretty sure of yourself." Everly turns and I see the heat in her eyes. My skin prickles under her gaze.

"I think I proved that last night... and I think you liked it."

Her eyes sparkle under dark lashes, her lips forming a shy smile. "I did like it... a lot."

I might have gotten carried away with the dirty talk too soon. I might have been too demanding. But I've always liked sex a little rougher, more adventurous, and even though I did tame it down from what I really like, I have no idea about Everly's level of comfort in the bedroom. I'm hoping she says she'd like to amp it up. "It wasn't too much?"

Her cheeks turn a rosy shade of pink as she pulls her bottom lip between her teeth. "Not at all. Maybe even not enough..." Everly looks down at the bedsheet, her ponytail falling over one side of her face, and inside I'm fucking giddy because it seems like our sexual preferences do match up.

"Ev, you don't have to be embarrassed with me. I want to make you happy in bed, that's what turns me on... turning you on, and for the record," I say, brushing her ponytail from her face. "I like it rough. I like it hard. I like turning you on with my dirty mouth. I like toys and trying new things. But I also like it slow and passionate too."

She smirks. "Me too. I like all of that. I especially liked it when you called me a good girl last night."

"You like to be praised. I love that. It's so fucking hot."

She draws her thumb across my bottom lip, eyes tracking the motion. "Are we going to stay in bed all day or should I make us breakfast?"

I lean forward so she's forced to turn in my lap to face me. "I wanna take you somewhere. Do you have a couple of hours before you need to pick up Birdie?"

"I do... where do you want to take me?"

My God, I can't get enough of her. It's been this way ever since that night I ran into her in the hallway at Catch 21. One look at her and I was gone.

I kiss her nose and scoop her up into my arms. I look around the room at the mess we made—clothes and pillows scattered across the floor, bedsheets and the comforter a pile in the center of the bed. Everything is out of place, yet everything feels so right.

"A shower, and then I'm taking you out."

Parking is not my friend today in Reed Point. But after driving along First Street three times, I finally snag a spot big enough to parallel park my F-150. It's a bit of a walk to where I want to take her, but it's gorgeous, sunny and 75 out today, so a walk-through downtown past the shops and trendy restaurants isn't so bad. I shift the car into park then round the cab of my truck to get her. I hold out my hand to her after opening the door. She looks at me with a quirk in her brow. "So sweet, Jake, but I can hop out of your truck on my own."

I smirk. "I'm sure you can, but you won't be when I'm around," I say tipping my forehead to my hand that I'm holding out to her.

Everly smiles, shaking her head, and hops down from my truck. I watch her, the way her plain white T-shirt clings to her breasts, short sleeves revealing smooth bronze skin. Her perfectly broken-in jean shorts emphasize her toned legs, and her hair is pulled up in a ponytail. She looks take-your-breath-away beautiful.

I meet her on the sidewalk for a chaste kiss because I can't help myself. I lace my hand in hers, hoping she's okay with it and she seems to be, so I hold her hand a little tighter, tugging her in the direction we need to go. It feels good to be out together in public, unabashedly. It was only a few days ago she was barely talking to me.

A minute into our walk, Everly slows down, veering towards the window of a book shop. She eyes the window display, a banner with a new release announcement. "Are you a fan of Emily Silver's?" The book has a couple on the cover in an embrace. It isn't overly steamy but it's clear from the title and the description that it's one of those spicy romance novels that girls like. I remember the stack of romance novels I saw on Everly's coffee table.

"I am. I've been waiting for her to release this one," she says as I stand behind her and wrap my arm around her waist. "Do you think it's weird that I read romance?" she asks, looking at me over her shoulder.

"Are you blushing? You are, aren't you?" I smile, holding her closer. "Why would I think that? It's hot as fuck. I'm pretty sure most girls read those books. All the hot ones anyways."

Everly tosses her head back against my chest and laughs before she turns in my arms to face me. "Can I ask you a question?" I nod. She has a thoughtful expression on her face. "Did you ever think about me after we ran into each other that night at Catch 21?"

"Every fucking day," I admit. It's the truth and there's no point in hiding it. She blinks, swallows thickly, her focus fixed on me.

"Me too."

My heart sweeps up into a loop in my chest. I've wondered the same thing. I've wondered if I made as much of an impression on her as she did on me. I love knowing that she's had me on her mind. "My turn for a question."

"Okay."

"Are you okay with the way things are between us? I'm not moving too fast for you, am I?"

I'm nervous waiting for her answer. I need to know if she's okay with the pace I'm moving at. When I showed up at her door last night, I never expected to be where we are today— a marathon of sex, a sleepover, and a morning-after breakfast— so I want to hear it from her that I'm not rushing things.

"No, Jake. I like the way things are." She searches my gaze, the flecks of gold in her irises sparkling under the sun. "I'm good. I will tell you if I'm not. Promise." My eyes dip down to her lips. Now that I know how good they feel and how perfect they taste, I'm an addict. So, I kiss her in front of everyone on First Street. Every reason I've ever had for hating PDA falls to the wayside as I grab her by the waist and pull her into me. She kisses me back, opening for me, our tongues softly gliding together. Neither of us move, my hands wrapped around her back, her chest pressed up against mine. A girl giggles as she walks by with her mom, dragging us back to reality. We break the kiss, remembering where we are, wrapping it up before we're putting on a show. It's for the best... my dick was starting to get ideas and the busiest street in the city is not the place for a hard-on.

Everly hides her pink cheeks into the curve of my neck, and I can feel her smiling. A few minutes later, we fall into step, walking the sycamore-lined streets, the sun warm on our skin. Nodding my head towards the restaurant I want to take her to for breakfast, I open the large pink door, motioning for her to go first. She raises an eyebrow at me when she notices the lineup outside of people waiting to get in, but she ducks under my arm anyways when I tell her it's fine. We inhale the delicious scent of waffles and coffee as we step inside.

"It's so cute, Jake," she says stopping in the entryway to admire the laid-back atmosphere with pink suede seating, wicker lamp shades, and rich green palm leaves in large ceramic pots. "I've heard of this place, but I haven't been. I've heard it's impossible to get in to."

The place is packed, and with good reason. Not only

does the food smell amazing, but the unobstructed view of the ocean is jaw-dropping. We wouldn't usually be able to just walk right in, but my good buddy owns the place, and I called him before we left Ev's house this morning asking if he could save me a table.

We are taken to the patio by a hostess where my friend Sam greets us with two champagne glasses and a twinkle in his eye.

"Mimosas on me," he says smiling brightly, clapping my shoulder. "It's good to see you, man. Thanks for coming in."

Everly and I sit down, and I watch her eyes go wide at the view from our table on the edge of the patio: turquoise ocean sparkling like diamonds under the morning sun, sea birds perched on a rocky bluff 50 feet away. I'm thankful to Sam for hooking me up with the best table in the restaurant.

"It's good to see you too," I say. "I guess I have to come eat here if I want to see you these days. You need to start getting out on the trails riding with us again."

"And show you guys up?" he laughs. "I wouldn't want to make you boys look bad."

I laugh, hand to my chest like he's killing me. "Yeah, yeah. I guess I need to be nice to you since you hooked us up with this killer table."

"Maybe you'll pay me back by giving me a deal on my porch reno." He smirks. "I'm going to be hitting you up in the spring."

"We'll see how good breakfast is, and then I'll let you know."

"Jake Matthews... you never change," Sam chuckles, before his eyes drift over to Everly obviously hoping for an introduction.

I'm not sure how to introduce her. I mean, it's pretty clear we're on a date, and after last night we are definitely seeing each other. But is she my girlfriend? Can I use the label? We didn't technically get that far last night. I was too eager to get my hands all over her. Without a lot of time to think on it, I stumble my way through an introduction.

"Sam, this is Everly. A good friend of mine," I say. It sounds all fucking wrong and I hate it. "Everly, this is Sam, my buddy I met in college."

The word *friend* tastes sour on my tongue. I want to take it back but it's too late. Friends is what we were weeks ago, but after last night she's so much more.

Sam offers a hand and Everly takes it. "It's great to meet you, Everly. You two look like great *friends*."

Everly laughs, blushes and then lets go of his hand. But there isn't any awkwardness. She seems to be rolling with it, unlike me. "It's nice to meet you too. Thank you for the mimosa."

"My pleasure. Check out the menu and I'll have Carrie take your order asap. I know you two have somewhere to be." Sam taps the table with his palm before walking away.

After Sam leaves, Everly looks at me with eyebrows raised. "We have somewhere to be?" she asks with a grin. I sip my drink, meeting her eyes over the rim of the glass. "Maybe," I tell her. "I guess you'll just have to wait and see."

When I called Sam earlier, I told him I needed a table as soon as possible and that we would be eating and running because I have some plans. I want to treat Everly today. I know how tired she's been, working so many late shifts at the restaurant and getting up early with Birdie in the mornings.

She's sipping from her champagne glass, a light breeze blowing strands from her hair across her face. Her cheeks are tinted pink, her skin sun-kissed. "I talked to my mom earlier," she says, setting her champagne glass on the table.

"We've got all afternoon, so there's no rush. My parents want to keep Birdie for the day, they're taking her to the pool."

"Perfect," I say as the server arrives to take our order. I decide on eggs benny while Everly orders waffles and strawberries.

"You are spoiling me, Jake. This view makes me feel like I'm on vacation."

"That was kinda the point," I tell her. "I wanted to take you somewhere where there aren't highchairs and crayons on the table. I thought you'd probably like it here."

"I love it. So much." Everly's eyes twinkle. "I haven't had a lot of time to get out and do things like this. I rotate between the grocery store, work, Birdie's school, the park, or the beach. There's so much I want to do."

"We can do some of the stuff on your list together."

"I like that," she says, looking adorably excited. "Where are we going after this?"

I shrug, trying to fight off a smile. "Nice try. It's a surprise, I'm not telling you."

Her expression turns more serious. "Jake, you're sweet, but you really don't have to do all this for me."

There's no one I'd rather do this for. Besides, it's not that big of a deal. It's breakfast and a little pampering. If her ex wasn't such a fuck-face she would be used to days like this. "I know I don't have to, but I want to."

Everly's brows tug together, her eyes on her napkin. I can tell she has something on her mind.

"What's up, Ev. What are you thinking about?"

She cocks her head, looking at me like she's debating what to say. "Have you dated much?"

"I haven't." I clear my throat. "I haven't been interested. Too busy at work to. It's been a big learning curve owning my own company."

There are other reasons too, like the fact that I find it hard to let people in. Then there's Jade, and the fact that I think I have been subconsciously waiting for her to come back from Italy. It's probably stupid. She broke up with me, and everything after that was beyond my control, but I loved her— like, really loved her— and I wasn't ready for things to end. But I can honestly say that for the first time in over two years, I haven't really thought about Jade since meeting Ev.

"It's impressive," Everly says. "I mean, to own your own contracting company at your age."

"Thanks," I shrug. "It kinda just fell in my lap. I started off working there after college and eventually was given the opportunity to buy into the company. Last year, I bought my two partners out."

"And are you happy?" her voice softens.

"I love what I do. I like building things. I like seeing a design come to life. So yeah, I'm happy."

Everly smiles, her warm eyes searching mine. "Did you always want to work in home building?"

"If I told you what I wanted to do when I was a kid you would make fun of me."

"Well, you have to tell me now."

"I always thought it would be fun to be a weather man."

Everly bursts out laughing. "Honestly, I think that's cute. I think you'd make an awesome meteorologist."

"Right," I smirk. "That's why you just busted a gut laughing."

Our server arrives at our table with our meals, sliding the plates in front of us.

I try not to devour the plate of eggs in front of me like a wild animal, but my stomach is growling with how hungry I am. A sex all-nighter will do that to a guy.

"This is so good, Jake," Everly says, taking a bite of her

waffles and letting out a little moan. My eyes are fixed on her as she eats, the joy on her face. It's official, I've lost my fucking mind.

"You are killing me," I tell her. "You can't moan like that."

"Why? Is it giving you ideas?"

"Yes," I admit, seeing how her eyes glimmer with amusement. "Ideas I can't act on in a public restaurant."

I shift in my seat. By the time I'm paying the bill, I've calmed down enough to thank Sam for everything.

"You ready for the next stop?" I ask her as we head out.

"Jake, you've already given me the best morning. You don't need to do anything else. But, yes! I'm ready."

EVERLY

THE MORNING JUST KEPT GETTING BETTER. AFTER THE BEST breakfast, the VIP treatment continued with a mani/pedi appointment at the cutest salon. The nail tech tried to get Jake to stay, offering him the massage chair next to mine to get a pedicure too, but there was no way he was sticking around. Jake is definitely not a mani/pedi guy. He politely thanked her then left, opting to get some work done at the coffee shop next door. Before he left, I saw him sneak his credit card to the girl at the desk.

"Your boyfriend is sweet," she said after he'd left. I didn't argue the label. She's right. I can't remember the last time I treated myself like this. Luxuries like the spa have not been in the budget for a while.

But it did make me wonder, what exactly *are* Jake and I? Back at the restaurant, he introduced me as his *friend*. It didn't bother me considering everything between us literally happened less than 24 hours ago, but still, this thing between us feels like... more. I mean, do friends whisper filthy things to each other or have the kind of sex that Jake and I had last night? Definitely not the friends that I know.

I felt a little guilty as I sat in the chair having my toes painted by one woman while another was painting my fingernails. But I could tell Jake really wanted to do this for me, so I decided to just relax and enjoy the experience. I would find a way to repay him in my own way another day.

I'm learning that Jake is a giver in more ways than one, and he enjoys making the people around him happy. It's one of the many qualities that I like the most about him. I see it in how kind and gentle he is with Birdie. It makes me happy, but it also kind of scares me.

I could really fall for a guy like Jake. If I'm honest, I'm falling for him already.

My heart was full and happy when he dropped me off at my apartment later, and when he pulled his truck away from the curb, I felt like I was already missing him. But I also couldn't wait to see Birdie.

I headed straight to my parents' place to pick her up, and for the rest of the day, Birdie hasn't left my side. We walked to the beach to throw the Frisbee around, and she danced all the way back home. She helped me cook dinner and then watched her favorite show while I painted her nails to match mine.

And now we're snuggled up in her bed under her bedspread, my hand stroking her hair as she drifts off to sleep.

Today was the perfect day. The best of both worlds. Time with Jake followed by a perfect day with Birdie. And I find myself thinking that maybe I can have it all.

In this moment, it absolutely feels like I can.

EIGHTEEN

YOU'RE A LUCKY BITCH

Everly

My good mood is ruined by Grant the next morning. It's like he somehow sensed that I found happiness and needed to find a way to crush it. I woke up to my phone ringing at 6:30 a.m. and when I checked the screen to see who would call me at such a ridiculous hour, I saw Grant's name and knew I better answer it. If I didn't answer it then, the calls and the texts would never stop. So, wiping the sleep from my eyes, I sat up and pressed the call answer button. I immediately regretted it.

He was livid, wanting to know why I didn't tell him that Birdie broke her arm. And when I told him that I left two messages on his voicemail and one with his assistant, it didn't stop him from losing his mind on me. I wanted to say, *maybe if you weren't so busy fucking random women every night, you'd be aware of what's going on in your daughter's life.* But I took the high road like I usually do. What would it matter anyway? Nothing I say will ever get through to him. It would just be a waste of breath.

After he finally finished yelling at me—and not *once*

asking how Birdie's arm is—he wanted to talk about the birthday party his mom is hosting. Apparently, he's planning on showing up, but I'll believe that when I see it. I told him I would drop her off at his house on Friday after school and pick her up on Sunday morning. That seemed to work for him. When I asked him if Birdie would be sleeping at his house or his parents', he brushed me off.

That phone call was several hours ago, but I'm still stressed as I get my things together for work.

"What's going on Ev, you have a weird smile on your face?" Willa asks. She's on a Facetime call, my phone propped up on my dresser. "You look like you're glowing or something. You better not be pregnant."

There's no point in denying it. I was going to tell her anyways. I know it's soon and I'm not sure where it's headed, but I feel like a giddy schoolgirl again and I have to tell someone. Willa has always been that someone. "Whoa. Not pregnant," I say, grabbing my phone. "But I met someone."

Willa screams, tossing her head back. "Stop it! I can't take it. I need to know everything. Don't leave a single juicy detail out."

I smile so hard my cheeks hurt. "His name is Jake. He's tall, has dark hair, tattoos, and muscles everywhere. You will approve, Wills. He is nothing like my loser ex."

"You had me at tattoos, tall and muscles. I'm already jealous. What does he do?"

I walk into the bathroom to do my hair, setting the phone against the mirror. "He owns his own contracting company. He renos and builds houses."

"That's so hot. He works with his hands. Does he wear a tool belt? Are those a thing anymore? Has he worn one for you in the—"

I laugh, grabbing an elastic off the counter. "I need you

to focus, babe," I say, pulling my hair to the nape of my neck. "There's something I haven't told you. You might think it's weird."

"Okay, now you're scaring me. Does he have weird piercings? A third nipple? Oh my God, he's been to prison. No wait, he's in prison right now!"

I shake my head and laugh. "None of the above. And you've been watching too much TikTok. It's that he's younger than me."

She gives me the biggest *who cares* look. "Well, that's not a big deal. Why would that matter?"

"Well, it's more than a few years." I pause. "He's seven years younger than me."

"Girl, you've still got it. Look at you!" She slaps her knee playfully. "That is so hot, Ev. Holy shit, you're one lucky bitch."

My mind drifts back to the moment when Jake stood at the edge of the bed taking his shirt off. His hard pecs, his perfectly shaped blush coloured nipples, all that incredible ink. The happy trail leading down to his gorgeous dick.

Willa calls me out. "You are daydreaming about him. Look at you. You're practically drooling."

You would too Wills, if you knew how big he is.

"He's just a really great guy, that's all. And he's great with Birdie too."

"He's met my Birdie-baby?"

"Yes." I sigh. "I normally wouldn't have introduced them so soon, but it wasn't planned. Birdie and I kept running into him wherever we went, and she took a liking to him quick."

"It sounds like it's kismet," Willa says. "Like it's fate."

I smile, and Willa squeals, then quickly turns serious again before asking, "Does Grant know?"

"No."

Just the thought of Jake officially meeting Grant gives me a headache.

"Probably for the best," she says, echoing my thoughts.

I sigh, feeling a little anxious, but then brush it off. I'm done letting Grant Billings ruin my happiness.

JAKE

It's been one of those days. I got up early and drove around to different job sites, gave an estimate on a big project I'd like to land and then spent a few hours in my office catching up on paperwork. I have a stack of work to do, but I'm distracted. The fight I had with my sister has been weighing on me. I'm still avoiding Grayson and her like the plague. I've been avoiding the guys too, so I don't have to see Gray. I'm still pissed as hell at them for lying to me—I feel like an idiot for being kept in the dark. I know the distance between us is killing Sierra, and it's starting to eat at me too. I've lost so much in my life, I can't stand the thought of losing my sister too, not to mention my best friend. Part of me gets why they didn't want to tell me—they knew I'd blow a gasket, and that's exactly what I did. I need time to work through it. It's how I'm wired.

It's no wonder I'm behind at work. The company is absolutely slammed—a good problem to have, but I need help at the office. I haven't given up hope that Everly will change her mind about the job. I know she is the perfect person for it.

When she texted me earlier today asking if I was free for dinner and a movie at her house, I right away said yes. Until she told me dinner would be at five and the movie would start at six. There's no way I'd be able to make it out of the office in time, so I had to opt for a rain check.

Now, I'm on my couch with a beer, exhausted and lonely, thinking about the two of them and everything I missed out on tonight. After flipping mindlessly through channels on TV for a while, I empty what's left of my beer into the sink and head to my bedroom. I brush my teeth and then crawl into bed, easing back against the pillows to shoot Everly a good night text.

> Jake: Sorry about tonight. I really wanted to hang with the two of you.
>
> Everly: It's okay. We can do it another time. Long day?
>
> Jake: The longest. But I'm home now. I'm already in bed.
>
> Everly. Me too.

She attaches a photo to the message. It's a selfie of Everly in bed wearing a thin tank, her hair piled up on top of her head. She's covered from the waist down with her bedspread. The same one I fucked her on two nights ago. I want nothing more than to be in that bed with her, naked, and fucking her so hard she can't see straight.

A photo isn't enough. I work up the courage to FaceTime her. My pulse drums in my veins as I wait for her to answer. She does, after two rings.

Fuck. Me.

She looks even hotter on my screen than she did in the picture. I'm not sure I will ever get over how beautiful she is.

"Hi, Jake." She's smiling, her head resting against the pillows she has propped up against her headboard.

"Hi." I soak her in. Fuck, I miss her, and it's barely been 36 hours. "I missed you today. Wanted to see your face before I fell asleep. I hope it's okay."

"It's very okay," she murmurs. She looks sated, a little sleepy but happy to see me. "I was just reading."

"One of your spicy books?"

Her cheeks pinken, and she brings her free hand to her neck covering the blush that is rising there too. "Yes."

"Were you reading a steamy scene when I texted you?" Just thinking about Everly in bed reading a smut scene in one of her romance books is enough to get me hard. I grip myself over my boxers to ease the ache.

"Maybe," she admits in the sexiest tone. "What do you think?"

"I hope you were."

"I was. The hero had the heroine pinned against the bathroom counter and... um... I guess... you can imagine what they were doing."

"Fuck, baby. Who were you thinking about when you read that scene? Who were you wishing was fucking you like that?" Everly's chest rises and falls, and she lets out a breathy exhale. She loves it when I dirty talk her. I've got her turned on.

"I was thinking about you, wishing it was you and me in my bathroom." Everly's hand slips down her sternum until it disappears from the screen. Her lips part and her eyes flutter closed. I slip my hand inside my briefs and fist my hard cock, wrapping my hand around the base and slowly shuttling it up and down my length. I'm so hard I can barely think straight.

"Are you touching yourself, Ev?" My voice is low and gravelly. "Let me see you. I wanna watch you play with yourself."

She angles the camera so I can see her from her thighs up. Her nipples are straining against the fabric of her thin pink tank top, begging to be worshipped. I wish like hell I was in her bedroom to touch them. "Take off that top, baby. Let me see those perfect tits."

Her hands move to the hem of her tank and then she's raising the material very slowly over her head revealing the most perfect pair of tits I've ever seen. I'm not sure if she's purposely doing it slowly to tease me, but it's working. "Fuck, you are perfect. You have no idea how badly I wish I was touching you right now. Now, be a good girl, baby, and take off your shorts too." I'm mesmerized as I watch her shimmy her shorts down her legs, then toss them to the side giving me a full view of her naked body. I quickly give her the same view, impatiently taking my shirt off and sliding my briefs down my legs. My cock springs free, bouncing against my stomach, hardening even more.

"Such a good girl for me. Now spread your legs wide and let me see you. Show me how wet you are."

I watch as her thighs fall to the side, revealing everything to me. She's pink and perfect and soaking wet for me. Groaning, I fist my shaft tighter, working the tip. "So perfect, baby. You were made for me. Look at you drenched."

She bites down on her bottom lip, as her hand trails slowly towards the apex of her thighs. I watch her hazel-eyes flutter closed as she dips two fingers inside herself, whimpering the most beautiful sounds. Heat pools at the base of my spine and my balls begin to tighten. I have to pinch the base of my cock to stop myself from coming too soon, because there is no way I want this to be over before it even starts. This is the hottest thing I have ever done in my life, and for a second, I worry this might be too much for her. My mind is put at ease when she asks me to move the camera closer to my cock so she can watch me work myself.

Happy to. I would give this girl anything she wants.

I adjust the camera so she can see how turned on she's made me, my cock harder than granite and leaking in my hand for her. Her tongue slides absentmindedly across her bottom lip, eyes wide. "You are so big, Jake. I love watching you work your dick. I wish it was my hand making you feel that good."

"I do too. Fuck. Trust me when I tell you I wish it were my fingers fucking you right now. Pretend your hand is mine. Imagine it's my hand fucking you."

I watch her play with her slick entrance, her other hand squeezing her breast. "Do you like watching me?" Her voice is breathless.

My admission is out of my mouth before I have time to stop it. "I have imagined what you'd look like with your legs spread wide while you touch yourself. I've jacked off to that image, I'm not sure how many times now."

Her eyes flare and she moans as she slips a finger inside of her, then another, slowly back out and then in again. I watch Everly's legs spread wide for me, drenched with arousal, whimpering the neediest sounds. Then her middle finger rubs tight, quick circles over her sensitive spot and I'm *this* close to coming instantly.

"That's it, baby. Imagine it's my tongue flicking at your perfect pink nipples."

I stroke myself a little faster, remembering how good she felt when I sank inside of her. Warm, wet, and tight. The images in my mind nearly unravel me. My cock is aching and swollen.

When have I ever been this hard?

I know the answer to this.

It was the last time I fucked Everly.

"That's it, baby. I want you to come all over your fingers for me." I stroke myself harder. "Be a good girl and let me see you come."

"Jake," Everly breathes, getting close. "I'm almost there."

I'm on the verge too. My pace increasing. "The next time I see you, I'm going to tie you to that bed and tease you with my cock until you are shaking and begging me to fuck you, baby. You'd like that, wouldn't you?"

Everly cries out my name. Her back arches off the bed and her mouth falls open as she rides out her release, and it's the sexiest thing I've ever seen. I follow right after, coming hard, my warm release spilling over my hand onto my stomach. I groan and shudder through my orgasm in a haze of my post-release high.

God, I needed that— so much, and it looks like Everly did too.

"Give me a sec, Ev, to get cleaned up. I'll be right back," I tell her, slipping off the bed to take care of the mess on my abs. When I return to bed, Everly is on my screen, lying on her side, her warm, mossy eyes sated and content.

"That was the best FaceTime call I've ever had in my life," I tell her, leaning back against my headboard. I pull the sheet over my softening cock to my waist.

She smiles. She looks a little sleepy. "I'm not sure I'll ever be able to forget that."

"Good. I don't want you to."

She sighs against her pillow, and I wish I was cuddled up next to her.

NINETEEN

BACK SEAT MAKING OUT IS SO OVERRATED

Jake

I'm in Gran's room at her assisted facility home watching her blow out her birthday candles. Sierra and Grayson are here too, and while I was nervous as hell to finally talk to them, I did, and I think we're good. It took Gran's birthday party for the three of us to be in the same room together. After stewing on their sneaking around for a good couple of weeks, I'm ready to move on. It also helps seeing my sister happy. And if she believes Grayson is the guy that makes her feel that way, then I won't stand in the way. But if he hurts her— and I will make sure he knows this—I will personally see to it that he never walks again.

Sierra dishes out slices of the bright yellow birthday cake that she made for Gran, and we all sit around the coffee table. The cake tastes as good as it looks. It makes me happy that Sierra didn't lose her passion for baking after our mom died. It's sort of like having a piece of her with us. One day, we may have to share Si's talents with the whole town. She's hoping to have a bakery of her own in Reed Point.

Now that we're talking again my sister doesn't waste a

minute—we've barely sat down before she's peppering me with questions about Everly.

"C'mon Jake. When can I meet her? You've been seeing each other for months now. It's my right as your sister to meet the girl who has you all lit up."

"First off," I shoot her a pointed stare. "I don't remember it going down that way when you two started sneaking around." I flick my fork between Grayson and her.

"Fine, I deserve that," she says. "But it would be really nice to meet her. I'd love to meet her daughter too."

I've told both Sierra and Gran a little about Everly and Birdie, but I haven't opened up a lot. It wasn't all that long ago that even a cup of coffee with Ev seemed like a pipe dream, so I guess I haven't wanted to jinx things. I also feel this need to protect the two of them after everything they've been through.

I still find it so fucked up that her ex is such a deadbeat dad to Birdie. I will never be able to understand how he can go months without seeing her. Birdie is the coolest kid I've ever met. I meant it when I told Ev that I want to be a part of *both* of their lives. I love spending time with them—watching movies together, cooking breakfast in the morning. When I'm with them, it feels like we're making memories. Part of me feels like my childhood was cut short the night my parents died. Sure, my grandparents were the best pseudo-parents a boy could ask for, but they weren't my mom and dad. Everly does an incredible job making sure Birdie feels loved and wanted. If she's willing to let me be a part of building a happy life for her daughter, I'm in.

Gran catches my eye and winks at me. "She must be something special for you to be so head over heels for her."

"Who says I'm head over heels?"

Is it really that obvious?

"You are mad about this girl," Gran scoffs. "I know when my grand-baby is in love. It's written all over your face."

I shake my head. I hate feeling vulnerable around people, it makes me feel antsy. I know that I have very strong feelings for Ev. Hell, she's all I think about, day in and day out. I want to be with her every chance I can get. I'm definitely falling for this girl. But am I in *love* with Everly?

"I'm not getting any younger and I'd like to be able to tell Angie that I have more great grandchildren than she does," Gran says, rolling her eyes. Angie lives down the hall, and she and Gran seem to be in constant competition about practically everything. "She rubs it in my face every chance she gets. I don't know why she has to be so competitive."

Grayson, Sierra, and I all look at each other and laugh. Gran is *the* most competitive woman on the planet. She once ate an entire raw jalapeno just because Tucker made the mistake of saying he didn't think she could. He lost $50 on that one.

"Your Gran is right," Grayson says. "You have this vibe thing going on, man. Like you have a happy aura around you."

"What the f—fudgsicles are you talking about?" I ask, catching myself in time. "What the hell does an aura even look like?"

"Don't worry, it's a good look on you. Your energy is way less grumpy."

Grayson is not picking up on my deep desire for this conversation to end. If Gran wasn't in the room, I'd have kneed him in the balls by now.

"You should bring her around," Grayson continues with a grin, clearly enjoying this. "We want to meet the girl who has you all gaga."

"You can be an idiot sometimes. Are you sure you know

what you're doing with this guy, Si?" I toss a look at my sister, who's giggling at the two of us bantering.

Sierra smiles, looking adoringly at Grayson. He kisses the tip of her nose and it's enough to make me lose my appetite. "Think about it, Jake," she tells me. "We'd all like to meet your girlfriend."

"She's not my girlfriend yet," I say before putting my empty plate on the coffee table.

"Semantics," Gray says. "It's just a matter of time."

I lean back into the couch, hands clasped behind my head, gaze pointed to the ceiling. He's right: it is semantics. We just haven't formally put a label on our relationship.

I intend to fix that.

EVERLY

THE KNOCK AT MY DOOR SURPRISES ME. JAKE IS AT WORK AND Franny is visiting a friend this morning, she messaged me earlier to let me know. I can't think of anyone else who would pop by unannounced.

I reluctantly open the door to find a box with my name on it sitting on my doorstep. I pick up the package and bring it inside, setting it on the counter.

"Who was that, Mommy?" Birdie calls from the living room. "Is Jake here?"

"No, baby. It wasn't Jake. It was a package. Can you grab me the scissors to open it?"

She bounds over to the drawer and then carefully passes me the pair of scissors. Sliding their edge along the packing tape, I open the cardboard flaps of the box. Birdie watches from the stool she climbed up on. "What is it? Open it."

I lift the brown packing paper from the top to find a beautifully wrapped gift topped with a pink bow. A smile tugs at my lips when I slip the ribbon and tissue paper off the gift. *The book.*

It's the romance novel by Emily Silver that I showed Jake the day he took me to breakfast. There's also a note inside.

Wanted you to be one of the first to read it, Jake xo.

Blinking back the blur in my eyes, I read the card again. I can't believe he remembered.

"What is it, Mommy?" Birdie looks at me with a curious stare. "You look like you are so happy you could cry."

"Aw, my sweetheart," I say leaning over the counter towards her, bopping her little nose. "It's a book I wanted. It's from Jake. Isn't that thoughtful?"

"I like Jake," she says with warmth in her eyes. "He makes you happy."

"He does," I agree. "And so do you."

That is what I want, I realize. For Birdie to see me truly happy with someone who treats me right. I've always worried about who I want to include in her life. After Grant, dating seemed a long way off, but just the thought of it made me nervous because it's not just me I have to think about. It's Birdie, too. But ultimately, I want her to know happiness, to be surrounded by joy and live in a house where two people adore one another. It's not hard for me to imagine that with Jake.

But I'm getting ahead of myself. Jake is still in his 20s. Would he even want to get married, to have kids? Is that even on his radar? I've thought about this at length, and I know without a doubt I want to give Birdie a sister or a brother. Maybe two. Which means my clock is ticking.

It might be too soon to be having these kinds of conversations with Jake, but if we aren't on the same page, there's no point in taking things further. We'd just be wasting both of our time. I decide I need to talk to Jake about all of this, and the sooner the better. But for now, I will just allow myself to enjoy this moment.

I flip through the pages of my new book before grabbing my phone from the counter to snap a selfie. I send Jake the picture of me with the book clutched to my chest.

> Everly: I got the book you sent. That was so thoughtful, I'm speechless. I'm also very excited to read it. Thank you, Jake.

My phone chimes with a reply a few minutes later.

> Jake: I'm glad you like it. I was pretty positive you would.

> Everly: It was sweet. You are very charming.

> Jake: Only for you.

I grin. If someone had told me a few months ago that I would be messaging with a guy seven years younger than me, I'd have laughed.

> Everly: My Lover Boy.

> Jake: Maybe we can read the steamy parts together.

> Everly: We'll see. Thank you again. The sweetest gift I've ever been given.

> Jake: I'm happy you love it. Are we still on for shopping tonight?

He adds a bicycle emoji to the end of the sentence. Jake offered to help me shop for a bike for Birdie for her birthday. The subject came up when I was lying in bed after the hottest FaceTime of my life. I've never done anything like that. I'm the girl who has never sent a nude. I still blush every time I think about what we did. It surprises me how fully in the moment I was. How I didn't hold back and did everything he asked of me. And the crazy thing? I loved it.

I loved watching how Jake stroked himself and how turned on I made him as he watched me. Every so often since then, I'll find myself zoning out, replaying the night in my head. I loved the way it felt to do something so out of my comfort zone, so naughty. I'm hoping we can do it again soon.

> Everly: We are. Franny is going to watch Birdie.

> Jake: Tell her not to wait up. I wanna get lucky tonight in the back of my truck.

I laugh out loud. I'm not opposed to the idea.

> Everly: Backseat making out is so overrated. Unless it's with you.

> Jake: I'd make out with you anywhere. Happily, all day.

I smile so big my face hurts.

I HOP INTO THE TRUCK AND JAKE CLOSES THE DOOR AFTER ME. We just left Dick's after an hour of looking at every kids bike they had in the store. I would have bought the first one we saw—pink with a purple stripe down the side — but Jake didn't like the wheels or the fact that it was heavy. So, I followed him around the store as he checked out every single one. In fairness, he knows a lot about bikes considering he's been riding mountain bikes all his life. I ended up spending more than I wanted to, but Jake thought it was worth it. He was cute, wanting to make sure the bike is absolutely perfect for Birdie. He asked if he could buy her a helmet, and after arguing with him for a good five minutes, I reluctantly agreed. It was sweet of him to want to buy her a birthday present. It actually made my chest feel all fluttery.

I told Jake about Birdie going to my mother-in-law's for the weekend, and how anxious I am about it. After talking it out, he came up with the idea of getting a hotel room in Brookmont so that I can be closer to Birdie in case she needs me. He knew I wouldn't be able to relax if she was two hours away. I love the idea, but two nights in a hotel is expensive, and I'm not sure I should be spending money on that right now. So, I told him I would think about it.

Once we're on the road, I can't help but notice that Jake seems nervous. He's distracted, his knee bouncing steadily up and down as he drives. He seemed fine when we were in the store, so I'm not sure what caused this sudden shift in his mood.

Should I ask him what's on his mind? We continue driving in silence, past the downtown boutiques and shops, then eventually onto the road that winds along White Harbor Beach. It's beautiful this time of night—golden hour. The sky is bathed in an ethereal glow, and everything feels like magic, as if the world seems to be holding its breath.

When we stop at a red light, Jake looks at me with a cautious expression, and my heart rate blips. "Can we park for a second?"

"Okay. Why do I feel like I'm in trouble?" I tease because that's what I do when I'm nervous. I say stupid things.

"You will be the next time I get you alone," he says, with one dark brow raised, causing a shiver to ghost over my skin. The tension in his jaw fades and any trace of unease in his eyes is gone when he smirks. He keeps driving until he finds a parking spot, backing his pick-up in. He only breaks the grip he has on my hand to get out of the truck and walk around to open my door.

I follow him to the back of his F-150, watching as he lowers the tailgate. Suddenly, Jake lifts me by the hips so I'm sitting with my legs swinging underneath me, and then hops up beside me. The sun is setting in a kaleidoscope of purple and pinks, and a salty breeze drifts up from the ocean.

Jake nods towards the horizon in front of us. "The sunset is pretty tonight."

"It is," I agree, listening to the sound of the waves. "But why do I feel like that's not why we're sitting here?"

An anxious feeling rises inside me. I can tell that he has something on his mind, and the longer he stays quiet, the more nervous I get. *Oh God, what hasn't he told me? What kind of secret is he keeping from me?*

Jake is silent for a moment, watching me with a small smile before he takes a long breath and sighs. Hesitating slightly, he begins. "It was my Gran's birthday the other day and I went to see her. My sister, Sierra, and her boyfriend Grayson were there too. That's a whole other story—Grayson is one of my best friends and I recently found out they're together. It weirds me out, but I'm dealing with it."

I laugh, because he can be so alpha sometimes and other times, he is sweet like honey. I watch him, waiting to hear where he's going with this.

"Anyways, they were on me all night. They want to meet you. They want to meet Birdie too... and I know it's early and it might freak you out, but I thought it would be nice for you to know a few more people here." He looks up at me through dark lashes. "My friends Beckett and Jules have a daughter who Birdie would get along with, and my buddy Liam has a couple of kids too. It would be nice for Birdie to have some new friends."

My brows dip. "Is that the only reason you want me to meet them?"

He grimaces, running his hand through his thick dark hair. "Fuck, I'm terrible at this. That's not why I want you to meet them. It's not the reason at all. It's just a bonus. What I'm trying to say is I'd love for you to meet my family, get to see where I live. But I understand if it's too much for you and Birdie."

I feel like I can breathe again now that I know what he wanted to talk to me about. It's a relief to know we're okay, but meeting his family is a big step—one I'm not sure I'm ready to take. Until I know where things really stand between us, and where they're going, I can't give him the answer he wants to hear. Jake waits for me to say something, rubbing the back of his neck nervously. I guess I'm bringing this up now. I swallow. "Can I ask you a question first?"

Jake nods. "Of course."

"Do you see yourself having kids in the future? Is that... um... something that you want? Because I want siblings for Birdie. One or maybe two. I want to get married again. I get that this seems like a lot, but I'm 34, Jake. I have to be thinking about this. And if it's not something you're ready for, I totally understand, but we have to be honest with each other. I don't think either of us should waste our time if we don't want the same things."

Jake leans in closer, reaching for my hand. His energy

feels strangely calm, considering the bomb I just dropped on him.

"Honestly, I've never seen myself having kids," he says, and my heart plummets to my stomach. I should have known a 27-year-old guy like Jake is not at the point where he's thinking about having a family. I don't know why I thought maybe he could be.

He squeezes my hand in his. "After losing my parents, I told myself I would never want to risk that kind of heartache again. But meeting you and Birdie has changed how I feel about having a family. Now I know that I want that for myself. I want what I lost, and that includes getting married and having kids one day."

"Really?" I ask, my voice shaky.

"Yes, Ev." He reassures me. "I love spending time with Birdie. I love having her around. Let me introduce you to my family. I want you to meet them. I wouldn't ask if I didn't see a future with you."

I blink at him, trying to take in every word he just said. Jake leans in and he kisses me. He presses his lips to mine, soft and lingering, before his tongue sweeps inside, mingling with mine. The kiss is passion mixed with something that feels a lot like love; a kiss that you'll remember for the rest of your life.

He slowly breaks the kiss but doesn't pull away from me, leaving only a few inches between our faces. "Say yes, baby."

I nod with a smile. "Yes."

It happens so fast, I'm not sure how I got here. But Jake's hands are on my waist, and my hands are wrapped around his neck. I'm straddling him on the tailgate of his pick-up truck, under the purplish-pink glow of the sky, my heart in his hands.

"You know what this means, right?" Jake asks, squeezing my hips.

"What does it mean?" I giggle.

"It means you are my girlfriend. I'm making it official." He smiles, and It's infectious so I'm smiling too, so hard that my cheeks hurt.

"I don't get a say in it?" I ask playfully. He can tell I'm teasing by the way I hold him a little tighter, move my body a little closer to his.

"Nope, you don't."

"I'm very okay with the label." I say, before my eyes dart down to Jake's lips. He leans forward, giving me a quick kiss. When he pulls back, his gaze is on me.

"I think I'm falling for you," Jake murmurs, his emerald-green eyes shining back at me. I feel my face flush.

I know without a doubt that I've already fallen for Jake Matthews.

JAKE

I watch Everly yawn from where I'm sitting at the bar at Catch 21. Her shift tonight is exceptionally long, which is why I'm waiting inside to walk her home instead of out on the sidewalk. After 20 minutes of standing around outside, I decided a Pilsner at the bar sounded better. And I was right, because watching Everly work in her black skirt that ends mid-thigh and a blouse that looks sexy as fuck on her is an unbeatable view.

I glance at my watch. It's almost midnight. I take a look around the restaurant, noticing that there's only one table left, and they look like they're getting ready to pay their bill.

Thank God. I'm tired. But I'm not the one who has been working on my feet all night, so I can't imagine how Everly is feeling.

She's behind the bar stacking a tray of clean glasses when she looks over at me and smiles. She looks exhausted. And it breaks me. She has been working so hard, picking up extra shifts at night to pay for Birdie's birthday and dance classes, then taking care of her daughter all day by herself. She never complains, but a person can only work so hard before they break.

I hate that her jackass ex isn't man enough to take care of his own daughter. Just the thought of that guy makes me grip my beer bottle a little tighter.

"Hey, Everly. After you've done that, get out of here. I'll handle the rest," Owen says to Everly from where he's wiping down bottles.

He nods at me, and I can't help but notice that he looks like he has more energy left in him than Ev and I combined. "The beer is on the house. It's good to finally meet you, man."

"Nah, you don't have to do that," I say, reaching for my wallet in my back pocket.

"You've spent enough money here. I recognize you. You come in with the Bennetts sometimes. Keep your money."

"Thanks, man. I appreciate it" I say, grabbing a few bills and leaving them on the bar. Everly walks past Owen, clasping him on his shoulder. "Thanks O. I'm beat. I'll see you Monday."

"See you Monday. Have a good weekend," Owen says over his shoulder as Everly stops in front of me, leaning her elbows against the bar.

She looks tired, her eyes glassy with exhaustion. "I'll

grab my things and we'll get out of here. I'm sorry it's so late."

"It's fine, babe. Take your time."

Ten minutes later she's changed into sweats and a pair of Converse. "Have a good night, Owen," Everly calls out as we're heading out the door to my truck. As I pull out of the parking lot, Everly rests her head against the headrest with a groan. "That was the longest night ever," she sighs, closing her eyes. By the time I've thrown the truck into park in front of her apartment, she's almost asleep.

"Come here, baby," I say when I open the door for her. "I've got you." Her tired eyes flutter open and I slip one arm around her lower back, easing her out of my F-150.

When we get to her door, I take her keys from her, quietly opening the door. Franny gives us a little wave from the couch, then stands up to gather her things. "You poor thing," she says to Everly, pulling her in for a hug. "You look wiped."

"She's working herself ragged," she tells me quietly with a shake of her head as she walks to the front door. "I'll get going. You get her to bed."

I nod at Franny as I kiss my tired girl on the crown of her head before saying, "Goodnight Franny. Thanks for watching Birdie."

I walk Everly into her room and sit her on the edge of her mattress then walk to her dresser to get a T-shirt for her to wear to bed. "Arms up, baby," I say, standing between her legs.

"Jake, you don't have to. I can do it—"

"Let me take care of you. I want to."

Her arms go up to the ceiling and I slip the workout top she's wearing off her body and then pull the T-shirt over her head. She shimmies back towards the headboard, and I slip her sweatpants down her legs, leaving her in just her white lace thong. I get her under the covers and into bed, tucking her in before pressing a kiss to her temple. "Goodnight, Ev. Sweet dreams," I say, sweeping her hair from her face.

"Where are you going?" she whispers as I move towards the door.

"I'm going home."

"Stay," she says softly. "It's late."

"Here?"

"Yes, here." She sits up a little in bed. "I want you to stay with me."

I walk back to her side of the bed, sitting on the edge. "What about Birdie? Are you sure you are comfortable with me staying?"

"Do you want to stay, Jake?"

"There's nothing I've ever wanted more."

"Then stop arguing with me and get into bed."

I strip down to my boxers and then crawl into bed, pulling her into my arms. I listen to her soft snores, breathing in the citrusy smell of her hair before I allow sleep to take hold of me.

TWENTY

DON'T MAKE ME BEG

Everly

The next morning, I wake up to the feel of soft kisses and the tickle of stubble gliding along my shoulder.

I sigh, curling into Jake, my back against his warm, hard chest, my ass nestled right up against his hard cock. He feels so good; every bit of him touching every part of me. I don't know how I will ever be able to go back to sleeping in this bed by myself when I know how good it feels to wake up in his arms.

I close my eyes again, savoring the way he feels as Jake's arm snakes around my chest and his leg drapes over my thigh. His erection nudges my entrance, sending a bolt of lust between my legs. I roll my hips back against the outline of him, his hard cock trapped behind the soft fabric of his boxers.

"Mmmm... good morning. Sleep well?"

"The best," I murmur. "I like having you in my bed with me."

"I like being in your bed with you." Jake kisses my neck.

"I like being anywhere with you. You are all I ever think about."

I smile against my pillow. "How are you real, Jake Matthews? You always say the sweetest things."

"Oh, I'm real. Want me to prove it?" He pulls me closer into his chest and I giggle.

"Is Birdie up yet? What time is it?" I reach for Jake's wrist, the one he wears his watch on, and I check the hour. We should have a little time. I wiggle my ass against Jake's groin, teasing him, showing him I'm definitely down for morning sex.

He whispers into my hair as his fingers trail down to where my ass is rolling against the hard length of him, hooking his fingers into the waistband of my thong. He slides the lace over my hips to my knees and I help him take the fabric all the way off from there. "I want to be so deep inside of you."

I swallow. "Then your boxers need to go," I say, gasping when I feel his cock spring free, tapping at my ass. We're both naked from the waist down now, and I'm desperate to feel him inside of me. I wiggle my ass against the head of his swollen cock.

He curses, nudging the tip of his erection against my wetness before pulling away and then nudging in just a little more once again. My hips greedily rock back against him, wanting him in the worst way possible.

"Ev, baby... condom."

"It's fine," I murmur, rocking into him.

Jake pauses for a second before gripping my hip with his big hand and thrusting into me. I gasp as he begins to move, his bare cock sliding deep inside me, feeling better than it's ever felt.

"Fuck, you feel so good like this," he moans from behind me as he continues to push into me in a quickened pace. He's entering me at the perfect angle, hitting me in just the right spot. I groan into my pillow to muffle the sound. The door to my bedroom is closed and locked, but I still don't want to wake up Birdie. As it is, this is reckless, but we both know this needs to be quick.

Pulling out of me, he turns us so he's lying on his back. "Sit on me." Jake grips the base of his hard cock, proudly pointed towards the ceiling, eager to be inside me. He takes me by my waist, lifting me on top of him so I'm straddling his hips before he slips my T-shirt over my head. He lines me up and slowly lowers me down the length of him until I'm seated, balls deep, and I ride him. He seems to know this angle takes him deeper inside me, and I'm still getting used to how big he is, so he starts slow.

"Look at you, baby. That's my girl. You look so good riding my cock," he says, voice low and husky as he reaches for my breasts.

Soon, my hands are firmly on his pecs and I'm picking up the pace, unable to stop moving up and down his length. With Jake inside of me, raw, all I can think about is being filled with his come. He feels better than I could ever have imagined. I feel a desperate need to have him claim me in this way that brings me closer to my release. I moan, throwing my head back, grinding my pelvis against his. "Don't stop, Jake. Please don't stop."

"Never baby. Not until you come first."

"You feel so good," I groan before biting my lip, realizing that was a little too loud. But then Jake is thrusting his hips up into me with a punishing force and that's all it takes before I'm coming undone all over his cock.

Jake curses through clenched teeth. "Such a good girl coming for me. You look so beautiful when you come for my cock."

I keep riding him as my orgasm fades, then I feel Jake's dick twitch and pulse inside of me before he's filling me with his warm release. He keeps fucking me through his orgasm, until his body goes limp and he's pulling me down for a kiss. His lips linger on mine for a moment before his green eyes open, my face hovering over is.

He brushes my hair from my face. "You know how to make me lose all control. You are addicting."

"I don't know where I found the energy. I'm under your spell, Lover Boy," I murmur, before kissing him chastely and slipping out of bed. I throw his T-shirt on over my head and walk to my dresser. I need to have a quick shower and get dressed for my shift before I get Birdie ready for school.

"About that," he says, sitting up in bed, looking for his boxers and tugging them on. "You can't keep up the pace you're working at. I know how tired you are. You just won't admit it. I want you to reconsider coming to work for me. I—"

"Jake…"

"No, Ev…hear me out," he says, sliding out of bed and walking across the room to where I'm grabbing clean underwear and a bra. His warm hands gently find my shoulders. "I can't keep watching you work yourself to the bone. And be honest with yourself… how much longer can you run at this pace? Besides, I need you. I need help at the office, and you would be perfect for the job. This could be great for both of us."

I know Jake is right; I can't keep this schedule up for much longer. I feel like I'm running on empty. And it's not fair to Birdie that I'm half-asleep when I'm reading her bedtime story, and that I have to miss her dance recitals and after-school activities. I've been looking for a day job, but there isn't anything that pays as well as what I'm making at the restaurant. I've also been regretting my decision not to fight Grant in court for child support. Stupid me, thinking he wouldn't be a petty asshole, and would provide for his daughter, but I'd rather work myself to the bone than ask him for a cent.

And then there is Jake, who wants to do everything he can to help.

"It makes sense. Listen to me, baby. There's paperwork, scheduling the team, orders, and planning that I don't have time for. I am drowning right now. I need you just as much as you need me."

I sigh. "Why haven't you hired someone? There are plenty of people out there looking, I'm sure, you could find someone."

"Because the position is yours. I've been waiting for you to realize that. I'm not filling the spot with anyone but you."

"Jake..."

"Please, baby. Don't make me beg. I've never begged for anything in my whole life, and I don't want to start now."

A small laugh escapes me, but then my expression turns serious. "But what if things don't work out with us?"

Jake flinches. He looks like I've physically hurt him, and I instantly regret that I was so careless with my words.

"I'm sorry, that came out all wrong," I say, sliding my hands over his chest. "It's just, I worry about providing for Birdie."

"I know you do, and I would never get in the way of that," he says, scratching his fingers through the scruff on his jaw. "But if you're not happy with the job, then you leave. I won't stop you. At least you tried."

I'm glad that Jake wants me to work for him, and I believe him that he needs the help, but I'm not sure it's the best decision for us as a new couple. On the other hand, he spends a lot of time out on job sites so it's not like we'd actually be working together all day long. Maybe I'm overthinking it. I have to admit that this *could* solve a lot of my problems.

"Okay. I'll do it," I say softly.

"Really?" Jake's eyes widen, like he wasn't expecting to win me over.

"Yes. I'll give my notice at Catch 21 today," I say, watching a thousand-watt smile takes over his face. "I'll let you know what they say and when I can start."

He presses a lingering kiss to my lips. "I'm so happy. Like, *so* happy, baby. I promise you it's going to be great. And Ev, I'm not going anywhere. I'm in this with the two of you."

I bite my lower lip, then smile and go up on my toes to kiss him. Jake might be seven years younger than me, but he's so mature for his age that it's easy to forget. On paper, we might not seem like a good fit, but I have more in common with him than I ever did with the 34-year-old man that I married. Jake is more of a man than Grant will ever be. He's supportive, protective, loyal to his family, and I'm not sure I've ever been with anyone who has made me this much of a priority.

But I also have to think about Birdie. She will always come first. She needs stability in her life, so I hope I'm not making a giant mistake. Something in the back of my mind is telling me that everything is going to be okay. "Thank you. I hope I won't disappoint."

"You have nothing to worry there. You could never disappoint me. Unless you decide you are sick of me."

A satisfied grin spreads across his face as his hands grip the apples of my ass, squeezing before I wiggle out of his arms and walk towards the ensuite bathroom.

"And Ev?"

"Yeah?" I ask, glancing over my shoulder at him as I slip into the bathroom.

"Can you wear that black skirt you wear at the restaurant when you work for me?"

I shake my head. "You are trouble," I laugh as I'm shutting the door.

I shower with a smile on my face. I'm ecstatic that I will no longer have to work nights. I can't wait to not be on my feet for hours. Best of all, I can work while Birdie is in school, which means I'll be there for her at night. And I have Jake to thank for all of it.

I GOT DRESSED AS QUICKLY AS I COULD SO I COULD WAKE UP Birdie while Jake made breakfast. When I told her Jake was in the kitchen, she shot out of bed like a rocket to see him. Luckily for me, she didn't ask when he got here so I didn't have to explain the fact that he slept over. Eventually, if Jake staying over becomes a reoccurring thing, I'm going to have to talk to her about it, for now I have another difficult discussion to tackle. I need to tell my manager at Catch 21 that I'm leaving. Even harder, though, will be telling Owen and Violet.

As I'm packing Birdie's lunch for school, I watch her with Jake in the living room. The two of them are sitting side by side on the couch, playing a quick game of Mario Kart. Jake agreed to play one game if she got dressed and brushed her teeth after breakfast. I've never seen her move so fast. Now, they're laughing and hollering at the TV. They've already become so cute together. Sometimes it feels like it's me against the two of them.

I'm just slicing the last of a handful of strawberries when I overhear Birdie ask, "Are you my mommy's boyfriend?"

My eyes shoot to Jake, just in time to see his expression change from playful to visibly anxious. He puts down his game controller.

"How would you feel about it if I was?" he asks thoughtfully.

Birdie smiles, turning on the couch to face him. "I would love it. Can I tell you a secret? And you promise not to tell Mommy."

"Of course," Jake says, holding his pinky finger out. "Pinky promise."

Birdie wraps her pinky around Jake's, and I smile, my heart expanding in my chest. She leans closer, thinking she's whispering but in actuality I can hear the whole thing from across the room.

"Mommy likes you. She's always smiling when she's with you. She talks about you a lot."

Jake grins at Birdie and then reaches over to lift her onto his lap. I melt. There is something about a big, broody-looking guy who is a softie for my daughter. "Can I tell *you* a secret?"

Birdie nods solemnly.

"I like your mom a lot too. She's pretty special to me."

"So, you *are* her boyfriend."

"Yeah, Birdie-girl, she is my girlfriend."

Birdie wiggles with a little squeal. "I'm the luckiest girl in the whole world. I love you, Jake!"

The knife in my hand slices the tip of my finger and I yelp, dropping it to the cutting board. "Ouch..." I say, breaking the sweet moment between them. Jake sets Birdie on the couch and then comes over to check on me.

"You okay?" he asks, gently taking my hand in his to get a look at the damage. My heart is beating like a drum in my chest, but it's not from the cut. I can barely even feel that. Birdie just told Jake that she loves him. I take a deep breath and try to play it off like Birdie's confession isn't an absolutely huge fucking deal. Jake goes with it, but I can tell he's shaken by it too.

"Where's the first aid kit?" he asks.

"Under the bathroom sink."

Jake returns to the kitchen and after applying Polysporin and a Band-Aid, I hurry to get dressed for work. I'm now behind schedule thanks to the unexpected injury, so I'm running around my bedroom trying to find my clothes when Jake walks into the room. He wraps his arms around me from behind and kisses my neck. I tilt my neck to the side, silently encouraging him to keep going even though I don't have time.

"You're in a rush, Ev. I'm not. Why don't you let me drop Birdie off at school for you?"

"It's fine. It's never a big deal if I'm a couple of minutes late. They know I need to get Birdie to school. Besides, I don't want to add to your plate."

Jake turns me around in his arms, shaking his head at me. "It's not adding to my plate. I love being with Birdie and I'd like to take her. That is, if it's okay with you?"

I don't know what to say. This man never ceases to amaze me. He's always looking for ways to make my life easier, to make me happy, and I know Birdie would love to have Jake drop her off.

"Okay," I say, wrapping my arms around his neck as his slip around my back. "But only if you're sure you have time."

"I have time, baby. And I want to," he says, pressing a gentle kiss to my forehead before his lips brush against mine in a slow, panty-melting kiss. I can't help the little groan that slips from my lips.

Jake rests his forehead against mine before letting me go. "Birdie!" he hollers as he walks towards the hallway. "Guess who's taking you to school?" Then he winks before disappearing down the hall.

I hear the two of them high-fiving, and when I peek my head down the hall, I see that Jake has Birdie in his arms. She squeals as he twirls her around, and for a moment I allow myself to imagine that this is what it would feel like if Jake, Birdie, and I were a real family.

It feels right.

Birdie is falling for Jake just as hard as I am, which is equal parts wonderful and terrifying.

I say a silent prayer for more good days like this one.

JAKE

THAT WAS ONLY THE SECOND TIME I'VE SPENT THE NIGHT WITH Everly, and I already know I want to do it again. Soon.

I know she's nervous about sleeping in the same bed as me with Birdie around, so I'm not going to push her. I know Birdie comes first with her, that's part of why I think she's so incredible. But that doesn't stop me from hoping it can become a more frequent thing.

I drove Birdie to school this morning, and it was the wildest experience ever. Everly had called to let the teachers know I'd be the one dropping her off, so in that way, everything went great and there were no problems. What I wasn't prepared for was the crowd of curious moms who introduced themselves, clearly wondering who I was. I was half-expecting Birdie to take off running to meet her friends as soon as we got there, but instead she took my hand and showed me the butterfly she drew that was displayed on the art wall. She eventually let me leave, but not before giving me a giant hug goodbye. I left the school with this fucked up feeling in my chest that I'm still trying to make sense of. How could such a simple, everyday thing like dropping Birdie off at school make me feel so happy? I'm not usually the type of guy who gets all charged up with emotions — especially not about dropping a 7-year-old off at school— but I liked the way it felt, and I find myself actually looking forward to doing it again.

The car ride to school was entertaining as hell too. Birdie wouldn't stop talking, and it was cute as fuck when she asked if she could be the DJ and choose a song from my playlist. Constant conversation doesn't come naturally to me, I tend to be pretty quiet—thankfully, Birdie seemed happy enough to do most of the talking.

After I dropped her off, I went home to shower and put on a change of clothes. In the car on the way to work, I thought about this morning, about having sex with Everly without a condom. It's not something I ever do. It's risky, even if she's on the pill, but when Ev is naked and in my arms, I lose brain cells. Fuck. I can't even say I regret it because I don't. My cock buried in Ev, raw, was better than anything I've ever felt.

All in all, it was a pretty perfect morning. I haven't even

had a chance to process the fact that Birdie told me she loved me. I'm pretty sure it freaked Everly out, even though she didn't admit it. It probably should have freaked me out too, but it didn't. Not even for a second.

I love that little girl too.

TWENTY-ONE
DO I EVEN WANT TO KNOW?

Jake

I've been on edge all day thinking about my Gran and Sierra meeting Everly and Birdie. I've invited the four of them for dinner tonight, along with Grayson because he's my sister's fucking boyfriend now, and I'm just a little nervous about how it's all going to go. It has been a long time since I've introduced a woman to my family, and I just want the night to go well.

I know that I'm stressing out for no reason. You only have to be in the same room as Everly for five minutes to like her. She has this calming way about her, she effortlessly makes you feel like you're the only person in the room with her.

Everly and Birdie came over early to help with dinner, and since she hasn't been to my house before, I wanted her to see it and feel comfortable before everyone got here. So far, we've been spending all of our time at Everly's apartment—it's just easier with Birdie. But I'd like to change that. I want them both to feel at home whenever they're here. Hell, I've even thought about making the spare bedroom into a room for Birdie, but I'm afraid that's moving too fast. I'd do it tomorrow, though, in a heartbeat if I thought Everly would go for it.

Instead, I went to Target on my lunch break yesterday and bought a few things to keep Birdie entertained. Board games, a stuffed cat she can keep here, some toys. I hope I did alright. I tried to remember what I've seen at Ev's so I could buy some of the same things. From the smile on Birdie's face when she saw everything waiting for her in the living room, I think I nailed it.

She's been kneeling at the coffee table working on a sticker book I bought her for over half an hour, while Everly and I sit together on the couch. Everly's tucked up into my side, her hair tickling my arm and the citrusy scent of her skin driving me mad. I love her scent so fucking much. I rest my chin on her head. It almost feels like we're a family. From the outside looking in, anyone would think we were. And I like the thought of that. Regardless, these two feel like mine.

"Birdie-girl, there's one more thing I bought you that I think you might like. It's in the cabinet under the TV if you wanna go see," I tell her with a grin.

She bounces over to the cabinet, then squeals when she opens the door and sees the Nintendo Switch. "Can we play, Jake? Can we play?"

"Birdie, mind your manners," Everly admonishes. "What do you say to Jake?"

She drops the gaming console on the floor and scrambles over to me, hopping up into my lap. She throws her arms around my neck. "Thank you, Jake. I love it. And I love being at your house. This is the best day ever."

"You're welcome, and of course Birdie-girl, we can play Mario Kart," I say, adjusting her cat ear headband on her head. This kid doesn't go a day without that thing. "Let me finish my lemonade first."

She kisses my cheek before slipping off my lap and skipping back to her sticker book. I watch her turn the pages, thinking to myself what a great kid she is and what a great job Everly is doing raising her. Suddenly Everly nudges my side with her elbow. "Ouch."

"Jake, you didn't have to do all this. You need to stop spoiling us."

"What? It's not a big deal. I wanted the Nintendo Switch too, so it's not just a gift for her."

"Still... you bought out the entire store," Everly says, sitting up on the couch beside me. She tilts her head, her eyes narrowing as she looks at me. "What's that look for?"

"What look?" I shrug, trying to hide my smile.

"*That* look. What are you hiding?"

"I didn't buy the entire store. I guess I'm lucky I didn't buy her what I really wanted to buy her."

She sighs, crossing her arms over her chest. "Do I even want to know?"

"Probably not."

"Well, you have to tell me now. I'm curious," she presses me, her soft hand squeezing my thigh. Birdie seems to be too focused on the sticker book to notice what we're talking about, but I answer Everly in a hushed tone to be safe.

"I saw a really nice swing set, and since I have a yard, I thought it would be perfect."

Everly's eyes go wide.

"Do you think I'm crazy?"

"My God, Jake, no," she says, her eyes misting over as she looks up at me. "Birdie would love that. It is so sweet of you to think about her. You have no idea what that means to me, but you have to stop spoiling us."

I can afford to buy her a swing set, so why wouldn't I? Now, I'm annoyed with myself that I didn't. I have a sudden vision of the three of us in my backyard, Birdie on the swing set. It's cheesy as fuck, and I love it. I am way more gone for these two than I thought. I need to slow the fuck down.

"It's nothing. And I like doing nice things for the two of you so don't expect it to stop."

Her shoulders drop and she shakes her head. "Something tells me I'm not going to win with you. Thank you for being the best boyfriend." She leans into me for a kiss, and I'm a little shocked that she's going to kiss me in front of Birdie. We haven't done that before, but I'm not complaining. I'm happy we're at the place in our relationship where we can be ourselves around her. My lips melt into hers. The kiss is still very PG, but it sends a shiver up my spine nonetheless.

"We're good?"

"We are... but I'm nervous to meet your family."

"You need to relax. My family is going to love you," I tell her squeezing her thigh. I can tell that she's anxious about this evening.

She looks gorgeous as always, her hair in long waves down her back, and her pale-pink dress showing off her lean, tone legs. But she's been a little antsy since she got here, which isn't like her.

"What are you worried about?"

"Oh, I don't know." She shrugs. "I'm a single mom who waits tables who is also seven years older than you."

"Baby," I say, cupping her jaw in my hand. "Don't sell yourself short. You're the best mom I know, and you work your ass off to give your daughter everything you can. And even if they did have a problem with our age difference, it wouldn't change the way I feel about you. Okay?"

"Okay."

"Good. I promise you, they're going to love you and Birdie."

I lean in and kiss her.

"Now, as much as I hate to leave you, I have a date to play Mario Kart."

EVERLY AND I ARE IN THE KITCHEN WHEN I HEAR MY FRONT door open. Sierra has always had a key to my house, even when she lived in Virginia Beach, but now that I have a girlfriend who tempts me at all hours of the day to fuck her, I'm considering changing the locks.

Everly wipes her hands on a tea towel and smooths out her dress. I mouth, *Ready?* from across the kitchen, and she nods with a smile before I lace my hand in hers as we walk towards the front door.

"There's my favorite grandson," Gran says, squeezing me in a tight embrace. She has her short grey hair curled and she's wearing her signature bright pink lipstick. Thankfully, with her dementia her memory loss is mild. She's forgetful, sometimes confused, and will repeat herself from time to time, but overall, she's the same Gran she's always been.

"Hi, Gran. Thanks for coming," I say before giving Sierra a side-hug and Grayson a clap on the shoulder.

"It's our first family dinner now that we're brothers," Grayson smirks. "This is a momentous occasion for us. We should take a selfie or something."

"I will stab you if you don't stop with that shit," I say so that only he can hear me. The fucker just smirks and then he lets out a laugh as we follow Gran and Sierra into the living room. I watch Gran's eyes widen the moment she sees Everly.

"It's so nice to meet you. Jake has told me so much about you," Everly says, embracing my Gran in a hug.

"He has, has he? I hope it has been all good things," Gran says, raising an eyebrow in my direction. "I can see why you like this one, Jakey. She's as pretty as a peach."

"Okay, my turn, Gran. You can't have her all to yourself," my sister says with excitement in her voice. "I'm, Sierra, and this is my boyfriend, Grayson." They both greet my girl with a hug. "We are really happy to meet you."

"We are," Grayson echoes. "And don't believe anything Jake has said about me. He's a big grump about me dating his sister, but he'll get over it."

"I probably won't." I say quickly. "I have no idea what she sees in you."

Sierra shakes her head with a laugh. "These two just like to give each other shit. Never mind them. We are also excited to meet your daughter too. She's here, right?"

Sierra and Gran look around the room eagerly. I can't wait for them to meet Birdie. They are going to love her just as much as I do.

"I'm here," Birdie says, popping her head up from behind the couch, where she's been busy playing with Lego. "I'm Birdie." And like the sweet kid she is, Birdie crosses the room and stands next to her mom. Gran's eyes sparkle. My heart rate picks up at the sight of the woman who raised me with the little girl who has quickly won me over.

"Oh, look at you, sweetheart. You have the prettiest golden curls. How old are you, my love?"

"I'm seven, but only for a few more days. I'm turning eight next week!"

"Well, my goodness. Isn't that exciting? What are you asking for?"

All eyes in the room are on Birdie as she breathes in a deep breath and begins to ramble off a list: "Well, I'd like a bike, or a doll I can feed or a cat, but my mom says no to the cat."

I laugh, because she's never going to give up asking for a cat and I know how Ev feels about having to take care of a pet. Gran runs her hands over Birdie's blonde curls as my sister eagerly bends down to meet her next.

"I'm Sierra, Jake's sister, and I've been so excited to meet you. I hear you are also a superstar at Mario Kart. I bet you beat him every time."

Birdie smiles and nods. "Did you know I can even beat him with my arm in a cast?" she says with a giggle. Sierra laughs too. "Good job, Birdie," she says, raising her hand for a high five. Birdie slaps her hand, and then holds out her other arm, still wrapped in a hot pink cast. "Will you sign this for me, all my friends have signed it." The two of them disappear into the kitchen to find a marker in my junk drawer.

"Come here, Gran. Let's have a seat on the sofa," Grayson says, taking her by the elbow and helping her to the armchair.

"Everly, come sit," she says. "I want to know all about you."

Everly's worries from earlier in the day seem to have disappeared already as she sits on the couch next to Gran looking perfectly at ease. I leave the three of them alone, going into the kitchen to get everyone a drink. My sister is sitting at the kitchen table next to Birdie, who is busy showing off her cast to my sister.

"This girl is tough. She told me how she fell off the

monkey bars then had to have it X-rayed. She said she was at the hospital way past her bedtime."

"She sure was. She was very brave," I say, watching Sierra find a spot on Birdie's cast to add her name.

"Do you think your Gran will want to sign it too?" Birdie asks, looking up at me with the Sharpie in her hand.

"I bet you she would. You should ask her."

"Okay!" she says, skipping out of the kitchen, leaving Sierra and I alone.

"Jake, oh my God!" Sierra says. "She is the cutest thing I've ever seen."

"Yeah, she's pretty cute."

"How have things been going with you and Everly?"

"Good."

She gives me a look before exhaling a breath. "C'mon, Jake, you gotta give me more than that. She seems really sweet. She's gorgeous too.""

"Things are good. Okay, they're great," I admit. "I'm happy. We're dating. Everly is a little cautious because she's worried about Birdie getting hurt, but everyday seems to get better than the last."

Sierra smiles before covering her mouth with her hand, eyes wide.

"What is that for?" I grumble.

"You're happy, Jake, and it's about time. You deserve this. Now just don't go fucking it up."

I laugh. "Geez, thanks for the vote of confidence. Now here, will you help me with the drinks?"

The dinner goes as smoothly as I knew it would. Everly and Birdie fit in seamlessly with everyone—it's almost like we have all known each other for years. I didn't remove my hand from Everly's thigh under the table the entire time, liking the way it felt to have her next to me at a family dinner. After we've cleaned up, we're talking in the kitchen while Ev is putting on a movie for Birdie in the living room to wind her down. I notice Grayson grab Sierra by the loops on her jeans and pull her down on his lap, kissing her temple. He lowers his mouth to her ear, whispering something that makes her blush. It makes me want to barf.

"You two are gross," I say with a roll of my eyes.

Everly walks into the kitchen just in time to notice the eye-roll. "What did I miss?" she asks, nudging me with her shoulder.

"Nothing. I'm just sitting here having to watch my best friend kiss my sister."

"Get used to it," Grayson says. "Your sister is a smoke show. I'm going to—"

"Finish that thought," I interrupt him, because I know Gray and he likes to push my buttons. "And you'll be leaving here in an ambulance."

"Oh my God, Jake. I am 25 years old," Sierra sighs. "The protective brother shtick has got to stop."

Grayson is smirking, his eyes flicking from me to Sierra. "Jake's bark is bigger than his bite. He just likes to hear his own voice. He's like a big ol' Golden Retriever behind that broody vibe he likes to rock. Just look at him with Birdie, who is the cutest thing on this earth, by the way, Everly."

Everly's eyes brighten like they always do when she's thinking about her baby. "Thank you. She's a spitfire. She's been a force to be reckoned with since she was born."

"I bet. You must have been really young when you had her," he says, sticking his foot directly in his mouth. "You don't look much older than 25." I haven't told anyone about our age difference. I'm not sure why. It doesn't bother me that Ev is older than me. I guess, it just hasn't come up.

Her eyes flick to me nervously before moving back to Grayson. "Well, I was actually 26 when I had her."

It feels like everyone in the room is doing the math in their heads, or maybe that's just me being overly sensitive. But beside me, I feel Everly stiffen a bit, so I know she's gauging their reactions as well.

"Older woman, Jakey. You're a lucky guy," Grayson says, breaking the ice. "Every guy's secret fantasy."

"Excuse me?" Sierra teases, elbowing him in the ribs.

"Not me, babe. You're my secret fantasy," Gray says, kissing her neck.

"Seriously." I shake my head at them. "Can you guys save that shit for when I'm not sitting *right here*?"

"Age is just a number. Everyone knows that." Gran adds.

Beside me, I can feel the nervous energy deflate from Everly's body. I hear the breath she was holding exhale. Now everybody knows about our age difference, and it turns out that nobody cares. I'm happy to have that over with.

"Do you have any plans for Birdie's birthday?" Sierra asks, getting up from Grayson's lap and taking their empty mugs to the sink.

"The birthday girl wants sushi and ice cream, so that is what we will do on Tuesday, then on Friday I'm dropping her off in Brookmont for the weekend. That's where her dad lives."

"*We're* dropping her off in Brookmont," I say.

Everly turns to face me, brows knit together. "What are you talking about?"

"I'm going with you. Thought we'd make a weekend out of it. I booked us a hotel."

"Wait, what? When did this happen?"

Grayson and Sierra share a look before Grayson gets up

from the table. "You guys should probably talk. I think that's our cue to go."

After everyone is gone, I shut the door before pushing my girlfriend up against it. "Are you excited to spend the weekend with me?"

"I thought I told you to stop spoiling me."

"I can't have you sitting at home all weekend worried about Birdie. Besides, this isn't about spoiling you. Spending two nights with you in a hotel room sounds too good to pass up. I have a list of things I can do to you to take your mind off of things," I say, nudging my thigh between her legs. I grip her hip in my hand, and she lets out a breathy moan.

"Sooo," I say, gripping her hip a little more tightly. "Birdie's asleep, and our company is gone. I finally have you all to myself. Tell me how you would like me to fuck you."

She moans as I run my nose across her jaw, stopping to nibble on her ear lobe.

"Surprise me."

I have her legs wrapped around my waist in record time before I'm carrying her down the hall and into my bedroom.

TWENTY-TWO

A HOT, SEXY DISTRACTION

Everly

Today is Birdie's eighth birthday, and I don't know who was more excited to wake her up—Jake or me. He stayed the night last night so he could be here for breakfast and watch her open her presents. We talked about it with Birdie yesterday and made sure she was comfortable with Jake sleeping over. Her answer? She loves sleepovers and she loves Jake, so of course it's the best idea ever. I agree, it is the best idea ever. I love falling asleep in Jake's arms after one or two orgasms and then waking up with him next to me, his limbs tangled up in mine.

"Wake up, birthday girl," I say, smoothing my hand over her mess of blonde curls.

Jake squeezes her toes over her bedspread next to me. "Good morning, Birdie-girl."

Birdie's eyes flutter open and a wide grin spreads over her face. My girl is like sunshine. There isn't a day she doesn't wake up with a smile on her face.

"I have an idea. Should I make you waffles with whipped cream while you open your presents?" Jake asks.

"Yes!" Birdie squeals, jumping out of bed. She wraps her arms around my neck in a tight hug before crawling down the bed to hug Jake.

"Hop on, birthday girl," he says, turning his back to her. She wraps her arms and legs around him and he piggybacks her to the hallway. "Close your eyes, no peeking."

Her presents are waiting for her in the living room, wrapped and set out on the coffee table. I watch her with her one tiny hand plastered over her eyes, bopping up and down on Jake's back, my heart fluttering with every step he takes.

When he reaches the coffee table, he lowers her down to the floor. "Mom, can she open her eyes now?" Jake asks.

"Yes! Happy birthday, baby."

Birdie's big brown eyes open wide when she sees the bike with a big red bow and the helmet from Jake. She opens up a few more smaller gifts from me and then we have breakfast. She bounces in her seat the entire time, shovelling bites of waffle into her mouth so that she can get outside and try out her new bike. When she's done, Birdie and Jake head out to give it a test run while I clear the breakfast dishes from the table.

"Look, Mommy, I'm riding my bike," she hollers as soon as I step out of the apartment building. Jake is holding the back of her seat while she peddles through the parking lot, a determined smile on her face. When she makes it back to where I'm standing, she hops off her bike and throws herself at me in a huge hug.

"Thank you for my bike. I love it!" she says into my cheek before taking off her helmet. "This is the best birthday ever!"

I smile as I watch Jake squeeze my baby tight in his arms.

It's Birdie's day to make a wish, but I make a silent one of my own: for a thousand more moments like this.

The rest of her birthday goes smoothly; the kids at school all sing her happy birthday, then it's back home for more bike riding before Jake joins us for sushi and ice cream, followed by a walk along the beach.

After a long day, she falls asleep in Jake's arms on our walk back to the apartment. He carries her to her room and sets her down on her bed. I pull the blankets over her before we both take turns kissing her forehead.

It's only after I close her bedroom door that I drop my head and exhale a deep sigh.

"I know what you're thinking, baby and I'm sorry. Your ex is a giant ass."

Grant forgot to call his own daughter on her birthday.

My heart is racing as I drive through the pristine streets of the posh neighborhood I used to live in. I am dreading leaving Birdie with Grant, but I'm trying my best to remain calm. I keep reminding myself that Ida will be there, and she would never let anything happen to my baby girl. She loves her, and if I was going to make a bet, I would say she will be the one keeping Birdie occupied for the weekend.

When I pull up to the iron gates in front of the estate, I roll down my window and wonder if my access code will still work. I punch in the four numbers and watch the gates swing open, admittedly surprised that he hasn't changed the code. Pulling up the long stone driveway, I see the house Grant and I once lived in together; large, opulent, with extensive manicured grounds and a four-car garage. The hairs on the back of my neck prickle as I get closer to the home that holds so many dark memories for me and my marriage.

This would be so much easier if Jake was here with me, but I dropped him off at the hotel before heading over. It felt like the best decision keeping Jake away from my ex. I can only imagine the fit Grant would throw if he knew I was dating Jake, not to mention the fact that Jake is still livid with Grant for forgetting to call Birdie on her birthday.

When I put my car in park, Birdie is unbuckling her seat belt and wiggling out of her booster seat. She grabs her overnight bag and the cat stuffy Jake bought her then swings open the door, Daisy the cat held securely in her hand.

"Ready, baby girl?"

"I'm ready," she says, excited to see her dad.

She hops out of the car and I meet her on the driveway, taking her bag from her hands. I take her hand and walk slowly towards the front doors. My heart is in my throat as I lift the heavy metal knocker. I never know what kind of mood my ex will be in. Will he pick a fight with me to ruin my day? Will he have a list of demands?

Thankfully, it's Ida who opens the door and scoops Birdie up in her arms. Birdie giggles as her former nanny holds her close to her chest. The two of them always had a tight bond, and I can't help but smile at how happy they look to be reunited. Ida was a good friend to me too. Near the end of my relationship with Grant, I would confide in her about my marriage and how unhappy I was. She was always empathetic and kind.

"I have missed you, my angel. You've gotten so big!" Ida says, taking a good look at my daughter.

"That's because I just turned eight," Birdie tells her.

"*That's* why," Ida says, running her hand down Birdie's blonde ponytail. "Come in, you two."

As soon as I step inside the foyer of the house, I pause. I swallow at the artwork on the walls, the grandeur of the double staircase with handmade iron railings, and gleaming oak hardwood floors. My eyes linger on the marble table at the base of the staircase where a crystal bowl still sits, a wedding gift from his parents that I later found out cost close to 5 thousand dollars. I remember wondering to myself what on earth we were supposed to do with it. Grant wanted it on display for everyone to see. Besides Miranda and Douglas's estate, it's the most opulent home I've ever stepped foot in. Suddenly, I remember everything I hated about living here. I always felt so out of place.

"Where's my daddy?"

The happiness drains from Ida's face, and I know what she's going to say before she says it— Grant isn't here. Of course he's not. He's probably out banging some chick whose name he can't recall.

"Your daddy will be here soon. In the meantime, I thought we could bake your favorite cookies. Good idea?"

"Yes!" Birdie cheers. "Can I go put my things in my room?"

Ida turns and looks at me, and I hesitantly nod. "Give me a hug first, my baby. I'm going to go. I'll pick you up on Sunday around lunchtime. If you need anything, you ask Ida and she'll call me, okay?"

"Okay, Mommy. I love you."

I crouch down in front of her. "I love you to the moon and back. I am going to miss you so much." My eyes blur with tears as I watch her run upstairs.

"She's going to be fine. I'll make sure of it," Ida assures

me, pulling me into a warm embrace that settles my nerves. "You look beautiful, by the way. I've missed you."

"I've missed you too."

I shift uncomfortably on my feet. Although I'm happy to see Ida, I'd like to get out of here before Grant comes home. "I better go."

I turn and walk to my car, blinking away tears. My rational side knows Birdie will be okay, but she's my baby and I'm still anxious to leave her. I take a deep breath and concentrate on driving back to the hotel and the only person I want to see.

Jake.

JAKE

THE SADNESS IN EVERLY'S EYES WHEN SHE WALKS INTO THE hotel room is more than I can handle. My instinct is to wrap her in my arms, but I don't. She looks like she's on the verge of tears, so I give her a minute, a little space to breathe.

The clock on the nightstand reads seven when I glance at it. It's been a long day. She must be tired, so I decide that instead of taking her to dinner like I had planned, I'll order room service, maybe draw her a bath. I want her to know I'm here for her.

I sit on the edge of the bed, holding my arms out to her. She comes to me, standing between my parted thighs, her hands at the nape of my neck, my hands on the skin at her lower back.

"How did it go?"

"It went fine, I guess."

I brush my hands over her back, down the curve of her

ass. She's obviously not fine, and I don't blame her. I hate that she's worried about Birdie. I hate her fuck-head ex-husband. I hate that there isn't much I can say to help.

"Do you want to talk about it?" I ask, watching her bottom lip start to quiver. My blood is now boiling, and an intense feeling of protectiveness flashes through me. "Did he do something? Did he say something to you?"

She trails her fingers down the side of my face softly. "No. He wasn't there. I saw Ida, his housekeeper."

Figures he wasn't there. I don't know why I thought he would be. "Come here, baby. It's going to be okay. I promise."

Instead of relaxing into my arms, she chews on her bottom lip before letting out a breath, moving from between my thighs. "We should get ready for dinner."

"Don't do that, Ev."

"Don't do what?"

I grab her hand before she has a chance to slip away. "Don't pretend that it isn't killing you to be away from Birdie. I saw your face when you came back to the hotel. I know you and I know it's killing you that she's with him. I also know that you miss her with your whole heart. So, don't pretend, for me, that everything is okay. Because I know you, and I know it isn't."

"How do you already know me so well?"

"I pay attention. I see you. I see you when you don't even realize it."

"Jake…" Her hazel eyes meet mine, sadness clouding them. She buries her face in my neck, and I cup the back of her head and hold her close.

"It's okay, beautiful. I've got you. Grab my neck," I say, wrapping her legs around my waist, carrying her away from the bed.

"Where are you taking me?"

"Did you see the tub? I'm running you a bath," I tell her, setting her feet down on the tile floor in the spacious bathroom. I turn on the faucet and check the water temperature before turning to face Everly.

"Come here. Lift up your arms."

I undress her, then order her into the tub. Before she lowers herself into the hot water, she removes the hair elastic from her wrist, tying her hair up on top of her head.

"Where are you going?" she asks as I move towards the door.

"I'm going to let you relax. I'll order us room service."

"I'm not hungry. I'd rather have you in here with me," she says with heat in her eyes. Her words vibrate right through me. The invitation is all I need to shed my clothes and step into the tub with her. I sink into the hot water and then turn her around by her waist so she's lying against my chest.

"As hard as today was, this feels pretty good," she sighs, relaxing into me.

"The three orgasms I'm going to give you tonight are going to feel even better."

She grabs my hand from where it's roaming her body, lacing our fingers together. "Thank you for this weekend. I don't know what I would have done if I had to sit in my apartment all weekend and stew on it. This is the best distraction."

"Is that what I am... a distraction?"

Everly turns in my arms. "A hot, sexy distraction. I see you too, Lover Boy. You're not the broody guy people take you for. You're a big mush on the inside. You're like a pineapple. Soft on the inside but prickly and rigid on the outside."

"I'll show you rigid," I say, forcefully lifting her onto my lap. Water sloshes over the sides of the tub as she giggles in my arms, seated on my hard-as-steel cock.

"How's that for hard?" I ask, lifting my hips against her center. She squeezes her eyes shut and then darts her tongue out to wet her bottom lip.

"Like stone."

"You're going to feel just how hard in a second." My erection is hard against her ass, eager and ready. "How do you want me to fuck you?"

She grins, mischief sparkling in her emerald eyes. "Like I've been a bad girl."

TWENTY-THREE
I ALWAYS KEEP SCORE

Jake

Everly sucks my dick into her mouth like she's made to. Her warm mouth wraps around my cock, taking me to the back of her throat. "That's it, baby. Suck me harder," I direct her.

Not that she needs direction the way she's taking me deep and working my cock with her tongue. I can barely breathe it feels so good. Everly's body is half under water, and every now and then her stiff, pink nipples appear over the bath water. I drop my hands to fondle them from where my ass is perched on the edge of the tub.

She pops off my dick for just a moment before she's licking her lips and sucking me again. Her tongue swirls around the head before licking a long stripe up the length of my shaft. My head falls back when she sucks just the tip of me. "Fuck," I curse when her mouth opens wider, and she takes me a little further. "Just like that."

Everly doesn't stop, each time taking me a little deeper with the help of my hands that are threaded through her hair. Her big hazel eyes look up at me through dark lashes.

The controlling side of me takes over, wanting to let her know I'm in charge. "Take every inch of me to the back of your throat," I command.

Her hazel eyes spark with lust, and I watch her take me as far as she can without choking. Everly likes it when I'm bossy in the bedroom, and I want nothing more than to make this good for her.

"Look at how pretty you look with my big cock in your mouth." Her eyes light up at my praise and I'm not sure how much more I can take. The combination of her mouth and the way she's looking at me is enough to make me come right this minute. Once my balls draw up against my body, I know I'm not going to last. I'm one lick of her tongue away from going up in flames when I grit my teeth and pull my shaft from Everly's warm mouth. I'm going to come.

"Show me your pretty tits."

Her hands drift from my thighs as she leans back bearing her perfect tear drop breasts with small, blush-coloured nipples. Unable to stop myself, I stand, tighten my fist around the base of my cock and pump my length.

My eyes stay locked on hers as I shoot thick ropes of liquid, painting her chest with my creamy, warm release.

My orgasm seems to last forever, the aftershocks shaking me to my core.

My caveman brain is intensely satisfied about seeing her marked with my come. I reach down, dragging a finger through the pearly white liquid until it's covered then I smear my release in a crisscross pattern over her tits. Her chest rises and falls with each pass of my finger before I leisurely bring my finger to her lips watching her suck the digit into her mouth.

"Such a good girl for me," I rasp, before dragging my finger once more across her chest and bringing it back to her pretty lips. Looking at Everly with the evidence of my arousal covering her torso is all it takes for my dick to come back to life. I stroke it up and down once then twice more to hurry it along.

"Now you get my cock." My hand tightens around my rock-hard dick. "I know how bad you need it. Am I right, beautiful girl? Is that what you want?"

"Please, Jake. You know it's what I want."

My lips twitch at the sight of her on her knees for me, begging me to fuck her.

I never would have imagined Everly begging me for my dick. Never. Not in my wildest dreams.

"I'd give you the world and you know it. You never have to beg." Looming over her, watching her on her knees with her eyes soaking me in. I wait until she's had her fill then gently take her jaw in my hands and pull her up to me. "I'm going to make sure you never forget tonight." I lean down and kiss her, swallowing the little noise she makes against my mouth. "I'm going to take my time with you, show you exactly what you mean to me until you can no longer take it and you're aching everywhere. You will never be the same after tonight. I'm going to make you feel better than you've ever felt."

Everly crashes her lips to mine, her tongue slipping inside, and I taste myself on her lips. I take control of the kiss, sliding my tongue against hers because I am in charge tonight. I nip at her bottom lip then run my tongue over the mark, soothing the pain. We last about two more minutes in the tub before I'm carrying her out to the bedroom, leaving puddles of water on the floor and the carpet in our wake.

"Up against the window, Ev. Stick out your ass for me." I order. She obeys putting her hands flat against the glass that overlooks the pool. We're on the eighth floor, high enough that someone would have to look up to see us. Something is telling me that Everly likes the thrill of getting caught.

"Are you going to come for me with all of Brookmont watching?" I push a finger deep inside her, savouring the tortured moan she lets free when I curl that finger inside her finding that spot. Her hips rock back and forth as she chases her pleasure and I grip her waist in my hands so I can hold her in place. "I want everyone to know who you belong to. You're mine, Ev." I say, adding a second finger. "I need to hear you say it. Tell me you're mine."

I'm so fucking bad because a part of me wishes her ex was outside watching us. Watching the way her chest heaves, her back arches, thighs shake. I wish he could see how she falls apart for me, how perfect she looks when I'm fucking her, and know it's me that makes her feel this good.

He will never get to touch what's mine again.

"Yours." Her breath hitches when I slip my finger all the way out and back in. "I'm yours, Jake."

I shut my eyes as I hear those three words. She's mine. Everly is mine and if I have my way, she'll be mine forever. Every muscle in my body tightens as I kiss my way up her spine, my other hand reaching around her to find that spot between her thighs that will send her over the edge.

I rub tiny circles at a relentless pace, whispering the filthiest shit into her ear. And when I take my fingers out from inside her, she lets out the most beautiful whimper.

Fucking hell, I can't get enough of Everly and the sweet sounds she makes.

I just came and there is already moisture leaking from the tip of my erection.

Two nights in this hotel room with her will never be enough. The rest of our lives will never be enough. All I want to do is make her happy, make her feel good, make her forget that her daughter is with her asshole ex-husband.

I kiss along her neck while my hands angle her ass up, spreading her legs so she's on display for me. My cock hardens to steel when I look down at her perfect pink folds glistening, wet and ready, the most beautiful sight I've ever seen. I pump my eager cock in my hand. "*Jesus*, Ev. So fucking ready for me. I will never get tired of seeing you like this, wet and begging to be fucked by me."

I tease her with the tip of my cock, before pushing inside of her. My self-control obliterated. I need to be inside her warm, wet, tight channel. Her body clenches my cock like a vice. My hands grip her hips as a groan rips from my chest. She feels so mind numbingly perfect I need to slow my pace.

"What if someone sees you up against this window with my cock buried 7 inches inside you? Would you like that, baby?"

She moans, grinding her hips back against my aching cock, my hand tightening around her throat. She's trying to take me as deep as she can, so I'll take that as a yes.

"That's my girl. You take me so good."

She nods in agreement as I begin to fuck her harder. My eyes move to where my cock disappears below her ass cheeks, and I'm completely enraptured. Out of the corner of my eye, I spot a couple walking across the empty pool deck towards the beach. I wait to see if they'll look up and see us. I keep rocking my hips into Ev's tight heat, feeling too good to even give a damn. Nothing could stop me from fucking Everly right now. She is heaven. Everly's body is flawless, and one that deserves to be worshipped. I plan on spending all weekend paying tribute to it.

"Hands and knees on the bed," I tell her, deciding I want

to taste her. I follow her to the king-size bed and watch her crawl onto the mattress. I tug her hips into mine from where I'm standing at the foot of the bed, spanking her ass cheek before soothing the sting with my palm. I kiss my way down to her ass and tease her center with one long, flat lick of my tongue that has her legs shaking.

"My god, Jake."

The next sweep of my tongue has her clinging to the bedspread, rolling her hips against my mouth. Fuck, she tastes so good. I'm going to make her see stars. She whimpers when I push my tongue into her, keeping my gaze on the side of her face that isn't pressed into the bed. I can't wait to watch her go up in flames when I finally make her come. I swirl my tongue in even circles over her most sensitive part next, palming her ass cheeks, spanking her once more.

"That feels so good," she breathes. I continue the relentless lashing of my tongue against the bundle of nerves until her legs begin to tremble and I need to hold her in place with my hand on her thigh. When I add a finger, tremors shake her body as she clenches hard around it. She comes hard on my hand, giving it all to me. Her body falls limp on the bed as I ease my finger out of her.

"That's one. Now you're going to come again," I say, kissing my way up her spine to her neck.

Everly's lips turn up in a sated grin. "Are we keeping score now?"

"I always keep score." I nibble on her ear lobe, hovering over her boneless body. She turns over onto her back, her green eyes sparkling back at me. I smile, settling in between the seam of her thighs.

"I want you, Jake. I need you inside of me."

"I need you more than you could ever understand."

"Please, just do it."

I sit up between her legs, pumping my cock. "I'm just deciding how I want you." I smirk, her eyes on my dick as I stroke it. "Do I put you up against the window again, so the world knows who you belong to? Or do I put you on all fours so I can spank you while I fuck you? Or maybe you ride me so I can play with your perfect tits?"

Her chest rises then falls in a heavy breath, her eyes going wider. Everly likes it when I dominate her. The control I have over her pumps pheromones through my system.

Everly's soft hands run up and down my thighs. "When you fantasize about it, what do you see? That's how I want you to take me."

Dammit this girl. Her and her mouth. Everything she says is such a turn on. I flip us so I'm on my back and she's straddling my thighs. I've already had her on all fours, so now I want to have her bouncing on my dick. I've imagined her this way a thousand times while I stroked my cock all alone in my bedroom. I can't be inside of her fast enough as I line myself up, notching my way in, then watching her sink down until our bodies are flush. We both let out a groan.

"This is what I dream of. I dream of you and those eyes. Those eyes are the death of me, Ev. I swear to God." I reach for the column of her neck, grasping with just enough pressure that she comes to me with a kiss. "It's only like this with you," I admit when she breaks the kiss. "I will never get tired of this."

Then she starts to move up and down my length. "That's it. Ride me. Such a dirty girl for me, aren't you, taking every inch of my cock and loving every second."

I watch Ev thrust her hips, using me, taking everything she needs, and fuck, it's the hottest thing I've ever seen. Her eyes are hazy, and they're locked on mine. Fuck. If she keeps moving the way she is now, looking at me with those eyes, I'm going to last another three seconds. But it feels too good to stop.

"Your body is perfect," I moan, reaching for her tits. Two perfect handfuls that I massage before plucking at her nipples. "Fucking perfect, Ev."

"Jake, baby," she says. "I'm gonna come." Her body begins to shudder as she's wrecked with her release. I feel my balls draw up at the same time, feeling tingles at the base of my spine. I groan through my orgasm as I fill her with my release, pumping my hips until I'm riding that post-release high. She milks me to the very last second before collapsing on top of me.

Slowly, my softening cock slips out of her, and I feel my warm come spill out of her onto my abs. There's something in me that wants to put it all back inside her with my fingers where it belongs, but I don't. Instead, I cup the back of her head and kiss the top of her hair.

"I wasn't too rough with you, was I?" I ask.

"No, not at all. It was perfect. I'll never forget it."

"I got two out of you."

She scoffs and shoves me in the chest. "I'm scared to think what the tally will be by Sunday morning."

I smirk. "You won't be able to walk."

She thinks I'm kidding.

I'm not.

"HAVE YOU EVER BEEN IN LOVE, JAKE?" THE QUESTION COMES out of nowhere the next day as we're walking hand-in-hand along a quiet strip of beach in Brookmont after meeting up with her best friend, Willa, for a drink.

Everly is in jeans and a tank top, and I admire her unreal body. Her skin golden, and her legs long. I haven't been able to stop staring at her all day.

I raise a brow at her. "I have been, it was a few years ago. Her name was Jade."

"How long were you together?"

"We dated for two years. She is my only long-term relationship. Kinda sad, right?" I think back to when we were together. I was 23, and I wasn't looking for a relationship, but we had a connection that was too strong to ignore.

"Why is it sad?"

"I'm 27 and I've been in love once." *Or twice, if I'm counting Everly.*

"What happened? I mean, only if you want to tell me. I'm just curious, that's all, how any girl could ever let you get away."

"I wondered the same at the time," I say with a self-deprecating laugh. "She wanted to see the world. Said we were too young. She was on a plane to Europe three weeks later after she ended things."

"And she broke your heart." Everly says it as if it's a statement rather than a question because she gets me. She sees me too.

"She did," I admit, looking back at her. Everly takes my hand in hers, going up on her toes to kiss me. "What was that for?"

"I felt like kissing you."

"I'm glad you did," I say, leaning down for another because one is never enough with her.

"Do you ever miss her?" She glances up at me, the ocean breeze blowing her hair around her face.

"I used to. Jade was a big part of my life. I was pretty messed up when I met her. I was mad at the world for taking my parents from me. I felt like nobody understood me." I pause. "I'd never met anyone who knew what it felt like to lose a parent, but Jade was different. She lost her mom when she was a kid too. She got me. It was easy. If I wanted to be angry, she gave me the space to be angry and she seemed to always know what I needed. I worked through my emotions when I was with her and became a better person."

"But you don't miss her anymore?"

"No."

Everly doesn't say a word. We walk for a few moments in silence, and then I stop and tug her gently towards me. "I stopped missing her the day I met you. I haven't thought about her since." I place my hands gently on either side of her neck. Her hands move to my chest. "I've fallen so hard for you, Ev, I can't think about anything else. I've never wanted someone as much as I want you. I've never felt this completely out of control."

How this girl has managed to knock me so off balance, I'll never know. I want nights with her, and I want to wake up next to her. I want breakfasts with her and Birdie, and bike rides after school. Our own little family.

"Birdie has me wrapped around her little finger too. I'd do anything for her. "

"You have no idea what that means to me."

"I think I do."

Everly looks back at me with warm, hazel eyes and places her palm against my cheek. "I love how sweet you are to Birdie. You are the best man I know. I'm not sure how I got so lucky to find you, but I want to keep you, Jake." She swallows. "I convinced myself that it wouldn't be possible to find a man who would accept my past, accept my daughter, and stay when times get tough. But you've been there for us in every way possible, and you'll never be able to understand what that means to me. I'm falling so hard for you too."

Dammit to hell, I want to push her into the sand and maul her. I'm crazed for this girl.

I lean in, bringing my lips to hers. She reacts instantly, her hand running through my hair, as I hold her close.

The kiss fades until it slows and stops. "Thank you for coming to Brookmont with me. I would have been a mess without you here."

"I'd do anything for you."

"I know."

I smile and kiss her forehead, then tip her chin so she's looking me in my eyes. "I'm coming with you tomorrow to pick up Birdie."

I am prepared for her to protest, but this really isn't up for discussion. I will not let her walk into a situation where she's talked down to. I will never allow Grant to hurt her again.

"Are you sure? You don't have to."

"I'm not letting you go back there alone."

She chews her lip nervously. "So that'll be it. Grant will know that we're together."

"Are you going to be okay with that?"

"Yeah," she nods. "I am."

Good. I want him to know she's mine.

THE SECOND GRANT OPENS THE DOOR, I KNOW THAT I MADE the right decision coming here. I can already tell nothing good is going to be happening here, but I remind myself to stay calm so that things aren't any harder for Everly than they need to be. The last thing I want is to say or do something stupid and have Everly pay the consequences.

"You brought security with you?" he sneers, nodding his head at me. "Overkill, Evy, even for you."

"Grant, this is Jake, my boyfriend."

I notice Grant's jaw click. "Into college guys now, I see... how cute."

I feel a flare of anger, but I look at him steadily, reminding myself not to take the bait.

"I'm not here to start anything with you, Grant. Can you please just get Birdie so we can go?"

"You're obviously here to start something if you brought him." Fuck, how was Ev married to this guy? Two minutes in his company and I'm ready to strangle him. Just then, Birdie rounds the corner and spots us in the doorway.

"Jake! Mommy!" she screams, running towards us, wrapping her tiny arms around both of our legs. "Are we going home now?"

"Yes, we are. Can you grab your things?" Everly asks, squeezing Birdie in a quick hug.

"She's all ready to go," says a woman who is following behind Birdie. "I can bring her stuff to your car and get Birdie in her booster seat."

"Thank you, Ida. That would be helpful." I put two and two together. Ida is Grant's housekeeper and Birdie's old nanny.

"Bye, Daddy," Birdie says, and Grant pats her head like she's a lap dog before Ida takes her hand and walks her out to the car. Then Grant's eyes lock on Everly and I ball my hands into fists. He glares at me next, and I can tell by the way he's looking at me that I have a target on my back.

"I talked to my lawyer, Evy."

"Because I won't move back in with you?"

"I never said you had to move in with me. I said I want my daughter back in Brookmont. I want her back at Brentwood Academy."

"Right. Because you're such an involved parent," Everly snaps back.

"You didn't even call her on her birthday," I add through gritted teeth.

"Since when was I talking to you? This is between me and my bitch ex-wife, College Boy, so I suggest you shut the fuck up," he growls, and Everly has to grab my wrist to stop me from lunging at the son of a bitch. Grant's gaze goes to Everly's hand wrapped around my arm and he lets out a wry little laugh as if he thinks it's funny that I want to clock him.

"If you value your life, you will never talk about her like that again."

"Grant, if you want to be mad at me, go ahead. But leave Jake out of this."

"Then you shouldn't be dragging him into it. It's not my fault that you are revenge-fucking a guy half your age. My bad for not being kinder to your new *boyfriend* who needs to learn how to mind his own fucking business."

I roll my eyes. Is this guy fucking serious? "It's fine, Ev. I can handle this idiot," I snap, and if he can't tell by the tone of my voice, I am three seconds away from knocking his teeth out.

"Let's not forget why I divorced you in the first place. I believe it was you who wanted to explore other people." Everly glares. "I seem to remember you parading them in and out of *our* house like they were trophies."

"They weren't trophies. I just didn't give a shit about you."

My jaw clenches as I grind my back molars into dust.

"Clearly. The same way you don't give a shit about Birdie. I'm done. We're going home."

"Good idea, your friend here is probably out past his bedtime anyways." Grant glares at me, and the only reason my fist doesn't meet his face is because Birdie is in the car and might be watching. This guy is mouthy for being half my size. I'm at least four inches taller and have at least 30 pounds of muscle on him.

"I want you and Birdie back in Brookmont, or I'll take you to court, and we both know I'll win."

"Goodbye, Grant."

"Don't play these games with me. You won't like the consequences."

The door slams behind us, and Everly flinches. Walking away without knocking that guy out is the most self-control I've ever shown in my life.

If I ever see Grant again, he will regret it.

TWENTY-FOUR
LOVED, PAST TENSE

E verly

It's been three days since we got home from Brookmont, and I have a million things rattling around in my head. I feel frazzled and on edge, and I know that it's starting to show. Yesterday, I dropped Birdie off at school and burst into tears watching her walk inside. Last night, I cried in Jake's arms after we tucked her in.

Grant has been threatening me for months and I've ignored him, but something in his eyes this time felt different. This time I actually believed him.

It's so frustrating that he thinks he can dictate what I do with my life. Coming to Reed Point was the best decision I've ever made, the fresh start that Birdie and I so desperately needed.

I throw a sweatshirt on over my head and walk into the kitchen, where Birdie and Jake are sitting at the table. Jake is teaching her how to draw—another one of his many talents.

"Are you going to stay tonight?" Birdie asks him, looking up from her notebook.

"Would you like me to?" Jake stops drawing to look over at her.

"Of course!"

"Then I will."

Jake has been sleeping here most nights. At this point, he only stops by his place to grab more clothes. We've fallen into this comfortable routine. The three of us wake up together and Jake gets breakfast started while I get Birdie ready for school. Then one of us drops her off. Jake has been picking her up from school some days too. Birdie loves it when he does the after-school pick-up because he usually takes her for a treat on the way home. Yesterday, the two of them went through the McDonalds drive-thru for caramel sundaes. He's promised to take her with him to one of the job sites later this week so he can show her a new house he is building. She's been talking about that for days.

I gave my notice at the restaurant, but in the meantime, I still have to cover some late-night shifts.

We spend the rest of the night watching a movie and by the time it's over, Birdie and Jake have both fallen asleep on the couch next to me. I grab my laptop from the coffee table and Google places for rent in Brookmont. I haven't figured out what I'm going to do, but I have to be realistic. Grant has no shortage of resources, and if he really wants to force me to move Birdie back there, he may be able to make it happen.

I glance over at my daughter, who is nestled into Jake's arms, and my heart lurches. How will we ever be able to leave him? I worry about what this will do to Birdie. The two of them have gotten so close.

"Are you going back?" Jake asks, startling me.

"You're awake."

"I have been for a while. Talk to me, Ev. Are you leaving?"

My eyes meet his. "I don't know. I just... I may not have a choice."

"When?"

"I haven't made any decisions. I'm just looking at options," I say, closing my laptop. "I know Grant, and he meant it this time. I can't lose her..."

"And you won't," he says, sounding certain.

"Jake, you don't know that, and you don't know my ex. I'm trying hard to stay calm about this, but I'm scared. I need to figure things out."

He sits up slowly, careful not to wake Birdie, and I have to fight the tears that so desperately want to fall.

"I'm going to put her to bed," he says softly. "I'll be right back."

Jake holds Birdie close to his chest and walks down the hall that leads to her bedroom. When he returns a few minutes later, he sinks to the couch beside me and gathers me in his arms, holding me against his chest.

"I'm sorry, Ev."

"What are *you* sorry for?"

"That you're in this position." He moves me so my legs are draped over his lap. "It's not fair. I know you've been happy here."

He's right. I haven't been this happy in a long time. I was lost when I came to Reed Point. Then I met Jake. We were only supposed to be friends, and somewhere along the way, I fell for him.

"I don't want to go." A tear finally falls, and he swipes it away.

"I don't want you to go either," he says, cupping my face in his hands.

"Will we lose you?"

"No chance. I care about the two of you too much to ever let that happen." Jake's lips part and he kisses me.

"Is Birdie sleeping?"

"Out like a light."

"Take me to bed, Jake. I need you."

He smiles softly, standing with me in his arms. "I'm going to make you forget about everything."

"I know you will."

And he does. For a little while.

"Don't be nervous. They're going to love you." Jake says, taking my hand as we walk the driveway to Sierra's house.

"I hope so."

He winks. "They will."

His sister is having us over for dinner along with a bunch of Jake's friends, and although I haven't been in the best frame of mind lately, I told him I would go. I know it's important to Jake that I meet his friends, and it's important to me too.

We dropped Birdie off at my parents' place on the way over, and Jake finally got to meet my mom and dad. We stayed for coffee and my mom's famous banana bread and ended up sitting in the family room talking for a while. My dad did most of the talking; my mom had difficulty wiping the smile from her face. As we were leaving, she took me aside and told me Jake was a keeper. Of course, I already knew that, but it still made me happy to know that she likes him.

"This street is a hidden gem. I can't believe I've never

driven down here," I say to Jake, taking in the expanse of beach right across the street from Sierra's house. I can see why she loves it here on Haven Harbor.

"This is where I grew up, baby. My gran and gramps raised Sierra and me in that little old house," Jake says as we pull up to the butter-yellow rancher that his sister moved into this past summer. "And right over there," he says, pointing to a bluff at the end of the road, "is where I would cliff jump into the ocean. I'd climb up there and just leap off. Gran used to want to kill me she'd be so scared."

"Always getting into trouble, even when you were little."

His lips tip up in that delicious smirk that I love. "I plan on getting into trouble with you later on tonight."

I swat at his arm. "That was so cheesy, but you look hot in this T-shirt, so I'll give you a pass." Jake knows I like it when I can see his tattoos. He is well aware of how much it turns me on.

"I know. I wore it for you." He takes two steps towards me, cradles my face, and slowly brings his lips to mine. "You look beautiful. I can't believe you're mine."

I sigh heavily. "There's no need to butter me up, Jake Matthews. I'm a sure thing tonight. Now, let's go inside before we cause a scene."

"The lovebirds are here," Grayson hollers to the room as he greets us in the entryway. All eyes turn our way, and I feel momentarily overwhelmed. I smile and then look up at Jake, who slips his arm around my waist and squeezes lightly. I'm relieved when Sierra appears at our side, a familiar face.

"Everly! I'm so glad you're here," she says, pulling me

into a hug. "Oh, and I guess you too, Jake."

She grins at her brother and then loops an arm through mine and starts making introductions.

I meet Tucker first, then Holden, and I'm taken aback at how handsome they both are. Holden is pretty with his perfectly styled hair and ocean-blue eyes, while Tucker is more rugged-looking. They're both really sweet, telling me how they've been pushing Jake to meet me.

Next, I'm introduced to Beckett and his wife Jules. Sierra and Jules work together at the hotel, and I can tell right away that they're close. Beckett asks about Birdie, and how she's enjoying Reed Point. He and Jules have a daughter too, he says, though she's a bit younger. His eyes light up as soon as he mentions her. Jake told me about Jules and Beckett this morning over breakfast, as he gave me a crash course in who I would be meeting tonight. The two of them work for competing companies, which I guess caused some complications in the early days of their relationship. It all worked out in the end—I can tell from the way they look at each other that they are head-over-heels in love.

"Okay, all of you," Sierra says, taking me by my elbow. "Let's give Everly some space. We don't want to freak her out." She winks at me, and then leads me to the kitchen, Jules following behind us.

I take a seat at the bar, and Sierra slides a glass of wine across the kitchen island to me.

"Thanks." I take the glass, feeling more comfortable than I was expecting to.

"I'm so glad you two finally get to meet. I've been telling Jules about you for weeks," Sierra says, raising her wine glass. "Cheers! To new friends."

We clink glasses, and then Sierra sets out a few appies.

"So," she says, leaning against the island. "I have so

many questions! We didn't really get a chance to chat on our own the night we met."

"I might need more wine for this," I joke, before taking a sip from my glass.

"Oh, there is plenty more where that Chardonnay came from," Jules chimes in. "Sierra has been waiting for this moment."

"Seriously, traitor," Sierra says, glaring at Jules. "I admit, I'm a little excited. Jake hasn't brought a girl home since... well, it's just been a while."

"It's okay," I reassure her. "I know all about Jade. He told me about her."

"Sorry, that slipped. I shouldn't have brought her up. It's just good to see him so happy again. Jake doesn't let many people in."

"I know. And I definitely get it. I guess we've both been afraid to get hurt again. That and the age difference," I confess. "It took some time to wrap my brain around it."

"Really? None of us have batted an eye about that," Jules shrugs. "Well, except for the guys congratulating him and giving him high fives. Guys love the idea of an older woman."

I take another sip of my wine, trying to hide the fact that I'm sure I'm blushing. Thankfully, the subject changes to Jules and her brothers. As I listen to Sierra and her chat, the puzzle pieces start clicking together and I realize that she's a Bennett, the wealthy family Violet told me about at Catch 21 the night I ran into Jake. He was having dinner with Liam, Jules' brother. Her other brother is the ridiculously hot Hollywood star, Miles Bennett. I'm dying to ask her about him, but I manage to resist. I'm sure she gets tired of fielding questions about her movie star brother.

I glance through the sliding door, where my eyes find

Jake's. *You okay?* he mouths. I smile and nod, and he winks. Jake is thoughtful and caring and everything I've ever wanted in a man.

"Gosh, you two are the cutest ever," Sierra says, noticing the stupid smile on my face. "And wait until you meet Birdie." She looks at Jules. "She is so freaking adorable, and her and Jake are so sweet together. My dumbass brother better not fuck things up."

My chest tightens. My heart will be broken when I move back to Brookmont, and so will Birdie's, and it will be all my fault. I try to hide the wave of sadness I feel, but Sierra notices my sudden shift in mood.

"Oh, are you okay?" she asks, reaching across the island to squeeze my hand. "Did I say something wrong?"

"No, not at all," I insist. I'm not sure how much I should tell them. It seems weird dumping my problems on them when we've just met. "Sorry. I'm okay… My ex is just making things difficult."

"I assumed there was an ex somewhere in the picture, but my brother hasn't said much."

"There is an ex. He lives in Brookmont, where Birdie and I lived until last March." I tell them a little about my history with Grant, my decision to move to Reed Point with Birdie, and his demands now that we return. I don't get into the really awful parts. Jules and Sierra listen intently with wide eyes. I can only imagine how they would react if they heard the whole story.

"My God, I am so sorry. You are dealing with a lot," Jules says with sincerity. "And now you've found Jake. I guess that further complicates things."

"It does." I pause. "I wasn't looking for someone. In fact, I had sworn off men all together, but Jake walked into my life, and he got it right where my ex-husband got everything wrong. It finally feels like I'm not the only one giving my all."

I just wish I could fully act on my feelings. I wish I could tell him I love him. But that will only make things more difficult when we have to say goodbye.

"So, what are you going to do?" Sierra asks softly.

I sigh. "I have to move back. I don't have another choice, and I can't ask your brother to come with me."

Jake owns a business; he has a family and great friends and a full life here in Reed Point. I could never ask that of him.

"If you two love each other enough, you'll find a way," Jules says with conviction in her voice. "Trust me. I know."

Jules tells me about her relationship with Beckett, about the obstacles they faced to be together—her family's disapproval, the fact that he had a very big job offer waiting for him in London. Sierra and Grayson also had to overcome some challenges, she tells me, but eventually, they figured it out. Their stories give me hope.

"I care about him a lot."

"He's a good one, Everly," Sierra says. "He's honest and giving, and he's obviously crazy about you. Guys like him don't come around often. Do everything you can to find a way to be together if that's what you want. He'll love you forever."

My throat gets tight at the thought. I've imagined a future with Jake and Birdie, and more babies with his green eyes and dark hair. I can picture a life with him.

But life doesn't always work out like you planned. I should know that better than anyone.

JAKE

. . .

"That's it! Keep peddling!" I holler at Birdie once my hand leaves the back of her seat. She rides without my help for a few beats before her handlebars swerve to one side and she plants a foot down to stop from falling. "That was great! A little more practice and you're almost there."

She drops her bike to the ground and snaps open the helmet buckle under her chin.

"You ready to have some lunch?" I ask, walking towards her, holding my hand out for a high-five. She winds up and claps my hand.

"Yeah, all that bike riding has made me hungry."

"Okay, let's go see your mom."

I carry her bike back to the apartment, Birdie skipping ahead of me. When we step inside, Everly is on the phone.

"I haven't said anything to Birdie, but I'll have to soon. I'm making decisions today." She pauses. "Thanks, mom. I know… I feel the same. I've loved living here so much." *Loved,* past tense. My heart aches hearing her say that. I understand she has to go; I would do the same if I were in her shoes. I only wish things were different. I prop Birdie's bike next to the door and walk to the kitchen for a glass of water. I don't want to hover, but I do want to hear what she has to say. "I gotta run. Jake's back with Birdie." There's another pause. "I will. I love you."

She ends the call and gets to her feet, an uneasy expression on her beautiful face. "Hey," she says, walking towards me. "Is Birdie in her room?"

"She is."

"How did it go?"

"She's so close. I give it another week and she'll be riding her bike without help." *But you won't be here for me to see it.*

I brush her hair back from her face, and Everly sighs as if she can read my mind. "You're going soon, aren't you?"

"I have to." Her forehead drops to my chest and my hand instinctively goes to the back of her head. She starts to cry.

"Don't cry, baby. Please don't cry. We'll figure this out." I hold her close.

"It's all so overwhelming. I don't know what to do first. I can't find a rental on such short notice. There's nothing."

"We'll take it one step at a time. I'll help you with whatever you need."

My hands are tied. The only option I have is to support her. We aren't married, and Birdie isn't legally mine, although, over the last couple of weeks, it has started to feel like she is.

I love that little girl like I've known her all her life. I still can't believe that an 8-year-old has made me this much of a mush. I want to be the one who teaches her how to ride her bike, helps her with her spelling homework and tucks her in at night.

I want to be the one who tucks her mom in at night too. But how can I tell Everly not to go? The hard truth of the matter is, I can't. Birdie comes first, and she always will. That's the way it needs to be.

"And what about us?" She takes a step away from me. "I can't expect you to do long distance."

"Brookmont isn't far. I'll visit you every weekend. Every holiday, until we can figure something out. You're not going to lose me. I promise you. I'm not going anywhere."

"Jake... it won't be easy."

"The good things in life never are." I reach for her, pulling her hips into mine, and then I lean down as she goes up on her tiptoes, meeting me halfway. I press my lips to hers, the words *I love you* left unsaid on the tip of my tongue.

TWENTY-FIVE

BUSY HANDS AND FRANTIC KISSES

Jake

Today is Everly's last shift at Catch 21. Ironically, she originally put in her two weeks' notice to come work for me, but that isn't going to happen now. Instead, she's moving back to Brookmont with Birdie.

My heart is already broken, and they haven't even left yet. I've grown so used to seeing them every day; the thought of there being hundreds of miles between us is gut-wrenching. I've been up every night this week, unable to sleep, trying to come up with a way that the three of us can be together in the same city, but I've come up short.

I finally found someone I want a future with, it seems so unfair that we can't just be together. Everly is smart, beautiful, thoughtful, and a good mother. She loves fiercely and gives her all in everything she does. I want a life with her and Birdie, and I hate the idea of going even one day without them. How I fell for the two of them so quickly, I don't know.

I'm getting dinner started when there is a knock at the door. I open it to find Everly standing there in a workout bra and leggings, her duffle bag on her shoulder. My mouth waters. I'm ready to scrap the pasta I'm making and take her to my bed and ravage her.

There's a smile on her beautiful face when she steps inside, and I pull her into my arms. "Last shift. It's official," I say, my heart squeezing with every word.

"Yup." She pulls back from my embrace, her long lashes fluttering.

"I wish it meant you were coming to work with me."

"It's probably for the best, Jake."

"How so?" I ask, surprised.

"I've never slept with my boss, but I mean, I'm sure it's grounds for an HR violation."

I chuckle before kissing her chastely. "I'd never tell. Now come on, let me feed you so I can get to the good part."

Everly giggles as I run my lips over the soft skin of her neck. "I'm going to go out on a limb and assume the good part is me?"

"It is." My hands drop to her ass. "I will be having you for dessert."

I suck on her neck before dragging her into the house with me. She has a quick shower while the pasta cooks.

Fifteen minutes later, we've fallen into a comfortable silence, working in the kitchen together. I finish off the pasta while she sets the table. It feels nice, being with someone who doesn't always need to make idle conversation. When we sit down together at the table we slip into an easy conversation, both of us avoiding the subject of her leaving. We have the night to ourselves—Birdie is at her mom's—and I think we both want to make the most of it.

After dinner, Everly and I are finishing off the dishes when we hear a knock at the door. "Expecting someone?" she asks, tossing the tea towel over her shoulder. I shake my head, then kiss her quickly before heading for the door. "Whoever it is, I'll get rid of them. I haven't forgotten about dessert."

I'm smiling when I pull open the front door. Then my jaw drops.

Jade. What. The. Fuck.

I blink once, then twice, thinking it can't be her.

I've dreamt of this day for so long. I've imagined exactly how it would play out, down to the last detail. It always ended with me taking her back. Every single time.

My heart pounds. Jade and I both stand in my doorway, silent, staring at each other. It feels as though time has stopped.

She looks a little different than she did the last time I saw her. Her hair is a little shorter, and her skin is a little more tanned. But her ice-blue eyes are exactly as I remember them. Her pillowy pink lips. Long, dark eyelashes. The freckle under her left eye that for some reason, always captivated me. She's as beautiful as she was the day she left me. That was two years and seven months ago. *I think.* I stopped counting.

"Hi, Jake. It's been a while." The moment I hear her voice, my pulse begins to race. I've dreamt of that voice. I've tried not to forget that voice. I open my mouth, but no words come.

I'm speechless. There was a time when I thought I would spend my life with this girl, and then she disappeared. Now here she is, standing in front of me with something that resembles hope in her eyes.

"I'm back."

"I see that," I manage to get out.

"How are you?"

"I'm fine." I shrug, wishing I had time to prepare for this. "You should have called."

"I should have done a lot of things differently," she says, shifting her gaze to the ground. The familiar vanilla scent of her perfume hangs in the air.

"This isn't a good time, Jade."

She cocks her head slightly, looking over my shoulder. I turn to see Everly standing in the doorway of the kitchen, looking from me to Jade and back again. She looks upset; angry, even. Is that how I looked when I saw Grant with Everly? I know that's how I felt.

Before I can think of what to say, she beats me to it. "I... um... I'll just be in your bedroom, Jake. I'm going to call Birdie." Everly crosses the entry way, quickly disappearing down the hall.

Once Everly is gone, Jade stares at me for a long moment, eyes wide. It's hard to believe that only four months ago I was counting the days she had been gone, keeping a mental tally. I'd have done anything to have her show up on my doorstep.

Looking at her now, I know without a doubt that I have finally moved on. I'm falling in love with Everly. Nothing about seeing Jade again—nothing she could possibly say—can change that.

"Is she your girlfriend?"

"Yes." I nod my head.

"And... it's serious?" she asks quietly.

"Yeah, it is. She's the one," I say to the woman that I once loved, needing her to know that there is nothing left between us. Everly and I have enough problems to deal with without adding my ex-girlfriend to the mix. "Why are you here, Jade?"

"I guess it doesn't matter now." Her expression turns icy, and she squares her shoulders. "It's good to see you again. You look good. I didn't know you were seeing someone, otherwise I never would have come here. I hope you're happy, Jake."

Jade studies me for a minute, her expression uncertain. "I guess I'd better go."

"Yeah, I guess you should. Bye, Jade," I say, raising my hand to the door.

"Jake, wait." She looks at me, taking a deep breath. "For what it's worth, I'm sorry that I hurt you."

"It's fine. It's forgotten. See you around, Jade."

And with that she walks away, and I shut the door behind her.

I stand there for a moment, trying to process what just happened. Then I walk down the hall to my bedroom. I really need to talk to Everly.

EVERLY

I'm sitting on Jake's bed with Birdie on Facetime when the door opens. Jake smiles when he sees me, but it doesn't reach his eyes. He seems anxious and upset—his energy is palpable and makes my pulse race a little faster.

I wasn't sure what to do when I saw Jade at the door. I knew immediately who it was. Should I have left, and let the two of them have time to talk? That would have meant walking right past her out the door, and I couldn't bring myself to do that. Instead, I hid out in Jake's bedroom, where I paced the floor, playing the moment over in my head. Jade is beautiful. She's also a lot younger than me. And she's the first girl he ever loved. How am I supposed to compete with that?

When my heart finally stopped beating a mile a minute, I pulled out my phone to call Birdie to say goodnight.

A lump forms in my throat as Jake comes and sits down on the bed next to me. What is he thinking? Is he happy she's back? And what does this mean for us?

Breathe, I tell myself. He told me that he hasn't thought about her since he met me. But maybe that's changed now that she's back.

Birdie spots Jake next to me and asks if she can see him, so I hold out my phone, noticing the way his green eyes soften when he sees her smiling face. "How's my Birdie-girl?"

"I'm good! Gramma painted my nails pink while Grandpa went to the bakery to get us donuts. I wish you were here to try one. They were the best donuts I've ever had."

"I wish I was too," he tells her.

"Are you coming to pick me up tomorrow or Mom?"

"We'll both be there. I can't wait to see you. I miss you just as much as your mom does."

"Okay, good. I gotta go. Grandpa says he's gonna water the garden without me."

I end the call with a tremble in my hands. I want to look at Jake, to see if I can read anything in his eyes, but I can't breathe, let alone speak. Suddenly the bedroom feels small. He turns me by my shoulders to face him.

Jake's expression softens as his hands move to my face, and I will his palms to stay there. "She means nothing to me, Ev. Nothing at all. It's only you that I want. I'm in love with you."

I'm in love with you.

I. Am. In. Love. With. You.

My heart thrashes inside my chest then it skips as my skin begins to tingle.

"Say it again, Jake."

I hold my breath as he gets off the bed and kneels on the floor between my legs, lacing my hands in his. His eyes meet mine. "I'm in love with you, Everly Billings. I love you so damn much."

My eyes flood with tears. I can't stop them from falling. Jake wipes them away with his thumb.

"I didn't mean to make you cry," he teases.

"I'm happy, Jake." I sniffle. "These are happy tears." I untangle our hands, reaching for his face. "I just wasn't expecting that. My heart is still racing," I confess, covering my heart with my palm.

"I should probably kiss you."

"You should... but first..." I murmur, my lips an inch from his. "I am in love with you too."

Then I crush my lips to his, holding his face in my hands, tears streaming down my face. His tongue slips inside, finding mine as I open for him. And I melt into the kiss. Jake has never kissed me like this before. The kiss is sweet, possessive, demanding and full of lust. I savor every second, wanting a lifetime of his kisses, wanting a lifetime with Jake.

Jake wraps my arms around his neck as he rises to his feet, my legs wrapping around his waist. We don't break the kiss. Then we're a mess of busy hands and frantic kisses, stripping each other out of our clothes.

"My God, I love you," he says, backing me up against the bed until the back of my knees hit the mattress and his strong body is hovering over me, his hard cock trapped between us. "Feel how hard you make me."

He shifts to his side when my hand wraps around his erection, stroking his length.

"Fuck." He moans, closing his eyes when my hand roams lower, cupping his balls. "Baby, that feels so good."

I squeal when he suddenly sits, picking me up and setting me down on his lap. "I want your eyes on me when I fuck you. I want you to see how much I love you."

I nod, reaching my hands around his neck, my fingers sinking into his soft hair. Then he's lining his erection up with my wet entrance and thrusting inside of me until I'm fully seated on his lap. His hands roam my skin, finding my breasts and pinching my nipples before rolling the stiff peaks between his thumb and finger.

He fills me so perfectly; I have to force myself to keep my eyes open and locked on his.

"Jake... oh God... baby... harder."

"I've got you, baby. I know what you like." Jake lies me down on the bed, never letting me go. He kisses me before taking his cock in his hand. I want him. I want him so badly.

"You know me so well. I'm so happy I met you. I can't imagine what my life would look like without you."

Jake kisses my shoulder, then my jaw, before gently sucking on my bottom lip. "I'm here, Ev. I'm not going anywhere," he whispers against my neck.

Then he's sinking into me again and there are no more words. I close my eyes as he begins to move, slower and sweeter this time, dropping his forehead to mine. My body begins to tremble, my heart pounding inside of my chest until my body shakes and I'm coming hard.

"That's it. You're such a good girl. You're going to make me come." Jake comes on a groan, pouring inside of me, before collapsing on top of me and burying his face into my neck. We both catch our breath as he falls to the mattress next to me.

I curl into Jake's chest, loving the warm feeling of his skin against mine. He brushes the hair from my face and then kisses my forehead. "I've never tried so hard to get a girl to go on a date with me. I have never thought about anyone as much as I think about you. I know you and Birdie have to go, but I promise you, I am yours. I'm not going anywhere."

"We're going to find a way, right?"

Jake smiles a lopsided grin. "You are mine. We'll figure it out. We just need time. But until then, I'm going to visit you ever chance I get."

He gently lifts my chin in his hand and presses the sweetest kiss to my lips. Every moment I have with him, I find myself falling even harder.

"I love being like this with you."

"Like what?" I whisper.

"Like this. Holding you in my arms."

I press a kiss to his pec then I lay my head back down, listening to the steady beat of his heart. I close my eyes, never wanting this feeling to end. Never wanting to let him go.

TWENTY-SIX

PERFECT LITTLE BUBBLE

Everly

"Why can't you come with us?" Birdie asks Jake as we sit in the middle of our living room, surrounded by boxes.

"I wish I could. There isn't anything I'd like more, but I have work here. People need me."

"But we need you more," Birdie argues, sadness all over her face. She loves Jake. It wasn't all that long ago that I was just hoping they'd get along. I never expected Jake to fill the void in her life that she was missing. But he has done just that and more.

I remember her big brown eyes and the way her face lit up when she saw him at the ice cream shop that night months ago. Despite my resistance, he had won her over instantly when they bonded over cat facts. She adored him right away, and since then, their bond has only grown stronger. It's going to make leaving him behind so much tougher.

An apartment in Brookmont had suddenly become available. I received an email from the landlord letting me know it was ours if we wanted it. She seemed nice and it was in my price range, and from the photos it looked like a decent space. But on the other hand, it made the move very real.

I broke the news to Birdie last week that we would be moving back to Brookmont. Her bottom lip began to quiver, and then she broke down in my arms. Through sobs and tears, she told me that she didn't want to leave Reed Point, that she'd miss Gramma and Grandpa, Franny, her friends at school, her pink bedroom and Jake.

My heart broke. She isn't handling it well, and I'm sure she is going to be a mess when we have to say our goodbyes. I feel the same way. This morning, I had a good cry in the bathroom before Jake woke up. But I need to put on a brave face for Birdie.

There is no avoiding it. Today, we are packing the last of our things. Tomorrow, Birdie and I are going back to Brookmont.

I crouch down in front of Birdie, forcing a smile as if my heart isn't breaking in my chest. "It's not that easy for Jake to move with us. If it was, he would."

"But it *is* easy. He can get a new job," she insists through watery eyes. "He won't be happy here without us."

Jake's eyes squeeze shut, and his chin drops to his chest. "You're right about that. I'm going to be very sad when I can't see you every day. That's why I'm going to visit you every chance I get."

"Will you take me bike riding?"

"I'd love to."

She smiles. "I'm going to miss you."

My heart cracks in two.

"I'm going to miss you too, Birdie-girl," he says with a sigh, pulling her into him for a hug. "But I'm just a phone call away, okay? And we'll see each other as much as we can. Now, are we going to play a game of Mario Kart before you need to get to bed?"

"Yeah!" She jumps out of his lap to grab the controllers. "I'm gonna beat you this time."

Jake is quiet the rest of the time I'm packing, and once Birdie is asleep in her bed, he turns to me, his hands moving to my face. "I already miss you. Is that weird?"

His admission makes me want to weep. "It's not weird. I feel the same way, Jake. You know how much I hate this."

"I know, and I've already cleared my calendar for next week. I told the team I'm away." Jake brushes his thumb over my jaw. "I want to be with you and Birdie."

My heart seizes in my chest as my eyes blur with tears. "You don't have to. I know you're busy at work. We'll be fine."

He lowers his face until his lips brush mine. "*I* won't be fine." He kisses me, and I melt into his arms. It kills me knowing this is our last night together.

"I'm sorry my life is so difficult." My gaze drops to the floor before my wet eyes flicker back to meet his.

"Baby, it's going to be okay. We're going to be okay. I promise."

"I know."

"Good girl," he says with a look in his eye that levels me. Goosebumps break out over my skin.

"You know I love it when you say that."

"I know everything you like."

I smile through the tears.

"Let me prove it to you." Jake pulls me up from the floor. "Tonight is our last night in this apartment. I need you."

He takes my face between his palms and kisses my jaw, my chin, and my mouth as he backs me down the hall into my bedroom. We take our time undressing one another, both painfully aware that we are running out of time together.

I'm leaving our perfect little bubble.

And somehow, I will have to learn to live without Jake.

TWENTY-SEVEN

FILTHY THINGS ON FACETIME

Everly

"Late night?" Miranda asks as she takes the coffee cup that I hand her. "That is the second time I've seen you yawn in five minutes."

Of course, she would point that out. Typical of Grant's overly critical mom. Fuck my life. I wonder what she would think if I told her the real reason I can't stop yawning— that I was up all night doing filthy things on Facetime with my boyfriend.

"The move has kept me busy, and Birdie isn't sleeping well."

Miranda frowns. "Is she not happy to be back at Brentwood Academy?"

I look at Birdie on the couch in the other room playing with her dolls. It's been three weeks since we moved. Three weeks of reminding myself daily that things could be worse. "She's having a hard time with some of the girls."

"Birdie? I find that hard to believe."

Miranda knows very little about her granddaughter. She's seen her a handful of times in the past year, and even then, she rarely *really* talks to her. "She does get along well with others, but that doesn't matter to mean girls, and Brentwood has its fair share."

Miranda harumphs. "There are mean girls everywhere. It's just a part of life. It will toughen her up. Birdie can be a little sensitive like…"

She stops before finishing her thought, but I know exactly what she's thinking. Why did I invite her here? She's been over for all of 15 minutes, and I already can't wait for her to leave.

We manage to be cordial, for two people who can barely tolerate one another. We talk about Thanksgiving coming up and she invites Birdie and I for dinner. I wonder what Jake will be doing. I miss him terribly. Not being able to see him after work or when I wake up in the morning is hard. He has visited a few times already, but it still doesn't feel like enough. Grant, on the other hand, hasn't asked to see Birdie once.

"Have you and Grant come to some sort of an understanding for Birdie's sake?" The way she asks that makes me want to vomit. How can you reason with Grant? It's like talking to a petulant toddler. No, we haven't come to any type of understanding. He insisted I move back here, and now he keeps making up excuses not to see her.

"I haven't seen him to be able to come to any kind of understanding, although it's not for my lack of trying."

"What do you mean? You've been here for three weeks, and you haven't spoken to him? Has he not seen Birdie?"

Why do you sound surprised? Your son is a dick.

"He hasn't seen her. Hasn't even tried." And because I am done playing nice, I continue. "Grant made it very difficult to be his wife; it's not easy when you're not the only woman in your marriage. Now he's making it very difficult for me to co-parent with him. He has seen her twice this year and it's already the middle of October. He didn't even bother to call her on her birthday."

Holy shit, did I just say all of that to my mother-in-law? A jolt of panic momentarily races through my veins. But when I look at Miranda, I almost think I can see empathy in her eyes.

"I knew there were problems in your marriage. I wasn't clear on what they were. I'm sorry my son put you through that. I'm sorry he has hurt you and Birdie."

Ummm, did I just hear her correctly? She has always taken Grant's side. She has never been kind to me. What has changed all of a sudden?

"Miranda, why did Grant come home early from North Carolina?" I ask carefully.

She doesn't answer. She just shakes her head before taking a sip of her coffee. All this time I've wondered what happened. I've wondered what he did to get himself sent back to Brookmont. But she's not going to tell me. Why would she?

My phone rings on the counter and I get up from the table to grab it, smiling when I see that it's Jake.

"Hi babe."

"Is that Jake?" Birdie hollers from the living room. "I want to talk to him."

"Jake, I have Miranda here, so I'll call you later, but Birdie wants to say hi." He asks me to put her on the phone, but not before telling me he loves me. My heart burns for him. I would do anything to see him in person right now. To see the intensity in his green eyes when he wants to undress me.

"Here baby, but don't be too long, he's at work," I say,

handing my phone to Birdie, who is basically climbing up my leg to grab the device from my hand.

She walks to the living room, jabbering away with bright eyes and a smile that reaches her ears. "Jake. I miss you. When are you coming to visit? I hate living this far away from you, and I really want you to take me bike riding again."

Miranda is listening with pursed lips, but surprisingly there isn't a single trace of anger.

"Those two are close," she remarks, and I brace myself for whatever judgemental comment comes next. But she says nothing.

"They are. He loves her." A warm sensation spreads through my body thinking about the way Jakes treats my daughter. She isn't his, but he chooses her. Birdie is his choice.

Birdie walks back into the kitchen with my phone, clutching the stuffed cat Jake gave her. "I miss Jake, Mommy. I want to go back to Reed Point. I hate it here."

I look at her pointedly. "Mind your manners, Birdie. We don't use that word in this house."

"Well, I mean it. I miss Reed Point. I want Jake. He tucks me in and takes me bike riding. When can we go home and see Jake?" she protests in her little voice, and I can tell that she is fighting back tears.

I do my best to explain that we *are* home. I silently curse Grant again for the way he ignores her. She doesn't deserve to be forgotten about, but I can't change that. I just need to love her enough on my own. I hug her to my chest until she's calm again, and then my little spitfire is gone running to the living room to play with her dolls.

Miranda and I sit in silence for a moment before she turns to me. "Everly?"

I nod.

"I want you to know I'm sorry Grant hasn't been a present father. It is not okay with me."

"It isn't?"

"How could it be? I like to think I raised him better than that, but now I'm not so sure. I obviously made mistakes along the way."

I inwardly wonder if she got anything right. "I'm sure you did your best."

"You're a good mom, Everly. You have always put Birdie first. It's admirable."

This is one of the hardest conversations I think I've ever had. Miranda has made it clear over the years that she doesn't like me.

"Are you sure about this guy?"

I sit straighter in my chair, looking her in the eyes. "If you are asking if I'm sure about Jake, the answer is yes. If I wasn't, he wouldn't be in our lives. I would never take a chance when it comes to Birdie's heart."

Her lips turn into a flat line before she sips again from her coffee cup.

I've known this woman for close to a decade, and I should know what that look in her eyes means... but I don't. In all honesty, I am done worrying about what she thinks.

JAKE

I TOSS MY IPHONE ONTO MY DESK, THEN MASSAGE MY SCALP with my fingers. My hair is long, falling over my forehead. I haven't bothered to get it cut. I haven't bothered to shave either. I haven't felt like doing much.

I also haven't been sleeping. I lie in bed every night, staring at the ceiling until I give up and turn on the TV. Last night, I fell asleep watching reruns of *Seinfeld*. The night before, I went for a run, hoping to clear my head. The only time I sleep well is when I'm in Brookmont with Everly. I've gotten so used to having her in my bed that when she isn't there, I can't turn my brain off.

I miss her. Fuck, how I miss her. And it only seems to get worse every day. I miss the way she snuggles in next to me when we're watching TV on the couch. I miss the scent of her body lotion that has faded from my bed sheets. If it wasn't for the fact that I own my own company, I probably would have quit my job by now and moved to Brookmont, but for obvious reasons I can't. I'm stuck here while she's stuck two hours away. And there's nothing either of us can do about it.

A yawn overtakes me, and I rub my blurry eyes. I have a contract to go over that will take me at least an hour. Then I need to meet with potential new clients to talk through a kitchen and bathroom renovation.

Work is what's getting me through my days, it is the distraction I need to stop thinking about Everly and Birdie. Ev says she is doing well at school, but she misses her friends in Reed Point. And me. I miss her too. So much some days it physically hurts.

Saying goodbye to the two of them was fucking hard. Will we find a way to be together? And how long will it take? My biggest fear is that she'll get tired of doing long distance. What if she decides it's not worth it? I hate everything about this arrangement. I just wish I saw a way to change it.

My phone rings. I check the screen hoping it's Everly, but it's not. It's Liam Bennett, and I'm a little surprised to get a call from him in the middle of a workday.

"Hey Liam," I answer. "What's up?"

"Hey, man. Can you talk?"

"Yeah, I'm good," I say, checking the clock on my desk. "What's up? Everything okay?"

"Everything's fine. Question for you. Did you say Everly's last name is Billings?"

"Yeah, why are you asking?" I sit up straighter in my chair.

"Is her ex-husband Grant Billings? He lives in Brookmont?"

"That's him. Why are you asking?"

"I was talking to a buddy of mine who knows him. He started to tell me about a guy that he works with and then I put two and two together and figured out he was talking about Everly's ex. He mentioned he has an ex-wife and a daughter, and some of the details seemed familiar. And Birdie isn't a common name, so I figured it had to be the guy."

"Get to the point, Liam. You're fucking killing me."

"I get it… you don't like the guy." Liam chuckles. "You're not the only one. He's a douchebag. Apparently, he was sent down to North Carolina to run operations for at least a year at his family's steel company and ended up lasting eight weeks. He drank too much at a company dinner and got handsy with the CFO's niece. She lodged a complaint against him with HR. Said he was saying inappropriate things to her all night and when she got up to go to the bathroom, he cornered her in the hallway where she had to push him off her. From what I've been told, she was going to file charges, but the family intervened."

It makes sense. Everly said that Grant wouldn't give her the whole story as to why he was suddenly back in town.

Turns out it's because he sexually assaulted someone. What a fucking sleaze bag.

I wonder who else knows about this. I would assume his parents are trying to keep a lid on it to avoid humiliating the family and their company.

The sad part? Grant is Birdie's dad. A man with no moral compass. One day she's going to find out who her father really is, and it will break her heart.

"They had no choice but to get him out of there," Liam continues. "The guy sounds like a total piece of shit from a few of the other stories my buddy told me."

"You have no idea."

By the time I end the call, it's nearly lunch, but I've lost my appetite. Instead, I clear my calendar for the next two days. I have someone I need to talk to.

EVERLY

The dizzy feeling in my head has finally eased up. Jake unexpectedly showed up at my house, and while I was thrilled to find him at my door, the reason for his surprise visit made me sick to my stomach. The news he shared about the real reason Grant came back to Brookmont left me in absolute shock. Grant being unfaithful in our marriage is one thing, but sexually assaulting someone is something I just can't wrap my head around.

Once the shock started to wear off, my emotions shifted to anger. How could he ever do such a thing? This was bad. It made me feel physically ill. We share a daughter, and Grant's actions not only affect me, they also affect Birdie.

What would happen if she were to ever find out? My skin crawls at the thought.

Jake and I talked about it for over an hour, trying to decide the best way to handle this. In the end, I decided that I needed to confront Grant about it. I needed to know the whole truth—and I wanted to hear it from him.

The car ride to his house seemed to take forever, the minutes ticking by slowly. My adrenaline pumps hard through my veins as Jake and I walk to Grant's front door.

This is it. I square my shoulders and look Grant in his familiar icy blue eyes when he opens the door.

He looks surprised. "What are you doing here?"

"We need to talk," I say, Jake's big hand resting on the base of my spine, giving me courage.

I expected to have the conversation on his doorstep, thinking he wouldn't let us in. Instead, he huffs and gestures for us to come inside. We follow him into the living room where we each take a seat, my hands trembling in my lap. I open my mouth to speak, but he goes first.

"I want to see Birdie this weekend. I'll pick her up on Saturday morning."

I shake my head. "We won't be here. We're going to Reed Point. It's my dad's birthday. I sent you a message about this weeks ago."

"Evy, why is everything always so difficult with you?"

I blink. Difficult with *me*? Is he joking? My shaking hands ball into fists as I explain to him that I can't always drop everything when he feels like seeing his daughter—which is basically never.

"For fuck's sake, Everly. I have a life, okay? A job. Responsibilities. You wouldn't know—"

"A job, right," I seethe, cutting him off. "Speaking of that, why did you really come back from North Carolina so early, Grant?" He pales—it's only for a moment, but it's all I need to know the truth. "Because I heard that it's because you forced yourself on a woman." I stare at him, waiting for his response.

He blinks. "What the fuck are you talking about?"

"You know exactly what I'm talking about." I glare. "It's the real reason you left North Carolina early. Admit it, Grant. You know what, never mind. It's too vile to even hear. I know you, and I can tell just by looking at you that it's true. You are damn lucky your parents own the company and are covering for you."

A vein in Grant's neck looks like it's going to burst as his posture stiffens. "Is this what you came here to talk about? Because if it is, the two of you can get out."

"No." Jake's voice bounces off the walls, a muscle firing in his jaw. The way he's looking at Grant— it's scary and hot all at the same time. "We're going to talk about this now." I've never seen Jake this mad. Grant is in trouble. "First, you cheat on your wife the entire time you are married. Then, you assault a female co-worker?" Jake glares. "You may have been able to silence that poor woman, but you will not be able to silence me. You won't speak to Everly the way you do ever again. You won't tell her how to live her life. Or you will have me to deal with, and believe me, I would like nothing more than to put my fist to your face."

I look at Jake next to me then at Grant, who just got his ass handed to him. I love Jake for this.

"You don't deserve a kid like Birdie," Jake continues, his voice low and steady. "And if I were you, I wouldn't be fighting Everly for sole custody. I wouldn't be fighting Everly on anything she feels is best for Birdie, including where she wants to live. Unless you'd like to have your name dragged through the mud. And trust me, we will take what you did to that girl public."

The anger on Grant's face is palpable. He opens his mouth, probably to tell Jake where to go, but Jake pushes to standing from the couch before he does, reaching for my hand.

We ignore him, walking towards the door. Then we walk out of Grant's house—the house I used to live in—and we get into my car.

My jaw hits the floor for the second time in 20 minutes. Jake left Grant Billings speechless. That must be a first.

A wave of intense relief washes over me as the reality of this sinks in. There is nothing else Grant can do to me. I will never allow him to make me feel small and unimportant again. I'm done playing his games. Jake has shown me how I deserve to be treated, he's given me my self-confidence back, and with him by my side I am stronger.

"Are you okay, baby?"

I nod. "I'm okay, but did that just really happen?"

"He isn't going to bother you, Ev. Never again."

With a smile, I lean over the console, and he meets me halfway. "I love you," I say, my hand on his jaw, my eyes locked on his.

"I love you too."

Then he seals his lips to mine.

The kiss goes on for minutes. And when his hand loops behind my neck pulling me closer, I feel a wild, burning sensation in my chest.

And I secretly hope Grant is watching from the window.

TWENTY-EIGHT

FATE WORKED ITS MAGIC

Jake
Three weeks later...

"You couldn't help yourself, could you?" Everly shakes her head with her arms crossed over her chest, staring at me.

"What was I supposed to do?" I ask her, an innocent look on my face. "My girl needed a swing set."

It took me at least 200 hours to put the damn thing together. I have been out here in the back yard until sun set every night this week, but it's all worth it to see the smile on Birdie-girl's face. "Last one to the slide is a rotten egg," I yell at her, taking off across the grass.

Birdie squeals as she chases me. I let her win. She scrambles up the ladder to the top of the slide, then turns to look down at me. "Come on, Jake! You have to come too!"

"Are you kidding? I'm going to be on this thing all the time," I tell her, following her up the ladder and then down the twisty covered slide, hoping like hell I don't get stuck.

"You are a big kid, Jake," Everly says, laughing as I pop out the bottom of it.

"It's your turn, beautiful."

Everly rolls her eyes, but she joins us, sitting on one of the swings. "Give me a push, lover boy."

"Oh, I'll give you a—"

"Jake!"

I grin at her, then lower my voice so that Birdie won't overhear. "Don't worry, Ev, I'll finish that thought later tonight."

She turns and playfully pinches my side. "Ouch!" I yelp, pretending it hurt. "You're going to pay for that." I take hold of the ropes and pull her backwards as far as I can before letting her go, sending her soaring through the air.

"Jake! If I fall off this thing, you are in so much trouble," she yells.

"My turn!" Birdie jumps onto the swing beside Everly, and I reach over to give her a push. She's wearing her cat ear headband as always and has a smile a mile wide on her face.

Everly and Birdie made the drive from Brookmont to stay with me for the weekend. I was dying to show Birdie the swing set I bought for her. I want her to feel comfortable at my place, I want it to feel like a second home for her. If I'm honest, I'm hoping to make this place *our* house very soon.

Everly's plan to move back to Reed Point is in motion and as much as I've wanted to ask Everly to move in with me, I've kept my mouth shut. I know how she works. She needs time before she takes next steps. But I'm running out of patience with the two-hour drive that separates us.

There's not a chance Grant will fight Everly on moving back to Reed Point. He's not even going to be in Brookmont for the foreseeable future. He sent Everly an email a couple of weeks ago letting her know that he would be in California for a while for work. When she brought Birdie to visit Miranda, she filled her in on the missing details. He had asked them for another chance in the company's West Coast division and they had agreed - this time on the condition that he commit to a therapy program. According to Miranda, he didn't fight them on it. Miranda also told Everly that she would understand if she decided to move back to Reed Point. She only asked if she could see Birdie a couple of times a month. Everly agreed.

Birdie takes off running when we hear the doorbell chime. Everly's mom and dad are taking her for sushi this evening, which means I get my girl all to myself for a few hours. I could kiss them both when I see them on my doorstep. It's been five days since I've been inside Everly. We still FaceTime every night, and while some of those calls are R-rated, it's not the same. After saying goodbye to Birdie, I close the front door and in a split second I have Everly pushed up against it.

"I missed you," I say, with my left hand on the door next to her face, my right-hand drifting over her hip to the hem of her shirt.

"I missed you too."

"I'm done missing you, Ev. I want to have the same address as you, here in Reed Point."

I'm done with the distance between us. I am hellbent on convincing her to move in with me. She doesn't stand a chance.

"Forget about Birdie's choir performance at the end of the month. Are you not dying as much as I am to be back?" It's a question I've wanted to ask her for days. The distance between us has been gut-wrenching, and I can't emotionally or physically take another second of it.

"To Reed Point?" she asks, playing with the collar on my shirt.

"Yes, to Reed Point."

"I do, I'm looking at places," she answers easily, eyes even greener than they usually are. I'm under her spell.

"Move in with me, Ev. I have plenty of room. I thought we could paint the spare bedroom pink for Birdie. Get her one of those loft beds and a desk to do her homework."

Everly goes quiet, pulling her bottom lip under her teeth. There's that look that makes my pulse spike every time.

"Ev." I scowl. "The distance is painful. Please, don't make me beg."

There isn't anything I wouldn't do to live under the same roof as her. This girl came into my life, fate worked its magic, and I've never been the same since. I can't imagine my life without Everly and Birdie in it.

"I don't know, Jake... I don't think your closet is big enough for my stuff." She smirks. Why am I not surprised she isn't going to make this easy on me?

"I'll build an addition on to the house if I have to. What else do you want? Name it, baby, it's yours."

She laughs. I kiss her neck. Then I nip her ear lobe. She moans. I have her right where I want her.

"Move in with me," I plead when I pull my mouth away from her, looking for an answer in her eyes.

"Okay." She smiles. "Okay, we'll move in with you."

I have no doubt she can see the excitement on my face. My heart pounds against my chest. "I want it to happen soon."

"Like tomorrow?" she says, laughing.

"Yes, like tomorrow. And do not tease me right now when I'm trying to be cute and win you over."

"I'll stop teasing you." She runs her knuckles over my jaw, then snakes her arms around my neck, love in her beautiful hazel eyes. "I hate living away from you. I never want to do that again."

"I won't let you." I answer. "Ev, I've been thinking."

"About?"

"I hope I can be a good influence in Birdie's life. I want to be that for her."

"You're the best man I know."

That. That right there makes the air rush from my lungs.

"I love you both, Everly."

"We love you too, Jake."

No matter how many times I hear her say that it will always feel the same. Incredible.

I lift Everly off her feet, her legs wrapping around my waist. I plant a kiss on her mouth. "You're my girl."

"I am, lover boy."

I carry her into the kitchen and lie her out on my kitchen table. I look down at her with a mischievous smile. "I have five days to make up for. I'm going to fuck you on this table before I tie your hands to the headboard and fuck you in our bed. Then I'm going to make love to you in our shower, and I'll decide what I feel like doing after that."

She blushes. She's perfect.

And gorgeous.

And mine.

And she loves me the way I want to be loved.

"Our bed, Jake? Our shower?" She looks up at me with a smile.

"Ours, beautiful. This house is ours." I kiss her, then I kiss her again. "You are my forever. You and Birdie. We're a family. Forever and always."

TWENTY-NINE
QUICK AND GREEDY

Jake
2 months later...

"I KNOW THAT LOOK IN YOUR EYES, JAKE MATTHEWS. YOU better not be thinking what I think you're thinking."

Everly bites her bottom lip and shakes her head, excitement shining in her big, hazel eyes.

"You are going to have to be quiet, baby, unless you want everyone in the office to know you're getting fucked by your boss." I turn the lock on her door, then cross the room to where she's sitting at her desk. Everly started working here last month. Best decision I ever made.

"Jake," she begins, eyes wide, but when I start unbuttoning my shirt she stops. I pull it off, tossing it on the chair, then waste no time leaning over her for a kiss. I watch her eyes flutter open when I pull back, pausing, until they meet mine.

"This is a bad idea," she says with lust-filled eyes.

"I like being bad with you." My mouth grazes the side of her jaw. "Stand up."

I take a step back, and I can tell by the look in her eyes that she's about to argue with me, which is okay because my cock loves it when she does. I also know my girlfriend. She loves knowing that we could get caught.

"Lift up your skirt," I demand. She's wearing that damn pencil skirt she used to wear when she worked at Catch 21, the one that drives me crazy. If she's wearing it to torture me, it's working. She paired it with a white blouse with tiny gold buttons down the front that have been mocking me all morning.

She pulls her skirt up slowly, the hem shifting from below her knees to mid-thigh. "How's this?"

"Not far enough, baby." I shake my head. "Lift it higher so I can see what you're wearing underneath it."

She pulls the fabric a little higher until I can see a glimpse of the white lace she's wearing, but it's not enough. "Higher Ev, or I'll do it myself."

She finally bunches the fabric around her waist so I can see what I want. My cock hardens.

Everly's eyes heat with lust when I move my hand to her blouse, slowly unbuttoning her. I watch a shiver roll over her skin when I slip the fabric over her shoulders, tossing it to the floor.

"Good girl. Now unbutton my pants and take my cock out."

She gets my pants and my briefs down far enough to get my dick out while I shimmy the lace down her thighs. She takes a nervous glance at the door while I take her in from head to toe. She's in nothing but a see-through lace bra, her peaked nipples giving away how turned on she is. "Sit on the desk," I command.

She does, and I waste no time dropping to my knees and flattening my tongue along her seam. She tastes like fucking heaven. I devour her, dragging my tongue back and forth through her wet folds, picking up speed before flicking my tongue over the place that sets her off like a rocket.

"Jake," she screams as I cover her mouth with my hand.

Once her head falls back and her body goes limp, I stand and suck on her neck to increase her pleasure. "Shh, baby. We need to be quiet. What if someone hears us? You don't want us to get caught, do you?"

She presses her teeth into her bottom lip when I remove my hand. I help her to her feet and then spin her around so she's bent over the desk. "Hands on the desk, baby." I push on her lower back until her chest is flush with the cold, wood surface and then I'm pushing inside her in one quick thrust. My eyes, I swear, roll back in my head when I feel her warm, wet heat. When I'm inside Everly, I'm fucking lost in her. I lose track of time. I forget where I am. I can't remember my own name. "You feel so good," I tell her as I push harder, slamming into her. I move in and out of her, slow and smooth at first before my pace changes to quick and greedy.

With her ass in my hands, I sink into her before flipping her around so I'm sitting on the desk and she's on my lap, straddling my thighs. "Please, Jake." She moans my name in a desperate plea. I grip the nape of her neck, pulling her mouth into mine, moaning into the kiss before lifting her up and lowering her down until she's seated. Everly sighs a groan of approval when I find that spot deep inside her.

"I had to be inside you. I couldn't wait until tonight," I growl against her neck, thrusting up into her until I feel her clench around my dick, finding her second release. "That's it, Ev. Let me feel you come all over my cock."

Everly's groans are muffled by my shoulder when I feel my balls begin to draw up and my cock begins to throb. And I'm done. I fall apart, spilling inside of her.

After several minutes, I slowly lower her to her feet. I pull her skirt back down over her hips before I smooth back her hair.

Everly starts to laugh. "I'm not sure there's anything you can do to make it look like we didn't just have sex."

"You should have thought about that before you decided to torture me with that skirt."

"You have no self-control," she says, buttoning up her blouse. "Now get out of here, I have work to do."

I give her a kiss before leaving her. Walking past my office, I grab my jacket from the closet and head out the door. I have somewhere else I need to be.

EVERLY

Jake must be working late tonight. I've tried to hold off dinner, but Birdie is hungry. I am starving too. I haven't seen him since he seduced me in my office earlier today, which was incredible, but made for a very awkward afternoon. I hid in my office for the rest of the day, too nervous to show my face around the team. I felt like it was written across my forehead— my boyfriend, your boss, just fucked my brains out on my desk. Thankfully, no one in the office gave me the side-eye or acted weird around me when I finally snuck out to grab a cup of coffee.

Birdie and I are sitting at the kitchen table at Jake's house—correction, *our* house—when we hear the front door open. We moved in when we returned to Reed Point, and living with my two favorite people has been even better than I could have imagined.

"Jake?" Birdie hollers from the kitchen.

"It's me, Birdie-girl," he answers as she takes off running towards the hallway. I peak my head around the corner in time to watch him scoop her up into his arms and twirl her around. Birdie giggles. My ovaries explode. His eyes find mine over her shoulder and he winks. I am so in love with this man.

"I have a surprise for you," he tells her when he sets her down on the ground. "Go have a seat on the couch," he says, then looks at me. "You too, Mom."

"I love surprises!" Birdie cheers, bouncing on to the couch as I sit down next to her. I watch him walk back to the front door, wondering what he is up to.

"Close your eyes, Birdie," he hollers, closing the door behind him. "No peeking, remember."

"They're closed." She has her hands covering her eyes.

When Jake returns, he's holding a tiny gray and white kitten in his arms, a red bow tied around its neck. I gasp, my hand flying to my mouth. "Okay, Birdie," he says with a grin. "You can look now."

"A kitten!" she screams, her entire face lighting up when she sees the cat in his arms. "Jake, is that for me?"

"It is, Birdie-girl. She's yours," Jake says, kneeling in front of her. "Do you want to hold her?"

"Yes! Yes, please. I'll be gentle, I promise," she answers softly before Jake places the kitten in her lap, glancing at me to make sure I'm not going to strangle him. How could I? This man has proven he would do anything for Birdie. He has a heart made of gold. He is truly one of the best things to ever happen to her life.

"Thank you," she weeps, hugging the kitten to her chest. "This is the best day of my entire life. I'm so happy."

"Are you mad at me?" He says the words quietly, his eyes finding mine. "She deserves the kitten. She deserves anything she wants."

My heart swells. I swallow down the emotion. "You shouldn't have, but I'm not mad. It was really sweet of you."

"Anything for my girls." He smiles.

"I know."

His eyes hold mine, an intense gaze, an invisible force pulling us closer. "I told you on our first *non-date* that it would be a matter of time before you fell head over heels in love with me and I meant it," he says, leaning forward for a kiss.

"Yes, you did. I remember."

"I was already falling hard for you that night." His eyes sparkle. My heart is his.

My whole body tingles, sending shivers down my spine, as he pulls me closer, until our lips are just millimetres away. "Have you been reading my romance books, lover boy?"

"Maybe." His hand moves to my jaw, the heat between us so hot, it feels like fire. "We got our happily ever after, baby."

"We did."

Like fate, Jake walked into my life and stole my heart before I even knew it was happening. I tried to resist. I tried to ignore the feelings he sparked inside of me. None of it worked.

The best kind of love begins without warning. It comes to you at just the right time: the time you least expect it.

It's how I found Jake, and I plan on never letting him go.

EPILOGUE

ABSOLUTE AFICIONADO IN BED

E verly
I look up to find Jake in our bedroom, bare-chested with a pair of perfectly faded jeans hung low on his hips. Those washboard abs and V-shaped muscle taunt me. I'm positive I will never get used to the sight of him.

"We can cancel our plans if you'd prefer?" he says with a smirk that slays me.

"Oh, believe me, I'd much rather stay in this room and appreciate my boyfriend's body than go to the aquarium."

"What do you have against fish?" he asks, stalking towards me. "What did they ever do to you?"

"They're like fireworks, everyone knows that. You've seen them once; you've seen them all."

"We'll make the best of it." He takes the romance book that I'm reading from my hands and sets it on the bed. I stare at my devastatingly beautiful man, eyes wandering shamelessly over his smooth, muscled skin. My gaze catches on the trail of soft hair that disappears into his jeans. My core heats, badly wanting to reach for him and undress him.

My heart races.

My skin pebbles.

My god, Jake Matthews is pure perfection, like chiselled stone. He knows just how to light a fire in me.

My heart flutters as I look at the bird tattoo on Jake's ribs. A simple sparrow for Birdie and the date Jake and I ran into each other at Catch 21 for me. He surprised me one afternoon while I was doing the dishes, removing his shirt, and telling me that he had been thinking about getting the tattoos for a while. My jaw dropped to the floor when I saw it. I ignored the dishes in the sink and with soapy hands I cupped his face and kissed him. After I finished kissing him, he told me that meeting Birdie and me was the best day of his life. He says the second best is the day Birdie told him she loves him. The fact that Jake wanted to honor Birdie speaks volumes about how much she means to him.

There's a bright twinkle in his eyes when he notices me staring. A playful smile flashes across his face. This man knows exactly how to get my heart racing. "You've been reading that smutty book for an hour. Has Hunter won Faith's heart yet?"

"Wouldn't you like to know?" I sass back, as he reaches for my hand, pulling me to stand. I lean forward and press my lips against his and he doesn't hesitate to slide his hand to the nape of my neck, deepening the kiss. I take his cheek in my palm, brushing my thumb over the scruff that covers his jaw. We only break the kiss when we hear Birdie bouncing down the hall.

"Are you ready?" Birdie asks, appearing in the doorway.

Pulling back, Jake shoots me a wink before slipping his shirt over his head.

"We're ready. The question, is are *you* ready?" He looks

her over from head to toe. She beams. I melt. "Cat ears, check. Teeth brushed, check. Pretty dress, check. You look ready to me, beautiful. Let's go."

"Are you sure you want to wear that dress to the aquarium, baby? It might be a little fancy," I say as Jake lifts her into his arms.

"I'm sure, Mommy. Now come on, let's go."

Minutes later, Jake deposits Birdie into her booster seat in the back of his F-150, and when he slips into his seat next to me, he takes my hand in his. He pulls the truck away from the curb, but instead of going south towards the aquarium, he heads north.

"You're going the wrong way," I remind him, shooting him a confused look.

Jake stifles a smile.

"Are you really not going to turn around?"

"I know where I'm going." He turns to face me with a smirk before my daughter hollers from the back seat. "Don't tell her, Dad. We're almost there."

The first time Birdie asked if she could call Jake "Dad," I froze. I didn't know the right way to handle it. After taking some time to think about it, I decided Jake is more of a father than Grant has ever been, so why not? He is a second dad to her, and he is always there for her. Jake might not be biologically related to Birdie, but he has earned the role of being her dad, and he loves her with his entire being.

Ten minutes later, he pulls into the parking lot at the beach, then gets out and opens Birdie's door. The two of them stand in front of the truck, all smiles, and Birdie motions for me to join them.

"What are you two up to?" I ask suspiciously, as Jake takes my hand and tugs me to the spot in the sand where we officially met for the first time. I cock my head his way, but he just smiles his sexy, serious smile. Birdie giggles with a cat-that-caught-the-canary gleam in her eyes.

Stopping in front of me, Jake takes my hands in his, making my pulse race a little faster. "Ev..." he says, dropping to one knee, and I stop breathing all together. "I fell in love with you in this exact spot and as crazy as it sounds, I knew that day that you were the one. I never believed I could be this happy. And I can't remember ever laughing like I do when I'm with you and Birdie. The two of you are everything to me." He pauses, glancing at my daughter. "I want to be the man you and Birdie deserve."

I press my hand to his chest. "Jake—" I murmur. "You are. You always have been."

"I want to love you both forever. Say yes, Ev. Will you marry me?"

When he slides the ring onto my finger, my heart pounds in my chest. Every cell in my body ignites. And every fiber of my being is present in this moment with him. "Of course, I say yes. Yes, baby, yes, I want to marry you."

I close my eyes as tears slip down my face. I never thought I'd be able to find anyone who loves my daughter like she is his own. And I certainly never thought a man seven years younger would be that guy. Jake has been the best surprise. But nothing surprises me more than the fact that I am going to marry him.

"I love you." I drop to my knees in front of him and gather his face in my hands. I capture his lips with mine, and Birdie giggles before Jake pulls her into the two of us. Just us. It's perfect. When the three of us are together I feel complete.

"I love you, too."

I kiss the top of my daughter's forehead. "Were you in on this, Birdie?"

She's all smiles as she nods while Jake brushes the tears from my cheeks with his gentle, solid fingers.

My heart bursts in a way I'm sure it never has before with my baby next to me and Jake's strong, protective arms wrapped around us.

We spend the next several months as a family of three, eating breakfast together in the mornings and dinners at night. Jake and I take turns driving Birdie to school and dance classes, and I haven't missed one of her recitals since I started working for Jake. Instead, Birdie has an entire cheering section in the audience. My parents, Sierra and Grayson and Gran all come to watch her perform. Franny often joins us as well. It feels like a dream. I'm positive it doesn't get better than this.

Jake and I flew to New York one weekend to stay at the very upscale Seaside Hotel. We toured the city, ate pizza, and went to a Rangers game, where we cheered them on to victory over the Florida Panthers. When we weren't busy sightseeing, we lounged in the jacuzzi tub on the private terrace overlooking Manhattan and made love for hours. It might have been the hottest sex we've ever had, and that's saying something. Jake is an absolute aficionado in bed. Sex with him is a dirty, wild affair.

A few weekends after that, we watched Sierra marry Grayson. It was a picture-perfect wedding and Jake stood beside Grayson as his best man. Tucker and Holden were at his side too. I was completely floored when Sierra asked me to be a bridesmaid; I remember hugging her profusely.

Back at home, the three of us have dinner with my parents on Sunday nights, where Jake is only too happy to sit and watch sports for hours with my dad. He has become a second son to my parents, they love Jake as much as I do. On weekends, Birdie begs us to take her to Sierra's new bakery, where there always seems to be a pink-and-purple cupcake waiting for her. Sierra quit her job at The Seaside Hotel to open Buttercup Bakery—a dream she has had since she was a little girl baking with her mom. And now it's a reality. Jake is so proud of her. He's always stopping off on the way to the office to pick up boxes full of croissants and muffins.

Time has flown by, and I still can't quite believe that tomorrow is our wedding day. It feels like just yesterday that Jake and I crashed into each other at Catch 21, but it also feels like I've been waiting my entire life for this.

The night before the wedding, we host a rehearsal dinner in our back yard, surrounded by everyone we love. We sit under twinkling patio lights and drink champagne as dusk casts a lilac-hued glow over a picture-perfect evening.

I gaze across the yard at our friends and family, everyone laughing and chatting, and it makes my heart expand in 10 different directions. Gran is here, looking like a dame with pearls around her neck and sequins sewn into her yellow sweater. She's chatting with my parents while my brother Adam and his wife stand to the left of them catching up with Willa, who made the trip from Brookmont to be my maid of honor. Holden and Tucker are getting drinks at the bar with Aubrey and Franny. We even invited Miranda and Douglas, who regretfully declined. They are in California visiting Grant. From what I hear, he is doing well. He calls Birdie every few weeks, which is more effort than he's shown in a while.

"No more champagne for you?" Sierra asks, tapping my shoulder with her clutch as she and Jules come to stand beside me.

"Nope."

"Birdie is the sweetest with Maya," Jules gushes. "You three should really join us for the weekend in Cape May next month."

"That sounds like fun," I agree. "I'll check with Jake."

"What, so Grayson and I aren't invited because we don't have kids? How is that fair?" Sierra asks, pretending to be offended. She bites her lip, looking from me to Jules.

"Okay, I'm going to tell you a secret, but this is not to be broadcast," Sierra warns. "We're not telling everyone just yet."

"Wait..." I say with wide eyes. "Wait... are you serious?"

Jules leans in closer, a huge smile on her powder pink lips. "You are pregnant?"

"Yes!"

It takes a real effort to stop myself from screaming.

"I am so happy for you!" I tell her in an exaggerated whisper as Jules pulls Sierra in for a hug.

I sneak a look at my fiancé. He is across the yard talking to Tucker and Holden, and as if he can sense me looking at him, his gaze finds mine. His greens blaze into my hazels, and my pulse races with lust. I almost forget how to breathe. Jakes walks my way in his navy dress pants, crisp white button-down, tan belt and shoes. His shirt sleeves are rolled up his forearms, and his skin is smooth with that sinewy vein that makes my mouth water. I couldn't stop staring if I tried. I don't really believe in magic, but the intense desire I feel to touch him, to press my lips to his mouth, it's almost like he's casting a spell.

"There you are." His voice is low and smooth. "Please tell

me you've changed your mind. Or are you really that determined to torture me?"

"You'll live, Lover Boy. It's only one night."

"Will I? I'm not so sure," he says, his eyes raking over me.

"My rules," I say, absentmindedly twirling my engagement ring around my finger. Jake has been pouting all day about Birdie and I sleeping at my parents' house tonight. I've reminded him it's tradition for the bride not to see the groom before the wedding. He's not buying it.

"But you'd have so much more fun if you were sleeping with me tonight."

"And years of bad luck." I press my hand to his cheek. "It's not happening."

Jake sighs. I smooth my thumb over his cheek, pretending to console him.

"Let me get you a glass of champagne. Maybe that will help to change your mind." He smirks.

"Nope. I'm happy with my punch. But nice try."

I feel his lips dust a kiss to the side of my hair as Tucker joins us. He claps my husband-to-be on the shoulder. "How do you do it, Everly. Seriously, tell me. It's like you have some voodoo magic. I've never seen this ole' grump smile so much." He squeezes Jake's shoulder who glowers at him in return.

"I love you too, man," Tuck says to him teasingly.

"Fuck off, dipshit." Jake swats at Tuck's head. "Your ass can be replaced tomorrow."

"You wouldn't," Tucker mutters, clutching his chest. "Don't even joke. I take my duty as your number one groomsman very seriously."

"Who said you are my number one?" Jake frowns. "I have three groomsmen, and if I had to choose between you, Beckett and Holden, I'm going with Holden."

"Geez. Ruthless," Tuck says, as I shake my head at the two of them.

As Tuck saunters away, I take Jake's hand and tell him there's something I'd like to show him. Pulling him with me, I move along the patio's edge, and we slip through the patio doors unnoticed. Once in the bedroom, I tell Jake to sit on the bed.

"Really, Ev in the middle of our rehearsal dinner? I mean, I'm not complaining, but..."

"I didn't bring you in here to have sex," I laugh, shaking my head at him. "You have a one-track mind, Jake Matthews."

"Are you sure? Because I can be quick. Fuck, Ev, you look so hot. It's killing me."

"I am sure it is," I nod, turning to open the dresser drawer.

I return to where he's sitting on the edge of the bed, moving to stand between his parted thighs with my hands behind my back. His hands immediately go to the back of my thighs, pulling me closer. The scent of his aftershave and the light eucalyptus of his shampoo floods my senses, intoxicating me.

"What are you hiding?"

"I've been keeping a secret from you."

"Okay." He frowns. The broody, serious face he sometimes wears is hot as fuck. "I guess we should talk."

"I'm pregnant," I announce, anxiously holding out the test I took this morning. I've been exhausted lately, but I chalked that up to everything with the wedding. I only suspected I might be pregnant when I was suddenly hit with a wave of nausea yesterday afternoon. The two pink lines that appeared on the test confirmed my suspicions. I was shocked at first. I've been taking the pill religiously, every morning after breakfast. I've never missed a day.

"Jake, are you okay? Do I need to get you a glass of water? A cold cloth..."

"You're..?" He doesn't finish the question, just looks down at the pregnancy test I'm holding in my shaking hands and then returns his gaze to me, his hand moving to my stomach.

"I am."

Jake rises to his feet, pressing a hard kiss to my mouth, and I taste the champagne he's been sipping on all night.

"We're having a baby," he says, his voice full of wonder.

"We are," I say, taking a moment to look into his eyes. "It's a surprise. Are you okay?"

"Are you kidding me, baby? I'm so much better than okay. You pregnant with our child makes me so happy. I just feel so... lucky." His green eyes pierce my soul.

"We are lucky," I say, fighting back silly, happy tears. It feels like a dream, like I have everything I've ever wanted and somehow more. We're going to have a happy life. I feel that in the deepest parts of my soul.

"I'm going to spend my life making you, Birdie, and this baby happy," Jake says, slipping his hand beneath my top, setting his warm hand on my belly. There is pure joy in his eyes. I think about this baby growing inside of me, *our baby*, and I'm positive that our little boy or little girl is fate.

"I'm thinking we have four more after this one."

"Four? Is that so?"

"Well, I really want ten," he says, eyes as serious as can be. "What do I have to do for you to agree?"

"Did you forget you are marrying an older woman? Ten little Matthews are not in the cards, but I *might* agree to one more after this."

"Two more?" he says, eyebrows raised with a wise ass smile. Jake slides his hand along a path from my pregnant belly to my hip. "You went from ten kids to two just like that." I laugh. "That was too easy. You've lost the fight."

"You fry my brain when I'm this close to you. And you just told me I'm going to be a dad to our baby. I can't think straight, I don't know what to tell you."

Jake growls and flips me around, laying me out on our bed and looming over me with a sexy grin. He gets on top of me and kisses me. "Can we tell Birdie together?"

I love how this man is always thinking about my daughter. "We can, but we'll wait a little longer."

"I'm so in love with you Everly Matthews."

"Not a Matthews yet."

Another kiss. "Fine. But almost."

"Almost."

He gets this ridiculously hot glint in his eye before he kisses me again, and I thank my lucky stars that I took a chance on Jake.

The End

CURIOUS ABOUT TUCKER? HE'S UP NEXT! His forbidden love, childhood best friend, frienemies-to-lovers, FOOTBALL romance is available now. Start reading Never Say Never today.

To find out release news and where you can find Lily, follow her on instagram, @authorlilymiller and on her website. Make sure to sign up for her newsletter.

· · ·

LILY MILLER

WWW.AUTHORLILYMILLER.COM

ACKNOWLEDGMENTS

Again the list is long, but I will do my best to keep it short and sweet.

To my readers— those who have been with me from the beginning and those who have just discovered my love of small-town spice—thank you for picking up my books. Thank you for supporting my dream of writing happily-ever-afters. Your continued excitement and passion for my books inspires me to keep dreaming up steamy stories. I hope you know how much I love you all.

To my Beta readers, ARC readers, bloggers and bookstagrammers who I have fallen in friendship-love with, I will always be grateful for every post, mention, reel and comment. I hope you know how much you mean to me. I couldn't get my books out to the world without you. A special thank you to Anita Walker, Dave Nakata, Lisa Johnson, Miriam Ehrlich-Schnider, Adrianna King, Dara Sorah and Hope Procops.

To my editor and friend of over 20 years, Carolyn, for being on this wild ride with me. Thank you for treating my stories as if they are your own, for pouring your heart into every one and for answering my frantic texts at all hours of the day. I love you, and there is no one I'd rather be doing this with.

To my girls, my other hype squad, who listen to me ramble on and on about story ideas and hot guys from Haven Harbor. Brandee, Carmen, Mary, Erin, and Leah, you are among my favorite people in the world, my chosen family, and if it wasn't for you, I wouldn't be half as happy. I love you all infinitely.

To my cover designer Kim Wilson, for killing my covers every time. You are a dream to work with and your patience is enviable. I am the luckiest to work with you.

To Asha Bailey of Asha Bailey Photography for answering my email and allowing me to use the stunning image you took for my cover. It is absolutely the cover photo Jake and Everly deserve.

To Ellie of Love Notes PR, for getting *Play For Keeps* out into the world.

To Emily Silver for being the best book bestie a girl could wish for. You keep me motivated, you keep me sane and you tell me where I need to be and what I need to do. I love celebrating our successes together and of course, I love you.

To my assistant Kait Miller for keeping me organized and celebrating my achievements by sending me the best voice messages. I love working with you.

To Anita Walker for being the best damn assistant at signings on the planet. I have so much fun with you, but more importantly, I would be a disaster without you by my side.

To my family who make my dream possible. You put up with a wife/mom who carts her laptop everywhere we go, sometimes forgets to feed you and has to watch my super cringy TikTok's. You love me fiercely and are always there for me when I need it most. Your love means everything.

Finally, thank you to the Pulse Dance Center parking lot where I sit in my car and have my best writing sprints. You are too good to me. :)

ALSO BY LILY MILLER

THE BENNETT FAMILY SERIES

Always Been You

Had to Be You

Heart Set on You

Crazy Over You

HAVEN HARBOR SERIES

One Good Move

Printed in Great Britain
by Amazon